The Waco Variations

Rhonda Rizzo

Dedication:

For my sister, Kelli

Author's Note

The Branch Davidian Cult Massacre

In 1981, David Koresh joined the Branch Davidians (a splinter of the Seventh-day Adventist Church). In 1983, he claimed to possess the gift of prophecy. By the early 1990's, he had assumed control of the Branch Davidian compound known as Mount Carmel in Waco, Texas. Responding to rumors of child abuse and weapons stockpiling, the U.S. Bureau of Alcohol, Tobacco, and Firearms (ATF) obtained a search warrant. The incident began when the ATF launched a raid on the compound. Koresh and his followers responded with violence. A siege ensued.

On April 19, 1993, after a 51-day impasse, the FBI attempted to end the standoff by initiating a tear-gas attack to force the Branch Davidians out, but that was met with gunfire. During the attack, fire engulfed the Mount Carmel Center. By the end of the siege, seventy-five had died from gunshot wounds or the blaze, including Koresh. Nine people survived.

Part I

"There is something in it of Divinity more than the ear discovers: it is an Hieroglyphical and shadowed lesson of the whole World, and creatures of God; such a melody to the ear, as the whole World, well understood, would afford the understanding. In brief, it is a sensible fit of that harmony which intellectually sounds in the ears of God."

--Sir Thomas Browne, "Religion Medici" (1643)

Aria

From the time she heard the first note, the Bach Double Concerto became the soundtrack of Cassie's life. She couldn't get enough of it. When practicing, she worked longer and longer hours at the keyboard, and when she was away from the piano each phrase wound its way through her every thought and experience. When she woke in the morning, it was there, and it was the last thing she heard as she went to sleep. The notes burrowed under her skin and started to feel like part of her blood and breath.

"Eric, your line answers Cassie's," Dr. White said. "Listen to her tone, listen to what she is saying, and answer her question."

Two concert grand pianos sat side by side on the stage in an auditorium dark except for a few stage lights. After working through several intricate passages in the first movement, they were a third of the way through the second.

Eric played his line again. Dr. White stopped him, took his glasses off, and caressed the bridge of his nose.

"A double concerto is an intimate conversation," Dr. White began. "This one is one of the most, um, intertwined of Bach's concerti." He looked at both of them a second. "It is a conversation between two people who are very close to one another."

They nodded and waited. He sighed, appearing to struggle for words.

"When you are really close to someone, you don't just hear the words he or she says, but you hear the deeper meaning in the words. It is only then that you can respond deeply to what the other person is telling you. When you play this music, you must hear the deeper meaning in each phrase, and you must answer with your own depth of understanding. "

He pulled up a chair and sat between the two of them. "You two need to have one mind when you play this. You must know what the other is thinking and feeling so you can communicate, not just push the notes."

He turned to Cassie and smiled at her. "Cassie said some beautiful things with her phrase, Eric. Did you hear it?"

Eric nodded, and Dr. White asked, "What did you hear?"

Eric shrugged. "It was really sensitive, and she had a beautiful tone," he replied.

Dr. White responded. "Yes, but what was behind the tone? What was the meaning?"

Eric gave both of them a confused look. Dr. White patted his arm and then turned back to Cassie.

"Please play it again."

Cassie put her hands on the keys, closed her eyes, and let the notes breathe out the ends of her fingers into the keys. At the end of the phrase, she stopped and waited.

Dr. White turned to Eric. "What did you hear?"

Eric looked at him, not at Cassie. "I heard someone trying to connect."

Cassie gasped and looked away, embarrassed. *Do I sound that desperate?* she thought.

Neither one seemed to notice her reaction. Dr. White reached over and flipped through Eric's score. "See what the orchestra is doing here? Pizzicato until later in the movement. They are the heartbeat, the passage of time. And the two pianos—you two—trade each phrase back and forth like caresses. You connect, but the essential loneliness never goes away."

At the word "caress," Eric looked at Cassie and raised his eyebrows. Cassie blushed and ducked her head.

Dr. White nodded at both of them. "Take it from the top. But this time, <u>really</u> listen to one another. Hear what's behind each phrase, and keep the conversation alive."

Cassie flipped the music back to the beginning of the Largo and then waited as Eric played the opening lines. Closing her eyes, she listened to each note. In them she heard tenderness and restrained passion combined in one big question: *may I?* Her entrance arrived, and her answer was longing and shyness wrapped in an unqualified *yes*. Eric's next entrance was bolder and more confident, and Cassie's answer expressed passion and surrender. In the next phrase, Eric held back a little, and Cassie's answer was bolder, with a slight flamboyance. In the caress of notes, Cassie knew nothing of fire, death, loss, or fear, just love plucked from Bach's hands, to Eric's, to her own—spoken in a language too deep for words.

Chapter 1

Day 0

When the world came to an end, Cassie and her grandmother watched it on TV. They watched with the same deadness they had felt every day since the siege began. There was no question of pain, or hope, or even anger—just numbness and a blank white noise in the brain that the TV images and sounds bumped into but never permeated. They watched the compound catch fire, and then they watched it burn to the ground. They watched reporters excitedly reporting the tragedy and officials smoothly shifting or placing blame. They heard the screams of the sirens through the TV, but most of all they heard the deadness of the silence behind the chaos.

Cassie felt no surprise, no grief, no anger, and no guilt. She sat on her grandmother's living room floor wrapped in a homemade quilt, barely breathing. Her grandmother sat on the sofa, a cross-stitch abandoned on her lap, with her feet firmly planted on the floor. When the fires started, they shared one brief, terrified glance, and then both turned back to the TV.

When the few survivors stumbled out of the compound, Cassie knew better than to search for the faces of her parents. They would have been right next to Him, guns firing, proclaiming their Messiah with bullets and martyrdom. The flames danced— red, orange, billows of black smoke—all of it visible fulfillment of the apocalypse He had prophesied was coming. He saw it, and now the rest of the world saw it too.

"That's it, then," Cassie said, her voice flat and cold.

When her grandmother didn't reply, Cassie turned and looked at her. Grandma sat perfectly still, her pumps neatly polished, skirt smoothed over her knees, hair impeccably set, hands folded in her lap, and tears making silent rivers down her cheeks.

Cassie turned away, and whispered, "It's over."

Later

Cassie woke in the middle of the living room floor, the quilt twisted around her. The sofa was empty, but she could hear her grandmother's voice in the kitchen.

"Well, she got out with a few other children at the beginning of the stand-off." A pause. "No, the FBI wouldn't let her back in." Another pause. "The other children went to Waco's Methodist Home." Another pause. "Well, of course she had to stay here! She's Jack's daughter; where else would she go?"

Cassie breathed slowly and evenly, kept her eyes closed, and pretended to be asleep.

"We haven't heard if they made it out." Silence. "I don't think they did." Her grandmother's voice cracked, and she took a moment before continuing. "The media is all over this like flies on poop. But I don't think they know she's here." Another pause. "Just me, and Janet's mother in Oregon." Pause. "She's sleeping right now, but I'll talk to her about it when she wakes up." Pause. "Thank you. I will. Goodbye."

The phone clicked, and then footsteps came toward her and stopped. She could feel her grandmother staring at her, so she pretended to wake. Her grandmother stood over her with perfect posture, immaculately groomed, and with no traces of tears on her face.

"Would you like something to eat?" she asked.

Cassie just stared at her, unable to respond.

"I can make us some macaroni and cheese."

Cassie kept staring.

Her grandmother's composure cracked, and for a moment her face crumpled like a tissue before it smoothed out again, leaving no trace beyond tears that threatened to overflow.

"We have to eat. And then we have to clean up. We have to brush our teeth, and we have to go to bed. And tomorrow we have to get up and do all this stuff again."

With that she turned and walked back to the kitchen. Cassie got up and followed her. She gathered plates and cutlery and set the table, while her Grandmother boiled water and opened a box of instant macaroni and cheese. When they sat a few minutes later, the bright orange noodles looked Day-Glo optimistic against the blue and white plates.

Cheerful, Cassie thought, looking at her plate. *They're cheerful.* And the thought of eating cheerful food—or even eating at all—on the day of the Apocalypse was so absurd that she had to stifle a giggle.

Her grandmother took a deep breath, as if to will herself into action, picked up her fork, and started eating with grim determination. Neither one of them said grace.

Day 2

Cassie woke to sunshine on her face, the smell of coffee, and the sound of the doorbell. She heard a murmur of voices, the slamming front door, and then a car crunching the driveway gravel as it backed into the street. Ignoring her grandmother's house rule of not appearing downstairs unless ready to accept guests, she wandered down barefoot and in the old-fashioned nightgown her grandmother had loaned her. She walked in on her grandmother slamming kitchen cabinet doors and muttering.

"What's going on?" she asked.

Grandma jumped, took a deep breath, and calmed down a bit. She gestured toward the kitchen table. "Sit. I'll get you breakfast."

"I'm not hungry." Cassie eyed the coffee pot, full to the brim with that forbidden liquid she always thought smelled like home on a cold day. "Can I have coffee?

"May you have coffee?" Her grandmother corrected automatically.

"May I have coffee?"

Grandma nodded, poured her a mug, and one for herself. She handed Cassie hers, then gestured to the cream and sugar. "I need to talk to you."

Cassie kept her eyes on her spoon as she added sugar and cream to her coffee. Her throat dry, she nodded and waited.

"I just had two reporters at the door," Grandma spit out. "Reporters! Parasitic vultures!" She stopped, took a breath, a sip of coffee, and then continued in a calmer tone. "They knew Jack is, was, my son."

Cassie couldn't breathe. Hands shaking, she lowered the coffee cup to the table and clenched her teeth to keep them from chattering.

"If they knew this in such a short time, it will not be long before they discover you are here as well. " She held Cassie's gaze, her blue eyes blazing. "You will not be their next news headline. You will not be paraded on the cover of every paper in this country."

Cassie's legs started shaking. When she tried to lock her knees together, the shaking continued up her whole body.

"We are Hardings. We do not air our dirty laundry in public." She glanced toward the front door. "We need to get you out of here."

"But where?..," Cassie's voice shook. She gripped the coffee cup with both hands and took a cautious sip. It warmed her a bit, so she drank some more.

"Your mother's mother lives in Oregon. She has agreed to have you go and live with her. She has a big house and…"

She kept talking, but white noise filled Cassie's mind, and she could no longer hear anything. When the shaking stopped, a cold stillness took its place. Cassie sat very straight, drank the rest of her coffee, and watched her grandmother's mouth move. When the movement stopped, Cassie nodded.

"OK," she said. And in her mind, even her own voice seemed to come from far away.

Day 6

It was raining when Cassie's plane landed in Portland. Gone was the broad blue sky, flat brown earth, and scorching Texas heat—and a monochromatic watercolor world had taken its place. Even her fellow passengers, dressed in black, taupe, gray, and nondescript blue jeans, matched the wet world outside the window. Cassie, dressed in a pink skirt, pumps, and a spring green sweater, looked out of place, and she knew it. She nervously smoothed her skirt and wished her grandmother had let her wear her old jeans instead of insisting on buying her new, dressy clothes for the trip.

"I want your grandmother to know you are a proper young lady," Grandma explained as she brought Cassie bags of new clothes. "I can't send you up there looking like white trash."

Now, looking at all the other passengers, Cassie knew she wouldn't be wearing most of the new clothes her grandmother had purchased and packed into her new suitcase. Reds, greens, pinks, floral prints—the clothes were those of a Southern minister's wife, not an Oregon teenager. The fashion magazines Cassie had read in-flight showed other girls wearing jeans, leather jackets, and high-high heels—clothes Grandma would have branded "Jezebel clothing." Cassie had a brief memory of sitting in meetings and seeing all the women dressed in floor-length skirts, their hair loose and long. Grandma's clothing choices were fashionable in comparison.

"Just try to fit in," her grandmother told her as she drove her to the airport. "Pay attention. Put all of this," she waved her hand at the window, "behind you. This is your fresh start; don't drag yourself and the rest of the family through the mud by talking about it."

There had been no tears at the airport. Grandma, determined to be part of a normal family saying a normal goodbye, had given Cassie a hug at the gate, and then turned and left before Cassie had boarded the plane.

Can they tell? Cassie thought, looking at the flight attendants and the other passengers. *Am I being normal?*

Of course she had never flown on a plane before. And she had never left the state of Texas before.

After a long flight, the plane arrived at the gate, and passengers began jumping up and grabbing bags just as the fasten seatbelt sign was turned off. Cassie followed the others down the aisle and off the plane. The cold, wet air of the causeway gave way to overheated airport air that smelled of coffee and too many hours on a plane. She stopped just inside the airport and looked.

Masses of people swarmed and teemed, and each one seemed to move with purpose. Other passengers pushed past her, jostling her to the side, where she froze and tried to figure out what to do next.

She said she would meet me here, Cassie thought, desperately searching the scurrying mass to find someone who looked familiar.

But the movement and the chaos were disorienting. She closed her eyes for a second and took a deep breath. *It's a fugue,* she told herself. *It's a Bach fugue. Just find one subject and follow it all the way through.* A middle-aged man in a business suit walked past her, and Cassie fell in behind him. One step, then the next, then the next. The crowd seemed to part for him. She kept walking until she nearly brushed past an older woman standing just outside the gate area.

"Cassie?"

Cassie stopped and turned to her. "Grandma?"

The woman had Cassie's mother's eyes. And as she searched Cassie's face, her eyes filled, and she stepped toward Cassie as if to hug her. Cassie froze. The woman dropped her arms to her sides.

"You look just like your mother," she said.

Cassie nodded and swallowed hard. The white noise had crept back into her mind, and the shaking threatened to start again as well. She looked at the crowd—the fugue was gone, replaced by random chaos. The businessman was gone. Even the sound seemed to have been muted. She pulled herself up to her full 5'2" and looked at her grandmother.

"Where do we get my suitcase?" she asked.

Day 8

Cassie got her period her second day in Roseburg. It surprised her that her body kept functioning when the rest of her had come to an end. There, in her JC Penney cotton underpants, proof that her body had gone on living even if she felt dead. All the normal occupations of life—eating, eliminating, sleeping, waking—felt like an affront. Embarrassed, she wadded up toilet paper and waited half the day before telling Maureen (Grandma insisted she call her Maureen, not Grandma) she needed some tampons.

"Oh, of course. I didn't think…" She gave Cassie a wry look. "It has been a few years for me." She smiled encouragingly at her. "Would you like to go to the store with me?"

Cassie shook her head. "No, thank you." Then, seeing Maureen's disappointment, she added, "I feel sorta headachy and crampy."

Cassie wandered through the house after Maureen's car disappeared down the street. It had been late when they'd first arrived, and Cassie, who had fallen asleep in the car on the way to Roseburg, woke just long enough to stumble into the house, remove her clothes, and crawl into bed before falling asleep again. She slept much of the next day, waking just to take a long bath and to have meals with Maureen.

Rain beat against the roof and through the windows, the sodden greens and browns seemed to merge with the gray sky. The house was so quiet Cassie could hear the hum of the refrigerator. Despite what her Texas grandmother had told her, Maureen did not have a large house. It was a two-bedroom, one-bath bungalow, surrounded by what looked to be wet greenery. Her room was on the back side of the home and housed a single bed, a dresser, a desk and chair, and a closet half filled with the Texas clothes. When

Maureen first showed her the room, she told her she could decorate it any way she wished. Beyond hanging her clothes in the closet, Cassie left the rest of the room as she found it. She had never had a room of her own before.

She prowled through the rest of the house—the small kitchen with its antique cupboards and tile countertops, the living room with a woodstove, sofa, easy chairs, and the TV and stereo tucked in one corner. The walls looked as though they were made of books. Cassie studied the titles and didn't recognize any of them. He wouldn't allow books. He wouldn't allow TV. He was the Word, and they needed no other. The only books Cassie had ever seen were the Bible and the textbooks Texas required as part of the state homeschooling program and she felt guilty even studying the spines of these books.

She walked back to her bedroom and paced the floor with a restlessness that she knew could be calmed if Maureen owned a piano. Her fingers itched to play. She tried not to think of the music and the piano she loved, now turned to ashes with the rest of the compound. She thought instead of the brand new sheet music Grandma had purchased for her during the siege. Opening her top dresser drawer, she pulled out the stack of books, sat on her bed, opened the Schubert, and entered the music. With no piano, she drummed the notes on her lap. But even this late, darker Impromptu seemed emotionally overwrought, and Cassie shut the music after the first page. She picked up Bach and turned to the Fugue in C Major.

This felt better—no emotions, no soaring melodic lines, just clean and clear lines, as clear and cool as glacier ice. The rain, the house, and even the bedroom disappeared as Cassie followed Bach's winding threads, his concise, decisive voice making each step inevitable but not predictable. She played through the middle section several times and then played the entire fugue. It bothered her that she couldn't always hear the inner lines in her head. Stopping, she played just the alto line, and then the tenor line.

Better. Starting again, she ran the entire fugue, and in her mind she could hear the bell-like tone of her Grandmother's Baldwin, as well as the out-of-tune upright Chickering she had learned on at the compound.

She played until she reached the end of the fugue. Looking up, she jumped as she saw Maureen standing in the doorway watching her. Maureen wiped her eyes. Cassie looked at her hands, unsure of what to say to this stranger who was now her family.

"I've put your things in the bathroom," Maureen said.

"Thanks," Cassie whispered.

"I didn't know you played the piano," Maureen said.

I didn't know you existed, Cassie thought. "Yes, one of the women at Mount Carmel taught me."

And then she was there, sitting at the old upright, with Ruby holding a pencil in her teeth and demonstrating right-hand fingering in the Impromptu. Ruby, with her dark flashing eyes and Master's degree in piano performance. Did she make it out? Cassie shivered.

Maureen sighed. "I guess we'll need to find you some piano lessons."

Cassie nodded. The magic of the fugue had disappeared. Outside, the rain shifted direction and pelted against the glass. Cassie closed the Bach with a sigh.

Chapter 2

It continued to rain, and behind the glass, there was a melting world of brown and green and gray. *The sky is weeping,* Cassie thought idly as she sat on the piano bench waiting for Dr. White to find a piece of music in his shelves of scores. She had been nervous when Maureen had told her that she had made an audition appointment for Cassie with the piano teacher at the community college where Maureen worked. According to Maureen, Umpqua Community College had an unusually strong music department because of Dr. White's leadership. It took Cassie several minutes to stop shaking when she first entered his studio.

Cassie watched him as he flipped through another stack of music, thinking that with his gray hair, gray cardigan sweater he should have been named Dr. Gray instead of White. She looked back at the window. It hadn't stopped raining since she'd arrived in Roseburg two weeks ago, and she was beginning to wonder if Oregon ever got sunshine.

"Ah, here we go." Dr. White brought the score to the piano. "Have you played any of Barber's music?"

Cassie shook her head. He opened the *Excursions* score and placed it on the music rack. "Would you like me to play a bit of it for you?" he asked.

She nodded and stood. He sat on the bench, adjusted his glasses, and started playing the first piece in the suite. With the first notes, the gray fell away and Cassie was on a train, rolling through a hot and flat Texas landscape with a sky as big as forever. He stopped playing in the middle of the second page, and Cassie opened her eyes.

"What do you think?" he asked. "Do you like it?"

"Oh, yes sir," Cassie replied. "It's neat." She coul\ word to describe the hot sunshine, dust, and motion of th\

A shadow crossed Dr. White's face. "Neat. Well, I'm ɔɩad you like it. Want to hear a bit of the other movements before you decide?"

Cassie nodded, her face red and hot. It was her first lesson with him, and she knew she had disappointed him. She had played her Bach Prelude and Fugue, and the Schubert Impromptu better than she'd expected, but had no other music to play. When he asked about the rest of her music, she told him it had been burned up in a house fire.

Fit in, she told herself, *fit in*. She listened closely to the other movements, shutting out imagery in favor of intellectual analysis. He finished playing the first page of the last movement and turned to her again.

"I, uh, like the cross-rhythms in the, um, third movement," she offered.

He nodded. "Do you think you might like to learn this?"

"Yes, sir," she replied. "Very much, sir."

He turned back to the score. "I have an extra copy of this, so you may work from my score until you can get your own." He looked at Cassie's book of Preludes and Fugues. "And start working on the D major fugue," he added. "We'll try to find you something Romantic and Classical next lesson." He handed the music to Cassie.

"You play very, very well," he stated with a smile. "What are your career plans?"

Cassie ducked her head. "I, uh, don't know. I haven't thought about it."

He nodded. "Plenty of time. You're young. In the meantime, please talk to Janice at the front desk and get yourself signed up for time in the practice rooms."

Cassie nodded. "Thank you, sir. See you next week."

She walked out of the office and smiled at Maureen, who sat waiting just outside the door.

"So? How'd it go?" Maureen asked. "Is he willing to teach you?"

"Um, Yeah, I think," Cassie replied. "It was good. I like him. And I got some new music." She handed Maureen the book. "He says we need to buy me my own copy."

"Not a problem," Maureen replied. "And did he say whether or not you may practice here?"

Cassie smiled. "He told me to sign up for practice times on my way out."

Maureen looked relieved. "I just wish I could afford to buy you your own piano," she said. "But this will have to do."

After signing Cassie up for practice times, they walked across the community college campus to the cafeteria. Cassie had the hood of her raincoat up over her head; Maureen and everyone else walked bareheaded as if it were dry. There wasn't a single umbrella in sight.

"Um, Maureen?" Cassie asked as she wiped a drop of rain off her nose. "Why doesn't anyone have umbrellas?"

Maureen glanced around and then laughed. It was a rich and deep laugh, which belied Maureen's stiff shoulders and usually tight lips.

"I think it's because it rains so much that drizzle is our natural habitat." She gave Cassie a small smile. "You'll get used to it."

Cassie wiped more rain off her face. "If you say so."

The cafeteria was mostly empty. Maureen ordered hot chocolates for both of them, and two enormous sugar cookies from a bored college student with shoe-polish black hair and so many piercings that Cassie thought she looked like her grandmother's pin cushion. They found a table close to the window and started snacking on the cookies while they waited for their drinks. Cassie looked at her shoes—bubble-gum pink canvas Keds thoroughly soaked through. She was beginning to understand why all the girls at the mall wore chunky black boots. Both Grandma and Mom had told her that black was too severe for her. But that was Texas, not Oregon. Maybe she would have to be severe to survive a world that never saw sunshine.

The memory came in a flash. For just a second, she sat in the shade of a cottonwood tree with Mom, sunlight dappling her lap as Mom braided her hair. Then all the air left her lungs, and the numbness crept back in. She stared at the raindrops and tried to count each one as they slid down the grass. The chasm that had opened beneath her feet closed, her breath returned, and the memory disappeared as if it had never been. Maureen, who had gone to the counter to pick up their drinks, noticed nothing. When she returned and placed the cup in front of her, Cassie wrapped her hands around it long enough for the shaking to subside.

"I hope you don't mind that I want to go to the first session with you," Maureen was saying. "We're both in uncharted territory, and I need some guidance as well."

Cassie stared at her. *Session? What session?* Then she remembered Maureen telling her a week ago that she needed to meet with a therapist to help "process the experience." She hadn't responded at the time, and she'd hoped Maureen had forgotten all about visiting a counselor. In fact, she had been making a special effort to be normal and friendly all week so Maureen would know she didn't need therapy.

"I thought I was being normal," Cassie said, shame snaking through her.

Maureen stared out the window, her lips tight. "I don't think it is about being normal. I just don't know how to help you, or me." She took a deep breath. "I messed up with your mother. I don't want to do the same with you."

They were silent for a few minutes. Finally Cassie nodded, her mouth dry. "OK. I'll go. For you."

The doctor's office—Dr. Giles, or Tim as he insisted on being called when he first met Cassie--was located in one of the old brick buildings in downtown Roseburg. Cassie shuffled into his office behind Maureen, sat on the overstuffed sofa, and stared at the new shoes Maureen had let her buy the day after her piano lesson. They were black leather, with chunky heels, and they gleamed against the tan carpet and the legs of Cassie's new blue jeans. With the shoes, jeans, and new brown sweater she wore, Cassie hoped she looked more like an Oregonian. The dark colors made her feel protected and powerful in a way the pastels never did.

"...I've got her enrolled in piano lessons, and I have spoken to the Department of Education about testing her grade level..."

Cassie tuned out and tried to hear the bass line of the Barber piece, hoping the memory of it would put her back on that train. But her knowledge of the piece was too sketchy to transport her, and she tried to go back into the white noise instead. Tim's voice pulled her out.

"Cassie?"

She looked up. Both Tim and Maureen were staring at her, obviously waiting for an answer.

"Pardon?" she asked.

"I wanted to know how you like Oregon," Tim asked.

Cassie gave him a polite smile. "I like it. It rains a lot."

Tim laughed. "That's an understatement. " He smiled at her. "Your grandmother tells me you're taking piano lessons. Do you like your new teacher?"

Cassie sat up straight. "Yes. He seems very professional. "

Tim and Maureen exchanged a look. Maureen opened her mouth to speak, and Tim silenced her with a glance. "What music are you playing?"

"Samuel Barber *Excursions* and the D Major Prelude and Fugue from Book I by J.S. Bach," Cassie replied, carefully folding her hands in her lap. "I get to practice at the college."

Tim crossed his legs. "Do you know why your grandmother brought you here?"

Cassie shot Maureen a glance. "Maureen said she needed me to be here for her, that she was having a difficult time dealing with, um, well the fire and everything. I am fine, but she needed me here so."

Tim gave her a gentle smile. "It's very generous of you to come in here today to help Maureen," he told her.

Maureen's eyes filled, and she bit her lip and turned away.

"It's OK to need help," Tim said. "The bravest people are the ones who ask for help when they need it. " He stopped as if waiting for a response. "Do you understand what it is that I do?"

Cassie nodded. "You work with crazy people." She shot a glance at Maureen. "Not you, of course."

Maureen's mouth twitched as she suppressed a smile. Cassie turned back to Tim.

"Well, most of the people I work with are not crazy," Tim replied. "Most of them are just having a hard time living with some tough life experiences. They talk to me, and I listen, and over time they start feeling better."

Cassie watched him without expression. *He's so earnest,* she thought, staring at the wrinkle between his eyebrows, *like a cocker spaniel.* She felt a flash of anger. He worked in this comfortable office, in a normal town, and was a normal person. For him and for everyone else, the Apocalypse had never happened—it was just some news story that Maureen switched off every time pictures of the fire or of Janet Reno showed up on TV.

"What am I supposed to do?" she asked politely, allowing none of her anger to show in her voice or on her face.

Maureen leaned toward her. "Tim and I want you to talk to him," she said. "You could visit him once a week, right after your piano lesson. You could talk to him about anything you want, and he wouldn't tell anyone—not even me. How would you feel about that?"

Cassie stared at her clenched hands. *Feel? I feel nothing,* she thought. She looked at Maureen and then at Tim. Now both of them wore that earnest, caring, cocker spaniel expression she was beginning to hate. They both wanted her to agree so badly. She swallowed hard.

"That would be nice."

Both Maureen and Tim smiled and relaxed. Maureen got out her calendar and checkbook while Tim stood and walked over to a desk tucked into the corner. Cassie looked at her jeans, her new shoes, and her soft brown sweater, and thought, *I really need to get some more clothes like these.*

That night she dreamed of Texas. She sat next to her father in the cab of the old blue pick-up truck, bouncing down a dusty dirt road. The heat was a palpable force—dry, heavy, and unrelenting. Both truck windows were rolled down and Cassie's hair whipped around her face. Dad hummed along with the country song playing on the radio, his weather-beaten fingers tapping time on the steering wheel.

Cassie didn't know where they were driving or where they had come from. It didn't matter. She smelled the dust and the heat and the Ivory soap her father showered with each day. He turned and smiled at her.

"You're getting to be just about as pretty as your Mom," he said, reaching over with one hand and pinching her cheek.

They came to an intersection and stopped. Cassie looked both ways for cars, and when she looked back at her father, he was no longer there. The roads were empty and there was nothing on the horizon except a huge blue sky and miles of sagebrush. She crawled into the driver's seat and stared at the dash. She knew she couldn't stay in the middle of the desert, but also knew she didn't know how to drive and had no idea where she was going, even if she could drive. She sat, paralyzed, as the heat and silence of the wilderness pressed her further and further into the dust.

She woke crying—great hiccupping sobs that seemed to come from a place that wasn't even human. The house was dark and silent, except for the sound of the rain running through the downspout outside her window. Cassie buried her face in her pillow until the crying stopped, and just as she started drifting back to sleep, she thought, *I need to learn how to drive.*

Chapter 3

The first thing Cassie noticed when she woke Sunday morning of her third week in Oregon was the silence. No rain pelted the window or ran down the spout. The second thing she noticed was warmth on her face. She opened her eyes to see sunshine seeping through the white cotton curtains, and to the sound of a bird chirping. She crawled out from under the covers, walked barefoot to the window, and pulled back the curtains.

The sunshine flooded her and for a second she closed her eyes, curled her toes into the carpet, and just breathed in the warmth. Then she peered through the glass at a world of green. Young, pale green tree leaves gave way to medium green grass thicker than carpet, rimmed by deep forest evergreens. Still wet, everything glistened. In the flowerbed underneath the window she saw hyacinths and daffodils, as well as some tulips that looked nearly ready to open. At the edge of the forest a deer stood staring in Cassie's direction. She watched it, transfixed, until it twitched its ears and stepped back into the cover of the evergreens.

Cassie remembered listening to the story of Bambi when she was little. With the deer, the forest, the grass, and the trees, it seemed for a moment that she had stepped into the world she'd only imagined back then. *An emerald world*, she thought, turning from the window and walking out of the bedroom.

Maureen sat in the living room, a steaming mug of coffee in one hand and the paper in the other. Her ruby-red reading glasses were perched low on her nose, and her short, steel-gray hair stuck up a bit in the back. Like Cassie, she wore pajamas and was barefoot. She looked up as Cassie came into the room, smiled, and put the paper down.

"Good morning," she said. "Did you sleep well?"

"I didn't know you got sunshine in Oregon," Cassie blurted and then blushed.

Maureen smiled and nodded. "We have a saying about spring in Oregon: if you don't like the weather, wait five minutes and it will change." She put her coffee cup down and ran her hands through her hair.

Cassie eyed the coffee. It smelled wonderful. "May I have coffee?" she asked.

"Where did you get this coffee habit?" Maureen asked, walking into the kitchen with Cassie. "I thought Davideans couldn't have caffeine. "

Cassie froze. Then Maureen froze. Neither of them spoke for a second. Maureen reached out and touched Cassie's arm. "I'm so sorry," she whispered.

Cassie shrugged. "It's OK. He was the only one who got coffee. The rest of us weren't allowed. After the, well, you know, Grandma let me have some."

A look of pure hatred crossed Maureen's face. "He had coffee? No one else?" She pulled another mug out of the cupboard. "Well. Then you get coffee anytime you wish!" She poured, handed Cassie the full mug, and pushed the cream and sugar across the counter to her. "Cream and sugar?"

Cassie added both to her coffee and then took a sip. Meeting Maureen's eyes over the rim of her mug, she felt a delicious thrill of breaking the rules and getting approval for doing it. The warmth of the coffee, the sunshine coming through the kitchen window, and Maureen's friendliness sent a jolt of pure pleasure through her, and in that moment she realized she was happy for the first time in months.

The rain returned a few hours later, and with it, guilt. The force of her self-loathing took Cassie's breath away. *You forgot, you forgot, you forgot.* She looked at the book she had been reading— F. Scott Fizgerald's <u>The Great Gatsby</u>—and fought the urge to hurl it across the room. Vivaldi played on the stereo. A fire crackled in the woodstove. Maureen sat across the room, a gardening magazine open on her lap. Cassie stared out the window and focused on breathing away the blackness that threatened to engulf her. In the glass she saw her mother's face. She didn't know she'd cried out until Maureen's voice broke the spell.

"Cassie? Are you alright?" Somehow Maureen had crossed the room and was now sitting beside her on the sofa.

Cassie jumped and noticed for the first time that her face was wet with tears. "I forgot."

Maureen looked confused. "Forgot?"

"They're gone and I'm here, being happy," she took a deep breath, "and drinking coffee." She looked at Maureen and watched the older woman struggle for something to say. *I don't even know who you are,* Cassie thought. "Everyone I know is dead."

The words she had blurted hung there. Maureen shivered. Cassie saw bleakness, fear, and finally determination in her face. *She doesn't want me here,* Cassie thought. *She's making the best of it, just like I am.*

"I almost met you once," Maureen said. "You were six months old. It was when your grandfather died and your parents came up to Oregon for the funeral." She took a deep breath. "I wanted to know you."

But they didn't let you, Cassie silently finished in her mind. "I didn't know anyone on the outside," she said.

Maureen reached out her hand and gave Cassie's arm an awkward, tentative pat. "We're going to make this work, Cassie. You're going to be fine."

Cassie heard the words, but the doubt in Maureen's voice spoke more loudly than any assurance she could offer. *She has no idea what to do*, Cassie thought. *And if she doesn't know, who does?* She fought more panic, focusing her attention on the lines of Vivaldi.

"I'll be fine," Cassie replied, her voice holding more conviction than she felt.

Monday morning, Maureen prepared to return to work and Cassie tried not to panic. The last few weeks had felt awkward and stilted, but at least she wasn't alone. Maureen wore a boxy business suit that made her formal manner even more intimidating. She greeted Cassie with a nod, poured herself coffee, and then handed Cassie a schedule she had written out for her.

"I've arranged for our neighbor Stella to take you to the college library today," Maureen explained. "Don't forget to meet with Matt for your tutoring at 11."

Cassie nodded, her mouth dry. Although they had discussed Maureen's return to work, and Tim had helped Cassie and Maureen construct the schedule, Cassie was sure she'd mess everything up. Maureen had introduced her to Matt several days ago, and now she worried if she would remember what he looked like. Was he a student? A young teacher? Cassie couldn't remember. She looked at the schedule, which Maureen had written on a map of the community college campus. Maureen had drawn highlighter lines among the music building, the library, the cafeteria, and the Dean's office, where Maureen worked as an administrative assistant.

"You have my number," Maureen continued, in between sips of coffee. "And don't forget to bring your music so you can practice after lunch."

Cassie nodded again, and tried to focus through the white noise starting to creep up on her. She focused on breathing in and breathing out. Had Tim said something about that? She couldn't remember. She just tried to give him the right answers when she dutifully visited him each week. Maureen picked up her purse and umbrella and then shrugged into her raincoat. Cassie's face must have mirrored her panic because Maureen stopped and gave her a gentle smile.

"It's all going to be OK," she reassured. "I'll see you tonight."

She walked out of the house, and Cassie listened to her start the car and back out of the driveway. The sound of the engine dissolved the white noise and Cassie listened until she could no longer hear Maureen's car and then pulled down a mug and poured herself coffee. The house was so silent it felt as if it was holding its breath. She took a sip of coffee, and then another. Her thoughts raced ahead to the day, and she tried to keep still and quiet as one "what if" after another hit her.

What if I can't find the library? What if I can't find Matt? What if I'm so stupid Matt thinks I don't know anything? What if I don't know anything? What if?

A truck backfired as it drove past the house. The sound ricocheted around the kitchen, and Cassie startled so violently that she spilled half her coffee all over the table.

It's not a gunshot, she reassured herself as she mopped up coffee with shaking hands. *It's not a gunshot*. It did little to stop the shaking or the memory.

Shots, screams, people running, people yelling. Cassie felt the broken glass crunching under her shoes before she forced the memory out of her mind and brought herself back to Maureen's kitchen. She stared at the creepy moving eyes and tail of the Kit-Kat clock on the wall until her breathing slowed.

You have to take a shower, she told herself. *You have to figure out how to be normal and fit in.*

The panic rose again when she realized she didn't really know what normal looked like. She thought of the girls at the mall with their blackened hair, multiple piercings, and dark, knowing eyes. They moved like packs of feral cats—slinky, sexy, and swaggering with bravado. If that was normal, Cassie knew she would fail. She stared at the table top and tried to pick out all the colors in the wood grain, and the more she focused, the more the panic melted away.

Of course, she thought. *It's like playing a piece from memory. Just focus on the notes you're playing.* The mantra in her head became, *focus on the notes, focus on the notes.* She kept repeating it as she showered and dressed, and she said it as she dried her long hair. She mentally rehearsed the new Chopin piece Dr. White had given her, focusing on hearing each phrase perfectly and expressively. Each time the panic started rising, she re-rehearsed whatever phrase she had been reviewing. In that way, the Chopin became an undercurrent of sound that carried her through breakfast, meeting Stella, the short ride to campus in Stella's Honda Civic, and into the library. With several hours to fill until her tutoring appointment, she settled into a chair in the corner of the periodical section with a stack of fashion magazines on her lap. The smiling, perfect faces of the models were a window into a world of sunshine, glamour, and non-stop fun. There were articles on applying eye shadow, articles on dating advice, and articles on how to dress. Cassie read them all, carefully memorizing each suggestion and noting the sleek glossiness of the women. They all looked perfect; they all looked happy; and they were surrounded by gorgeous men.

They're popular, Cassie thought. *That's what popular looks like.*

She looked down at her jeans, her chunky black shoes, and the nubby texture of her gray sweater. The outfit matched what most of the other girls in the library were wearing, but looked clunky and awkward compared to the models. They were perfect. Their skin and teeth and hair and eyes seemed to glow with well-being and beauty. They were at the center of everything, and they knew it. And surely nothing bad ever happened to people who lived in the center of everything. They had normal parents and normal neighborhoods and went to normal schools and went to proms and clubs and had dates with boys. The sun was always shining in the center of everything. Cassie looked around the library and began to realize that Roseburg was nowhere near the center of anything.

I'll get out of here, she promised herself. *I will be pretty and popular and in the center of everything, and then I'll be safe.*

She turned back to the magazines and continued reading with renewed determination.

Chapter 4

On the day of Cassie's first performance in Dr. White's piano master class, the temperature hit 90 degrees. The cool, dark interior of Jacoby Auditorium provided relief from the freakishly warm June day, and within ten minutes of entering the hall, Cassie was glad she had brought a light cotton jacket to wear over her tank top.

A semi-circle of chairs surrounded the keyboard end of one of the 9-foot grand pianos on the stage, and most of them were filled with students who all seemed to know each other. Cassie took a seat at the end of the row and tried to look inconspicuous. Dr. White had not yet arrived, and she hugged her music to her chest and watched the other students. She guessed they ranged in age from fifteen to twenty or twenty-one, and there seemed to be an even split of boys and girls. A few of them glanced at Cassie, but no one said anything to her. She shrank back in her chair and looked anxiously about for Dr. White. Two boys sat at the piano playing something jazzy that Cassie didn't recognize.

"Sorry I'm late everybody," Dr. White announced as he rushed into the room.

He sat down next to Cassie. The two pianists left the piano and sat back in their chairs while all the other conversations quieted. He smiled at the group before continuing.

"Before we get started today, I want to introduce our newest pianist, Cassie Carlyle."

Everyone looked at Cassie. She blushed, gave a little wave, and said, "Howdy." She had taken Maureen's last name a few weeks ago and was still getting used to hearing it as her own.

"Cassie comes to us from Texas. She is a fine pianist and will be taking classes here fall semester." He smiled at Cassie, then turned back to the group. "Now, who would like to play first today?"

No one said anything. Cassie held her breath. *Am I supposed to volunteer?* Ruby had told her about recitals and master classes, but Cassie had never been part of either one. Cassie glanced nervously around the room and avoided eye contact with Dr. White. Finally a girl with bleached hair and a lip ring raised her hand.

"I'll go," she said as she stood. She handed her music to Dr. White and walked to the piano. "I'll be playing Rachmaninoff's Prelude in C-sharp Minor."

She settled herself on the bench and launched herself into the first three notes. Cassie jumped. She had never heard anyone play the opening notes so forcefully; when she had learned the piece herself a year ago, Ruby had insisted on her keeping a round, elegant tone, despite the dynamic marking. The girl played the rest of the page beautifully, but started the triplets at breakneck speed. They fell apart in the middle, and the rest of the section was a muddy mess of missed notes and over-pedaling. She got through the last double-staff section with lots of fire but questionable accuracy. At the end of the piece, the girl released the notes, scowled, took a half-hearted bow, and slumped into her seat.

"Thank you, Shanna," Dr. White said, appearing to notice nothing of Shanna's scowl or how she was furiously picking at a hangnail on her right thumb "Who would like to start the discussion?"

A timid girl seated two chairs from Cassie raised her hand. "I thought it was really good," she offered. Shanna smiled at her.

"Thank you, Chloe. Anyone else?" Dr. White looked at the group.

One of the guys who had been playing the piano before class raised his hand. "I thought it was really powerful," he said. "I think she just needs to work on those triplets."

"Good point, Eric," Dr. White said.

Cassie listened with growing confusion as student after student said the piece was wonderful and offered little or no advice on how to fix what was, in Cassie's opinion, a musical train wreck. If she had played it like that for Ruby, there would have been no end to the suggestions Ruby would make to clean up the piece. Did these students have no idea of how the Prelude was supposed to go? And how was Shanna supposed to fix the problems if she didn't even know what they were? When the last student finished praising the performance, and giving crumbs of suggestions for change, Dr. White turned to her.

"Cassie, would you like to offer Shanna any feedback?"

She gave him a startled look. "Me? But I'm new here."

"Yes, but in my master class, everyone contributes by both playing and giving suggestions to the other players," he responded.

Cassie gulped. Shanna gave her a challenging look. She gulped again. "OK. Well, I thought it was..." she searched for a word that would be honest but not insulting, "forceful."

Shanna smirked. Dr. White nodded and said, "Do you have any suggestions for improvement?"

"Um, well, it's a really hard piece," Cassie began, warming as Shanna smiled again. "I played it last year, and my teacher suggested that I practice the triplets in chords first so I really learned them, and then never took that section too fast once I went back to playing the notes as written so I wouldn't lose control of it." She paused and took a breath. "And the last section with the double staff is easier to play cleanly if you learn it really well one hand at a time before trying to put them together."

There was silence in the room as she finished speaking. No one looked at her, and no one looked at Shanna. Shanna looked straight at Cassie, fury making her brown eyes glitter like rocks.

"Whatever, Miss Texas," she drawled, and then scanned the room for the nervous laugh she got from several of the other students.

Cassie gasped, "I didn't mean—"

"Cassie's suggestions were correct," Dr. White said, interrupting Cassie's apology. "And she stated them in a respectful manner. She gave the kind of critique I want all of you to give—practical advice that each of you can take to your practices to improve the music."

No one spoke. Shanna looked at the floor and shrugged. Cassie held her breath, alternately fearing she would pass out, throw up, or both. Dr. White looked at the tall boy sitting next to Shanna.

"Eric, would you like to play next?" he asked.

Eric nodded, and handed Dr. White his music as he walked to the piano. "I'll be playing Bach's Prelude in C-sharp Major, Book One," he announced before sitting down and adjusting the height of the bench.

He started playing, and the notes flew from his fingers with what Cassie could only describe as a shimmery sound. It was dancing light, crystals throwing prisms around the room, she thought, and each note was perfectly balanced with the next. Tall and thin, Eric was all limbs and big hands, but the touch was as delicate as anything Cassie had ever heard. When he stopped playing and the applause started, she realized she had been holding her breath.

I want to play that Prelude just like that, she thought as class members started commenting on the performance. And when Dr. White asked her opinion of the piece, all she could think to say was, "It was stunning."

Eric smiled at her, and for a brief second they made eye contact before Cassie dropped her gaze. She listened as two other players ran through movements of sonatinas, and then Dr. White turned to her and asked her to play. She didn't look at Shanna or Eric, and she tried to avoid eye contact with any of the other players in the room. Handing her score to Dr. White, she walked to the piano, announced that she was playing the first movement of the Barber *Excursions*, put the bench where she wanted it, and then closed her eyes.

The train was there waiting for her, its dusty, creaky wheels rolling through the hot and flat Texas landscape. She heard the first measure in her head, opened her eyes, placed her hands on the keys, and started to play. She thought of everything Ruby had told her about how to tell stories and paint pictures with the notes, and she focused on the motion of the train, the smell of dust and sagebrush, and the flat pressure of a hot sun. Except for a few notes dropped at the top of the C-minor scale passage, the movement seemed to play itself. She finished the last notes, put her hands in her lap, and then waited through a brief silence before the class started applauding.

I just played my first public performance, she thought as she stood, bowed, and then walked back to her chair. *That was so much fun!* Eric met her eyes again, an impressed half smile on his face. Shanna crossed her arms and stared at the ceiling as if bored. Dr. White started the bid for suggestions, and the first three students gave glowing responses. Then Dr. White asked Shanna for her opinion.

"Well, it was good and all," she drawled. "But the ending was a little, you know, abrupt. And I've found that if you practice scale passages slowly, it is easier to play them cleanly." She held Cassie's gaze, a challenge.

"Thank you, Shanna," Dr. White responded. "Cassie played the ending as Barber wrote it, but the suggestion about the scale passage is a good one."

Cassie nodded, "Thanks, Shanna."

The rest of the class passed quickly. After Dr. White dismissed the class, Cassie stood off to the side as students put away folding chairs and stood talking to each other in small groups. She had just turned to leave when Eric walked up to her.

"You're amazing," he said. "How long have you been working on that?"

Cassie smiled and blushed. "Just since April, when I moved here. " She forced herself to make eye contact with him. "You're really good too," she added. "You played that Bach like a dream."

He shrugged. "Thanks. But I've been working on it since January. I'd better be able to play it by now."

Shanna walked up and tugged at Eric's arm," Hey, a group of us are going to the cafeteria to get coffee. Wanna go?" She didn't look at Cassie, and it was clear the invitation did not include her.

Eric shrugged again. "Sure." He turned to Cassie. "Wanna come along?"

She blinked, surprised. "Um, sure."

Shanna gave her a fake smile, "Oh, yeah. You can come too, if you want." She pulled Eric with her, leaving Cassie to follow with a skinny, pony-tailed girl whose name she had forgotten.

"I'm Naomi," the girl said, and when she smiled, Cassie noticed she had a mouth full of braces. "Ignore her; she's a bitch."

In all her nearly seventeen years of life, Cassie had never heard anyone call anyone else a bitch. She was both stunned and thrilled. It may not have been nice, but it was accurate, and at least Naomi was willing to call a spade a spade, as her Grandmother would have stated it. Just for a second she had a mental image of Grandma, with her Ann Richards hair, pastel dresses and suits, and perfectly polished shoes. Maureen made her call Grandma every two weeks—conversations Cassie found very uncomfortable as both she and Grandma had to spend the whole conversation trying to appear happy and normal to the other.

They stepped outside the auditorium, and the heat and sunshine caressed Cassie's face and made her want to stop and drink in as much of both as she could.

"I've missed sunshine," Cassie said to Naomi as they followed the rest of the group across the lawn.

"Is it really hot down there?" Naomi asked. "I've never been to Texas. I've never been anywhere except California," she admitted.

"It's hot," Cassie said. "And dry. By July you can fry eggs on the sidewalks."

Naomi gaped at her. "No!"

"Yes," Cassie replied with a slight laugh. "The ground gets so hot that it feels like being baked top down and bottom up."

"What part of Texas are you from," Eric asked as he slowed down to walk beside Cassie and Naomi. Shanna gave them a disgusted glance and then walked on with two others girls as though she didn't care.

"Waco," Cassie replied automatically, then froze. She and Grandma had decided she would tell people she was from Dallas, but somehow she'd forgotten, and now the truth was out there, ugly and dangerous, and she could do nothing to take it back.

Shanna stopped and turned around, "You're not one of those Waco Whackos are you?"

Cassie couldn't breathe. Her mind raced, and she fought to keep the white noise from flooding everything. "No," she lied.

One of Shanna's friends slapped her arm, "Great one, Shanna! Waco Whacko!"

"Well, I think the government really fucked that situation up," Naomi said. "Their civil rights were abused!" She turned to Cassie. "What were they saying about that in Waco?"

Cassie was shaking, and all she could think to do was put down one foot and then the other, and keep breathing. Words she had hardly ever heard and never dared voice left her lips before she could think to stop them. "They said Janet Reno is a fucking bitch," she replied with more heat than she had intended.

The whole group, even Shanna, started laughing.

"And she looks like a bull-dyke lesbian," Shanna added. "I mean, what the hell is up with that hair?"

Everyone laughed again, this time harder. Cassie felt relief pour through her with so much force that her knees nearly buckled. They believed her! And they thought she was funny. And she had said "fucking bitch" in front of everyone and no one got mad at her. She ran the phrase over in her mind, fucking bitch, fucking bitch. It felt so liberating to just say it.

"If I ever look like that, shoot me," Naomi added. Her wiry frame and long, dark pony tail made such a contrast to Reno that everyone laughed again.

Eric reached over and patted her on the head. "Don't worry," he reassured her, "you're going to grow up to be a good lipstick lesbian!"

"Asshole!" She swatted at his hand, missed him, and then clobbered him with her book bag.

The group was still laughing as they entered the cafeteria. Cassie ordered a latte, iced, and joined the rest of the group huddled around two tables they'd pushed together. The conversation moved to the upcoming Umpqua Symphony concerto competition.

"I'm playing the first movement of the Schumann," Shanna announced. "It's so passionate. Dr. White thinks I have the right temperament to play it."

"Have you started working on it?" Eric asked.

"Just got it yesterday at my lesson," Shanna replied. "I've been listening to it non-stop since then."

"Which recording?" Naomi asked.

"Richter, with the Warsaw National," Shanna replied. She turned to Cassie. "Are you planning to compete?"

Cassie shrugged and looked at her fingers resting on the table top. "I don't know. I don't have anything in my hands right now."

Eric smiled at her. "It's OK. The competition isn't until the end of September."

Cassie nodded. "I guess I'll wait and see what Dr. White suggests," she said. But inside she could feel a flicker of excitement that caused her to first try to squash it because she probably wouldn't be allowed to compete, and then euphoria at knowing that He wasn't there and couldn't tell her what to do about anything anymore.

Later, as she sat in the library waiting for Maureen to finish work, Cassie thought of Him and the hot Waco summers--and most of all of her parents--and felt sick. She knew she had betrayed them, and in some small way it seemed as though she had betrayed herself as well. Just as quickly as she thought it, she remembered Grandma telling her to fit in, to tell no one about Him or the Apocalypse, and to be normal. She looked at the fashion magazines on her lap; in the two months since moving to Roseburg, she had read and nearly memorized them. Every one of them promised that anyone could make over their lives, start fresh, and be someone new. She thought of her new friends and wondered what they would want her to be. The magazines offered the perfect teenage template.

I am pretty, popular, and normal, Cassie decided. *In Waco I dated a football player*, she thought a moment, *named Ryan. I dumped him when I moved to Oregon because I didn't want to be tied down.* She smiled. *My parents were rich. Dad ran a car dealership, and Mom stayed home. They were killed in a house fire, and now I live in Oregon with my grandmother, Maureen.*

She slid into the new persona, trying it on and embellishing it with descriptive details and daydreams. In it she had a normal childhood in a rich neighborhood. She went to (she thought a moment) Catholic schools (Cassie didn't think she would be able to fake the high school experience). She had great clothes and said "bitch" whenever she wanted to.

A person can choose who she wants to be, she thought. *And this is who I will be.* Every time the sad face of her mother twisted her stomach into knots, Cassie replaced the image with her revised history. *Act as if, fit in, no one loves a loser.*

Chapter 5

"I passed my GED in Writing, Interpreting Literature, and Mathematics, and my tutor says I'll be ready to take the Science and Social Studies sections in August."

Cassie sat in Tim's office, flip-flop-clad feet splayed on his fleece area rug and her sundress smoothed carefully over her knees. The hot July sunshine made window-sized patches of warmth in the air-conditioned room.

"And the best part?" she bubbled on. "Dr. White assigned me a concerto. I'm learning one of the Bach double concertos—the one in C minor that Bach transposed from the famous Double Concerto for Two Violins in D minor. Eric, this really great pianist, is playing the other part."

Tim sat back and watched her, a gentle smile on his face. Cassie could tell he wasn't impressed. She knew he had to be impressed at how well she was doing in order to get out of a lifetime of counseling, and she grabbed another accolade to display before him.

"Maureen is starting me in driving lessons this month," she added.

She sat back and waited for him to say something. He waited a few seconds before responding.

"That's very good, Cassie," he said. "I'm very proud of you. You're doing very well adjusting to life here."

Her face flushed as she felt a rush of relief and pleasure at his words. But it quickly faded as he continued speaking.

"What concerns me is how you will not discuss what happened to you in Waco." He took a deep breath. "You have been coming to see me for almost two months, and every time we come close to the topic, you skirt away from it."

Cassie stopped breathing for a second as shame and rage rushed through her in equal parts. The white noise returned, and she fought it back with the rage. "I thought I was doing OK," she said, quietly and very evenly.

"Yes, you are doing remarkably well," Tim assured her. "But I fear you are burying your pain rather than working through it."

Fuck you, she thought, keeping her mouth tightly closed, her eyes focused on the carpet. *Fuck you and the horse you rode in on.* He appeared to be waiting for an answer, so she shrugged.

"Things like this never go away, Cassie," he said gently. "When they're buried, they grow into monsters that can come back later and destroy you."

She shrugged again, her rage growing to the point that her jaw was beginning to ache in her attempt to clench back everything she wanted to say to him.

"I can't help you if you won't let me," he said.

She took two very deep breaths. "I never asked for your help," she finally whispered.

"Pardon?"

She raised her chin and looked him straight in the eyes, her rage giving her courage to risk his wrath. "I said, I never asked for your help!"

He held her eyes. "No, you didn't," he replied, his tone gentle.

"I came here to help Maureen," she continued, the words pouring out of her now, faster and faster. "I told you that in our first visit. I didn't need you, and I don't need you now. I come here because Maureen wants me to and because you tell me I need to. I'd rather be practicing the piano or hanging out at the mall with my friends." She stopped, her breath quick and shallow.

"Maureen and I know that what happened to you was so horrific that it shouldn't ever happen to anyone," he replied, holding her gaze. "You lost your religion, your savior, and you lost your home. You lost your parents and everyone you knew and loved. This isn't something anyone walks away from without pain, Cassie. Not even strong people. Not even you."

She stared at him a second, and in her mind she let the rage erupt. *FUCK YOU!* she screamed in her head, all the while keeping her face impassive. *Fuck. YOU! It was the fucking Apocalypse, OK? The fucking WORLD came to an end. He was EVERYTHING—the Alpha and Omega. And I should have been there. Where was I? Oh yeah, the FUCKING government took me and the other kids out after the first attack and then they went back to murder the rest a few weeks later. He died, Mom died, Dad died, EVERYONE died, but I'm alive. And now you sit in your FUCKING office with your FUCKING platitudes and tell me to spill my pain. There is NOTHING you can do to fix this. There is NOTHING you can say that will make anything better. Stop it*, she told herself. *Stop it!* She forced herself to stop thinking of it, and put herself into the opening notes of the Bach Double. The anger began to dissipate and she started breathing more deeply.

She sat tall, held her head high, and even succeeded in putting a strained smile on her lips. "I'm fine." She smiled a bit wider. *And you're never going to get anything more out of me than that*, she told him silently.

He held her gaze a moment, then his shoulders slumped, and he sighed. "When do you start your driving lessons?"

Later that evening Cassie sat with Maureen on the back porch, drinking iced tea and watching the shadows lengthen across the grass and the forest. Maureen had what she called her summer drink—a G&T that she mixed heavy on the G and light on the T. Cassie, who had been given permission to try a sip, thought it tasted like carbonated bile and wondered how anyone could call it refreshing. After they talked about their days, Cassie put her glass down, looked across the lawn, and tried to look nonchalant.

"I want to quit going to see Tim," she said in her most matter-of-fact tone. "I don't think it's doing any good. I'd rather spend that time practicing."

She could feel Maureen grow still beside her. "What makes you feel this way?" she asked.

Cassie shrugged. "He just wants to convince me I'm not doing OK, and I am doing fine. He's really nice and everything, but I don't want you to waste your money." She was particularly proud of adding the bit about money, as she knew Maureen was always worried about cash flow, even when she tried to hide her fear from Cassie.

"Do you mind if you and I go in and talk to him together before making this move?" Maureen asked. Cassie could feel her worry and her disappointment, but steeled herself to stay strong.

It's the last thing on Earth I want to do, Cassie thought, and then said "Sure" out loud.

Maureen sighed. "I didn't know what to do. I still don't know what to do. I thought counseling would help." Her defeated tone nearly melted Cassie's resolve.

"I'm fine," Cassie insisted, looking at her with her most earnest expression. "I passed those sections of the GED, I'm studying, I've got a concerto to learn, and I'm going to learn to drive. I'm making friends." She smiled winningly. "I'm doing just fine."

Maureen took a sip of her drink. "Yeah, but at what price?" she mumbled.

"What do you mean?"

"I mean, I'm so worried that you are trying so hard to be good that you're not letting yourself process what happened to you." Maureen held her gaze. "And I am very, very worried about what happened to you. No one just bounces back from that. No one."

Cassie's eyes filled. "I have to be normal," she said quietly. "That's the only thing I can do right now."

Maureen looked at her for another moment and then sighed and looked back at the tree line. "What does it mean to you, to be normal?" she asked.

"Normal is to get up and do normal things like having friends, going to school, learning to drive, and wearing cool clothes," Cassie said slowly. "That's all I want to do right now. That and play the piano. You and Tim talk about damage and everything, but that doesn't help me figure out how to be a normal person."

She stopped. It was the most confrontational thing she had ever said to Maureen, and she was terrified that Maureen would be mad at her. She sneaked a look at her out of the corner of her eye. Maureen caught the look and gave her a small smile.

"Go on," she said.

"It's sad. I know it's sad. Sometimes I cry about it. But most of the time, Maureen, I'm just trying to figure out how to not be a freak. And then Tim wants me to sit there and do something he calls 'processing my grief,' and I don't know what to say to him. He doesn't understand." She gave Maureen a small smile. "At least you do, a little."

Maureen's eyes filled with tears and she nodded. "I lost your mother years ago, and I thought that was the worst it could get. But in April..." she didn't go on.

Cassie reached out and grabbed her hand. Neither of them spoke for a few minutes.

"I'll call Tim tomorrow," Maureen finally said.

A week later Cassie started driving lessons. As luck and small towns would have it, she found herself enrolled in the same class as Naomi, and together they were the only two girls in a class of eight students. They sat in the corner of the classroom and talked while Naomi simultaneously chewed her gum and wrapped her hair around her fingers.

"I mean, of course he had to say he liked her because she, like, totally put him on the spot," Naomi said, rolling her eyes. "But I was, like standing right there and he knew it so it like, really pissed me off. But then she went—"

"Hey Naomi," a shaggy-haired blonde guy in jeans and a ripped Ramones t-shirt called from across the room. "Heard you're giving Jenkins head. Nice!"

Cassie blinked. *Head?* Naomi didn't even look at him, preferring instead to extend her right middle finger in his direction. The other guys laughed.

"You wish," shaggy guy said.

She whipped around and gave him an icy stare. "Yeah. Right. I wouldn't fuck you with a stolen cunt!"

Laughter erupted, accompanied by a single whistle. It stopped as abruptly as it started as an authoritative male voice cut through the noise.

"Interesting image, but nothing to do with learning to drive an automobile."

Everyone whipped around to the front of the classroom, where a diminutive, balding man stood sweating in a white short-sleeved button-down shirt and a pair of Wrangler jeans. Cassie held her breath and was too afraid to move. Naomi kept twirling her hair and chewing her gum, but with a little less nonchalance.

"I'm Mr. Hogg."

No one dared laugh, but Cassie could see Naomi's lips twitching a bit, and somewhere a few seats over one guy coughed.

"During the school year most of you know me as Roseburg High's math teacher. During the summer it's my job to teach you miscreants to drive, although I can't imagine why the rules of the land put lethal weapons in the hands of sixteen-year-olds."

"He looks like a garden gnome," Naomi whispered.

Cassie gasped, then choked back a laugh. Mr. Hogg stared at her. Their eyes met, and Cassie froze, laughter gone, and waited for a blow or slap. For a second she could see His face—the angry one He showed the time she fell asleep in one of His Bible lectures. He beat her so hard she was sore for days. After that she found ways to be as invisible as possible.

"Something funny?" Mr. Hogg asked, his nostrils flaring a bit.

"No sir," she whispered, shrinking down in the seat.

'I'm sorry, I can't hear you," he replied.

Cassie wanted to die. "No sir," she said, louder this time. Her legs shook so hard her knees knocked together.

He shook his head and then continued talking about the importance of safety and following traffic laws. Naomi leaned slightly in her direction.

"Are you OK?" she asked.

Cassie nodded and tried to take a deep breath. Naomi gave her a puzzled look and then shrugged. Mr. Hogg turned to write on the board, and Cassie took several more breaths as she looked around the room. The shaggy-haired guy caught her gaze, winked at her, dropped his eyes to her chest and then slowly down the rest of her body. Naomi, catching the whole exchange, hissed at Cassie.

"He's an animal!" she whispered.

Cassie nodded, but she couldn't stop blushing, nor could she stop the little shiver of excitement that ran the length of her. No one had ever looked at her that way before. Now it seemed everywhere she went, they were there, with knowing eyes and insolent smirks. She stole a look at Naomi and felt envious of her confidence and swagger.

She isn't afraid of anything, Cassie thought. *And I'll bet she has kissed boys and had boyfriends and everything.*

For an instant she felt a flash of anger that she had never been kissed and had never had a boyfriend. He forbade it. She was to be His, if He wanted her. Cassie remembered her friend Linda, who had matured early and was made one of His wives by the time she was fifteen. Linda went from being a friend to being a mysterious, powerful stranger who smiled enigmatically whenever Cassie tried to ask her questions about what He was like.

She threw shaggy-haired guy another look. *Well, He might not have wanted me, but other guys do*, she thought, raising her chin. *Fuck Him!*

Mr. Hogg handed out driving manual booklets and pencils. Cassie accepted hers with a smile and a flip of her long blonde hair.

In her peripheral vision she saw several guys watching her, and another shiver went through her. Naomi noticed both the guys' and Cassie's reaction.

"They're not worth it," she whispered. "They're stoners."

Cassie stared at her, confused.

Naomi rolled her eyes. "They smoke pot, like, a lot."

Cassie still didn't know what she was talking about, but pretended to understand. "Oh, sorry. Yeah. OK. Thanks for letting me know."

Naomi gave her an appraising look, shook her head, and then opened her booklet. Cassie felt a little flutter of panic.

"Pot wasn't big at my school," Cassie added. "People drank instead."

Naomi smirked, her expression back to normal. "They do that too. They'd be fucking too, if anyone would let them close." She elbowed Cassie. "Be careful. They're totally checking you out."

"Oh, I'm out of their league," Cassie said, quoting something she had picked up in one of her magazines.

Naomi stifled a laugh. "Totally!" she whispered.

Cassie didn't realize she had been clutching her pencil in a death grip until after Naomi laughed. She slowly uncurled her fingers, opened her booklet, and started listening to Mr. Hogg's instructions.

Chapter 6

"Beautiful," Dr. White said as Cassie and Eric finished playing the final movement of the Bach Double. "From this point on, I want the two of you practicing together. I will get you access to the pianos, but you will need to check the office to see when the hall is available. And we'll look at this again next week, OK?"

Cassie nodded and smiled at him. After he left the room, she turned to Eric. Every nerve in her body felt as though it was humming—so much so that even the feel of her breath on her bare arms sent little shivers through her. Eric was studying his score with apparent concentration.

Dr. White had been coaching them for over an hour on the second and third movements, and now Jacoby auditorium felt alive with the notes of Bach. The intimacy in the middle movement had been so breathlessly intertwined that Cassie was blushing by the time they got through playing it. She kept pushing a picture out of her mind—an image of sitting on Eric's lap as he trailed kisses down her neck—and she had an irrational fear that both Eric and Dr. White could read her mind.

He's gorgeous, she thought as she watched Eric mark something in his music. *I hope we get to practice together every day*.

When Dr. White had first assigned her the concerto, Cassie thought he gave it to her because she wasn't good enough to play a solo concerto. But when she told her friends, Naomi had squealed and jumped, and Shanna made a snarky comment about how she would never share the stage with another pianist. Now, looking at Eric, Cassie didn't care why she got the concerto—she just wanted to play it every day, with Eric.

"Um, when would you like to schedule our practice times?" Cassie asked.

He kept looking at the score as he answered. "Mornings or evenings," he replied, not looking at her. "I work the afternoon shift at Jim's Burgers."

Cassie looked back at her own score. Eric seemed angry or upset, and Cassie felt as though it might be her fault. "Do you want to practice this some more today?" she asked timidly.

He shook his head and closed the music. "No, I think this is enough for today." He turned and looked at her, his eyes a burning blue intensity.

Cassie met his gaze and held it. Neither of them spoke. Cassie could feel herself blushing, but she couldn't drop her gaze. Finally the sound of the stage door slamming shattered the tension, and both of them looked away as Shanna walked in.

"You guys done in here?" she asked Eric, not looking at Cassie.

He nodded. "Sure. All yours."

The moment had passed. Cassie sighed, stood up, and packed her music into her tote bag.

"I'll meet you at the front office," she said to Eric. "Have a good practice," she added to Shanna.

"Wait, I'm on my way," Eric called. He packed up his own music and followed her off stage. A thundering passage of Schumann followed them out the stage door.

"She's really good," Cassie offered.

Eric shrugged. "Yeah, I guess." He caught her gaze again. "But you're better."

Sheer pleasure shot through Cassie. "Well, I don't know--" she got that far before he leaned over and kissed her.

She stood completely still. Eric's lips were softer than she'd imagined, and nothing prepared her for the intensity of that electric first contact. She now knew where the term "weak in the knees" came from. It was over as soon as it started; Eric brushed his fingers gently down the side of her face just before they heard footsteps coming down the sidewalk, and they jumped quickly apart.

One of the voice people—a guy Cassie had seen in the practice room but had never met—came toward them, his purple Mohawk glistening in the sunlight.

"Are you guys done in there?" he asked.

"Yes, but Shanna's got the stage now," Eric replied, in a normal-sounding voice.

Cassie was glad he had responded because she wouldn't have trusted her voice. *I've had my first kiss!* she kept thinking. *I've had my first kiss!*

"Fuck!" Mohawk guy said. "I am so done with singing in those little rat-hole practice rooms. How can I sing "Nessun Dorma" in a box?"

"We're going to the office to schedule our rehearsal times," Eric replied. "You might check and see when the hall is available."

"Well, I suppose," Mohawk replied. "But how would I know if I would be, you know, inspired when the hall was open?" He sighed and gave a dramatic eye roll.

Cassie noticed his eyeliner and suppressed a smile. In Texas, a guy wearing eyeliner would not be long for this world. Texas. For a brief second she was sitting in one of the many services listening to His hypnotic voice. He always preached about purity. Every girl knew they were to keep themselves pure, and maybe one day He would see them worthy enough to be His wife. She thought of the kiss Eric had just given her and could see Him in her mind calling her a Jezebel, a whore of Babylon.

"I've got to caffeinate and motivate," Mohawk added with a wave of his hand. "Toodles!" He sashayed down the sidewalk in the direction of the cafeteria.

"Tenors," Eric muttered to Cassie with a low laugh.

Cassie giggled. *Do I feel guilty?* Cassie thought as she walked next to Eric. *Did I just behave like a Jezebel?* She waited for the expected guilt to kick in. When it didn't, she smiled. Eric, seeing her smile and interpreting it as being for him, reached out and took her hand. Her fingers intertwined with his as if they had always belonged there. They walked the rest of the way to the office without words, the rightness of their clasped hands being all the communication they needed.

A few days later Naomi called and invited her to go to the mall with her. She always sat next to Cassie in master class and driver's ed, but this was the first time she had suggested doing something without the rest of the group.

"I'll get my brother Joel to drive us," Naomi promised when Cassie told her Maureen would be at work so she had no way to get there. "He owes me because I totally covered for him when he had his girlfriend stay over last weekend."

"How'd you do that?" Cassie asked. She remembered a time when her friend Jordan got caught lying to Him and she shivered. Jordan was locked in the basement for twenty-four hours without any food.

"Joel has a different girlfriend every week," Naomi said. "My parents can't keep track of them. I told them she was my friend. They had been at some stupid food and wine event, so my mom was too loaded to notice anything anyway."

Loaded? Cassie thought a second. *Oh, she must mean drunk.* "What time will you get here?" she asked.

"Around one," Naomi replied. "See you."

"Bye," Cassie replied, but Naomi had already hung up the phone. Cassie looked at the shorts and t-shirt she was wearing and knew she needed to change. An hour and twelve changes of clothes later, she sat on the living room sofa wearing a sundress and sandals and waited for Naomi. Ever since the first master class Naomi had been pretty friendly, but Cassie was a little afraid of her. She still remembered the time when she was ten and she said "crap" in front of her mother. She could almost taste the Ivory soap Mom had used to clean up what she referred to as Cassie's "potty mouth." Naomi used "fuck" as a noun, a verb, a modifier, an adjective, and an adverb. Cassie was beginning to wonder if she might find a way to use it as an article as well.

At 1:15 a beat-up Toyota truck pulled up outside with its windows down and the stereo blasting a bass line so loudly the front window vibrated with the beat. Cassie grabbed her purse and opened the door just as Naomi knocked on it.

"Can I see your room?" Naomi asked, peering around her.

Cassie shrugged. "Sure." *It's the last thing I want you to do,* she thought as she stepped aside to let her in the house. She was suddenly ashamed of the little house and her Spartan bedroom.

Naomi took quick surveillance of the living room, her gaze both curious and assessing. When they got to Cassie's room, she looked at the pile of discarded clothes on the bed, the small dresser, and the lack of pictures or any personal items other than a brush. She moved the clothes to one side and sat on the bed.

"Don't you have any pictures of your parents or your old boyfriend in Texas?" she asked.

Cassie felt the panic, took a deep breath, and leaned against the doorframe. "They all got burned up," she said. "Everything got burned up in a house fire."

"Oh my god," Naomi said. "Really? Is that why your parents...?" her voice trailed off.

"They died," Cassie said. "In a house fire," she added. There was a brief memory of watching flames engulf the compound before she pushed it away.

"Gawd..." Naomi said. "That's fucked up."

"Yeah," Cassie said. *Breathe, breathe, be normal, be normal, breathe, breathe.* She noticed she was absently pulling at a loose thread on her sleeve and made herself stop.

Naomi opened her mouth to say more but was interrupted by a series of horn blasts from the truck in the driveway. She rolled her eyes.

"My brother," she said, getting up. "He's an asshole. Let's go before he takes off and leaves us here."

Cassie led the way to the front door and locked it behind both of them. The fire image was gone, but an earlier memory crept in. She was three, or maybe four, and had wakened crying from a bad dream. Dad carried her back to their bed and tucked her in-between them, and she had gone back to sleep cocooned in warmth and safety as she listened to the gentle breathing of both her parents.

Grief slammed into her like a presence, and for a moment she hoped it would just go all the way and stop her heart. No tears, just a full body ache so intense she wanted to moan.

She thought again of her parents. Were they ever normal? Maybe once, before He convinced them He was the Christ, before the compound, before her Dad got quieter and quieter and her Mom got thinner, and before the fire. But normal joined a cult and that was most definitely not normal.

She followed Naomi to the truck, where they were greeted with a scowl from the dark-haired guy behind the wheel.

"Could you two have moved any slower?" he said to Naomi.

"Could you be any more of a dick?" Naomi replied. She climbed into the truck and sat in the middle. "This is my friend Cassie," she added as Cassie sat down beside her.

"Hey," he said, making brief eye contact with Cassie. "I'm Joel."

"Hey," Cassie replied. *Gorgeous*, she thought. *Too bad he doesn't even see me*, she added mentally as his gaze left hers without a flicker of interest. He threw the truck into reverse and they backed out of the driveway in a cloud of dust.

"Do you drive like this to make up for being an asshole or for being a clarinet playing geek?" Naomi snapped as dust rolled into the open window.

Joel simultaneously flipped Naomi off and stomped on the accelerator. "Maybe you ought to consider sticking a clarinet in your mouth rather than every guy's dick that crosses your path." He threw Cassie a quick glance. "Sorry."

"It's OK," Cassie said.

Naomi rolled her eyes and then leaned over and whispered in Cassie's ear. "Let me tell you about this guy I met at the mall yesterday. His name is Tony and his dad is a winemaker. He's at U of O which is why I never met him before and—"

She kept talking but Cassie barely listened. Naomi was always meeting some great guy who was so hot and amazing, but Cassie never met them. She was beginning to wonder if these guys existed at all.

"So, what do you think?" Naomi asked her.

Cassie hadn't listened to a word, but it didn't matter. "Oh, I think he likes you," she replied.

Naomi sat back with a satisfied smile and twisted the leather bracelet on her wrist. "Yeah, I think so too."

Chapter 7

Cassie was in her favorite practice room, with the Barber *Excursions* open to the third movement. A theme and variations on the old cowboy tune "The Streets of Laredo," the notes were easy when played one hand at a time and a nightmare when both hands played together.

Who writes seven beats in one hand and eight in the other, Cassie wondered, glaring at the music. She tapped the rhythm on her lap. It seemed to work. But as she applied the same rhythm to the notes, it sounded technically correct but stiff and choppy. Somewhere in another practice room she could hear a soprano singing warm-up exercises. She tried to block the sound out by humming the right-hand part of the Barber. Then she tried to play the left hand on the piano while humming the right-hand part. Things fell apart by the end of the second measure.

She sighed, closed the keyboard cover, and rested her head in her hands. The first two movements presented themselves to her with complete pictures—the first movement was the train, the second was a slow, sexy strut. The third just felt like a bunch of notes. She closed her eyes, hearing the melody in her mind, and let her imagination wander. Cowboys, no, swirling women's skirts, close, but still not quite right. Dr. White sometimes tried to get students to feel a rhythm by dancing it, so she swayed back and forth on the piano bench while hearing the melody. The seven again felt swirly, and when she tried to put a picture on it, that swirly feeling reminded her of seeing riptides at the beach.

She had first seen them on a trip she and Maureen took to celebrate her birthday. Right after dinner, she took a walk on the beach, and the waves came in at different speeds, sweeping the dark sand and then swirling together. Sunlight shimmered and danced on the water and the foam—sparkles as brilliant as diamonds. Within seconds, the waves were one, indistinguishable from one another.

The image felt right. Cassie opened her eyes, opened the keyboard cover, and started playing. With waves in mind, she played through the first page and a half flawlessly, the irregular time-feel swirling together like water on a beach. She stopped and smiled. Then she tried to play it without the image and the music fell apart again. She laughed and shook her head.

This thing is either easy or impossible, she thought.

She finished her practice time by drilling several new measures, and then packed her music bag and left the room. The image of the beach stayed with her, along with the Barber, which she hummed to herself as she walked out of the building and over to Maureen's office. The fountains in front of the administrative building sparkled with the same shimmer she remembered seeing on the waves, and she paused just a moment to watch and listen to the fountains cascade into pools of water.

Before her birthday weekend, Cassie had never seen the Pacific Ocean. The wide beaches in Florence seemed to invite her to walk forever, and Saturday afternoon she had tried to do just that. Maureen preferred to take a nap. Cassie, glad to have some time to herself, headed south on the beach and walked barefoot, her flip-flops in one hand.

She walked in and out of the shallow waves, the cold making her feet ache until they became numb and she no longer felt the cold. An ever-present breeze kept the sun from feeling too hot. Thirty minutes into her walk, she realized that this was the first time she had been really alone anywhere since she came to Oregon. And then she remembered that other than her piano practice time, she had rarely been alone in Texas either.

She looked at the other people on the beach. Families sat on blankets, tossed footballs, and created sand castles. An older couple walked slowly up the beach. Dogs—ecstatic to be off leash and near the water—zigzagged across the sand and occasionally into the surf. No one seemed to notice Cassie.

No one here knows me, Cassie thought. *No one knows about the Apocalypse, no one knows that I play the piano, and no one knows my name.* The anonymity felt both disturbing and liberating; never before had she been free from having to be something to someone.

This is what the real world feels like, Cassie thought, quickening her steps. It was just her, some strangers, miles and miles of sand and surf, and a limitless horizon. She walked until her feet started to hurt, and then she turned around and started heading back up the beach.

The rhythmic roar of the ocean seeped into her, and in the middle of the sound she began to fancy that she could hear words or notes. She listened more closely, with equal parts of hope and pragmatism, but caught nothing more than what seemed to be a passing whisper. In her gut she felt the rightness of this place and knew she belonged here, with this ocean, anonymous, yet part of everything.

Home, she thought. Her mother's face flashed into her mind, and she was eleven years old, in bed with the flu. Her had mother spent two days with her—reading, singing, bringing her soup, and praying with her. They had created a little world of two in the middle of the compound.

"Oh, Mommy, I wish you could have seen this," Cassie whispered, feeling all the breath leave her body. She stopped and stared at the water, tears running down her face.

It still seemed as though her Mom and Dad would come back--as though this was just a long trip from the compound, and in a day or two everything would be the way it used to be. Cassie went through each day doubting that anything was real, except for the music. And in these moments now, grief crashed into the present and drenched everything, before disappearing as if it had never been--disappearing like the past, like Him, like Mom and Dad, like everything that had ever made any sense.

"How do you just disappear?" Cassie asked aloud. "Where did you go?"

The rhythmic, anonymous ocean responded with the same pattern of approach and retreat that she had seen and heard since starting her walk. She willed the memories back into the past and slowed her breathing. When the tears dried, she turned and walked the remaining miles back to the condo. It was only when she got back that she realized she had been gone three hours.

Cassie listened to the sounds of people talking, a car engine starting, and tree leaves rustling in the wind. She tried to recapture the feeling of home that had come over her at the beach, but this time she felt nothing. As she thought again of the Barber, she knew music was the place where she felt any sense of home, and it was the only place that seemed to make sense. The music was safe, predictable, and produced order from chaos. Each measure provided structure, and Cassie was dimly aware that the bar lines between the measures provided her with some structure as well.

It's the only place I belong, she thought, as she turned to the administration building and opened the door. She chose a chair outside Maureen's office, sat down, and looked around. She had passed the last sections of her GED and was registered for fall classes at the community college. She looked out the window at the campus.

I want to belong here too, she thought. *I just wish I could.*

She tried not to think about classes. When Maureen helped her register, she had reassured her she would be able to pass all of them without too much trouble. Cassie wasn't convinced.

"You're taking music theory, piano lessons, creative writing, biology, and math," Maureen said. "You know all this stuff. You'll be just fine."

Cassie had politely agreed with her, but inside her stomach knotted up every time she thought about going to class. She had her routine, and it was comfortable: piano lessons, practice, master class, driver's ed.

This is also what normal people do, she reminded herself. *They go to classes and get grades.*

For a moment the panic subsided; then she thought of the upcoming concerto competition. Everyone wanted to win it, and master class had become a polite battleground as everyone tried to outplay each other. Even Naomi seemed to be pulling away as she worked on the cadenza of her Mozart concerto.

Shanna's probably going to win, Cassie thought, bleakly. She had to agree that Shanna's playing was stunning at the last master class, making Eric even more determined to win with their Bach Double. Now, in addition to wanting to win for herself, Cassie feared losing the competition and making Eric mad.

"Shanna's the one to beat," Eric had said at their first rehearsal after Shanna's spectacular performance in master class.

They sat on Eric's piano bench, Cassie's legs draped across Eric's lap. She looked at him from under her lashes in a way she hoped was seductive.

"I thought you liked her," she said coyly.

He shook his head. "No. She liked me. I always thought she was a bit, well, grunge. Besides, she's not Christian."

Cassie cocked her head. "What do you mean?"

"My parents are really into religion," he said, not meeting her gaze.

Cassie felt her stomach start to churn. She held her breath and waited for him to continue.

He ran his fingers down her arm. "So, do you go to church or anything?" He tried, and failed, to sound nonchalant.

Breath, just breathe. "I used to, in Texas," Cassie finally replied. "I haven't found a church up here yet," she added.

He looked at her and tangled his hand in her long hair. "Maybe you could come to mine sometime," he said, right before he kissed her.

His tongue entered her mouth, and his right hand drifted down to cup her small left breast. Every time he kissed her she never wanted him to stop. The kisses, and his caressing hands, blotted out all thought, and even the memory of them could dispel panic.

Later that evening, Maureen and Cassie had their usual cool drink on the back patio. The days were starting to get shorter, and the evenings were cool enough that Cassie put on a sweatshirt. She sat with her iced tea and listened to Maureen talk about her day. The last few weeks of summer and the first few weeks of the semester were busy ones, and Maureen found it exhausting.

"I didn't even have time to take a lunch break," she complained, taking a deep sip of her G&T. "I know it's like this every year, but it seems to get harder each year." She gave Cassie a wry smile. "I'm not as young as I used to be."

She noticed the question Cassie was too polite to ask.

"Sixty-five," she said. "I'll be sixty-six in December."

Cassie smiled, surprised that Maureen was so quick to read her. "I didn't ask!"

Maureen shrugged. "I don't mind. "

Cassie studied Maureen's profile. She looked much younger than sixty-five, and Cassie had guessed her age to be somewhere between fifty-eight and sixty. In this light, she could see where her mother got her looks. She closed her eyes and tried to imagine her mother at seventeen. *Do I look like she did?* All she could see was her memory of her mother in the compound, her long, blonde hair loose, a devout expression on her face as she sat listening to Him speak. Cassie shuddered. *Was she ever normal?*

"What was my Mom like at my age?" Cassie asked.

Maureen set her glass down before responding. "Beautiful. Musical—she had a lovely voice—" she stopped a moment. "She was very sensitive and emotional." Maureen's voice was measured and controlled.

Cassie turned to her. "What do you mean?"

"She was very creative and had an artistic temperament." Maureen stopped again.

Cassie put her own glass down and waited. The silence stretched to nearly a full minute before Maureen continued.

"Your mom had some challenges in life," Maureen said, turning to Cassie and taking her hands. "She did the best she could to live a good life and to love and care for you."

Cassie pulled her hands away. "She and my dad brought me into that place."

Maureen closed her eyes. "It's not her fault. I failed her."

Cassie shook her head angrily. "She failed herself. And me."

"I was not a nurturing mother," Maureen said, speaking almost more to herself than to Cassie. "More than once she accused me of not supporting her. I was raised Methodist. I fought your mother when she became Seventh-day Adventist. When your parents joined up with the Davidians, your mother tried over and over to get your grandfather and me to join as well. We had terrible fights. I kept thinking she would come to her senses." Her voice trailed off, and Cassie could see tears pooling in her eyes.

Cassie felt the beginnings of panic, a little white noise at the edge of her mind, and she pushed it back by focusing on the drops of moisture sliding down the outside of Maureen's glass.

"And when you were born," Maureen continued. "She didn't want me to have anything to do with you—" Maureen's voice broke, and she paused a beat before continuing. "She was afraid I would contaminate you."

In Cassie's mind, she could hear her mother's voice, telling her to remain pure and devout, and to be really, really good because if she was really, really good He would make her His wife. Mom never explained anything more. For a brief second, Cassie remembered the feeling of absolute belonging and absolute faith and certitude. Those feelings were replaced just as quickly with the memory of shooting flames and the smell of acrid smoke.

"Yeah, well she was wrong about a lot of things," Cassie said out loud, the bitterness in her voice surprising both Maureen and herself.

Maureen's tears threatened to fall. Cassie's eyes remained dry. They sat in silence until the mosquitoes forced them back inside the house.

Chapter 8

It rained the day of the concerto competition. In less than twelve hours the weather went from its usual 78 degrees September balminess to 60 degrees and gray slop. Cassie had Maureen drop her off at the fine arts building doors to avoid ruining her new black pumps, and once inside, she walked straight to the ladies room to make sure the rain hadn't destroyed her hair-do or caused her make-up to run. The mirror assured her that both had survived the weather. Her hair, which she had pulled up and off her face, hung down her back in long ringlets, and her eyes were startlingly blue in their frame of mascara and eye shadow that Naomi had taught her to apply.

She smoothed her simple black dress and wished she had thought to buy something a little fancier. And she couldn't help noticing that the v-shaped neckline would have been enhanced by a bigger set of breasts. She sighed, gave herself one more look in the mirror, and left the restroom.

She found Eric standing just outside one of the practice rooms. Cassie noticed that his black suit and dress shoes made him look older than he usually did, and for a second it was as though she didn't know who he was. He turned, spotted her, and smiled.

"Do you know how far along they are?" he asked, giving Cassie a hug.

She closed her eyes a second and just breathed in his scent. He always smelled like detergent, soap, and an indefinable something that always made her want to get closer to him.

"I don't know," she replied, her voice muffled by his jacket. She drew back. "I just got here."

He gave her a quick kiss. "It's almost our time. Let's go wait in the dressing room."

Cassie followed him back into the rain and around the back of Jacoby Auditorium. The first door they tried was locked, and she could feel her hair getting wetter and wetter in the rain. They found an unlocked door and entered the hallway backstage.

Eric walked over to the auditorium doors and listened. "Mozart. It's Naomi." He said.

Cassie joined him and then winced as she listened to Naomi's tempo. It was too fast. And the sixteenth notes seemed to be rushing as well. She could hear Dr. White trying to slow the tempo for Naomi as he played the orchestra parts on the other piano.

"Maybe she'll slow down as she goes into the cadenza," Eric whispered.

She didn't. If anything, she got a little faster. And partway through, she started dropping her left hand. A memory slip came a few measures after that. Pause. Restart. Another memory slip. Another pause. Restart. This time she kept going, but the expression and fire had gone out of the notes.

"Oh, she's going to be pissed," Cassie whispered. "She's been working really hard on that part."

She and Eric made eye contact. In his eyes she read the fear, pity, and triumph that she feared was in her own.

"I can't listen to any more of this," he said. "It's making me nervous just to hear it."

They entered one of the dressing rooms, and Cassie rechecked her hair and makeup. The hair was getting curlier and she noticed just a bit of frizz that completely ruined the sophisticated look she thought she'd achieved when she first styled it. She ran her index finger under both eyes and cleaned up slight mascara smudges.

I look like melting ice cream, she thought in disgust.

Eric came up behind her and wrapped his arms around her waist. "You look gorgeous," he assured her.

"I'm a mess," she said, leaning into him.

Naomi entered the dressing room with her eyes red and her mascara smudged. She barely looked at Cassie and Eric, who separated as she walked in. Cassie tried to think of something—anything--positive to say.

"Hey Naomi," she finally said, hoping her voice sounded normal.

"Hey," Naomi replied, not meeting her eyes.

Shanna walked in before Cassie could reply. In honor of the occasion, she wore a dress, albeit with combat boots, and had taken out her lip ring. Cassie stared at Shanna's hair. Had she curled it?

"Hey guys," Shanna said, balancing her music on one hip. She looked at Naomi. "How'd it go?"

Naomi looked at Shanna like she wanted her dead. "Great!" she said with a big, plastic smile.

"Wow, cool," Shanna replied. "Even the cadenza? I know that part is so hard!"

Everyone froze, and no one made eye contact with anyone else. Shanna gave a tentative giggle.

"I just got here. Did I say something bad?" she asked.

Naomi gave her a disgusted look and shook her head. "No. It's just that I totally fucked up the cadenza. I couldn't remember shit." She lifted her chin, a defiant gleam in her eyes. "It's not like any of this shit matters anyway," she added. "It's just fucking Roseburg, for Gawdssakes. It's all bullshit."

A murmur of "oh yeah, totally, sure, you're right" rose from Cassie, Eric, and Shanna.

Naomi shrugged her shoulders, her tough-girl persona back in place. "I'm blowing this joint. Got a hot date. You losers have fun." She turned, left the dressing room, and strutted down the hall with as much attitude as she could get into her slim hips.

Shanna blew a tendril of hair off her face. "Oh shit. I had no idea."

Yeah, sure, Cassie thought looking at her with disdain. Then, seeing the embarrassment in Shanna's eyes, she realized she was telling the truth.

"She'll get over it," Eric said. "You didn't know."

Shanna nodded. "Yeah." She turned to Cassie. "You two on next?"

Cassie nodded. "We're just waiting for them to come and get us."

"Good luck!" Shanna said. This time Cassie could see she didn't mean it.

"Thanks, you too," Cassie replied, with the same amount of sincerity.

Dr. White entered the dressing room. "You two ready to go?" he asked Cassie and Eric.

They both nodded. "Yes," Eric added.

They followed him out of the room and down the hall to the stage door. He held the door open for them and then led them onto the stage. All the stage lights were on, making it difficult to see the faces of a single row of judges seated several rows back. She swallowed hard, her mouth dry, and tried not to think of them.

"Here are contestants numbers 3 and 4," Dr. White announced. "They will be performing the Bach Double Concerto in C Minor. In the absence of a third piano, they will perform without orchestral accompaniment. Please be advised that the performers will skip the tutti to save time."

He nodded and smiled at Cassie and Eric before exiting the stage. The walk to the piano looked impossible, and Cassie suddenly feared sliding on the smooth stage in her high heels. The pianos were nestled together with the keyboards facing each other, and Cassie's was the one farther away.

Her steps echoed in the hall. Everyone seemed to be waiting for her. She wanted to hurry, but the fear of slipping was growing stronger, so she walked with mincing, careful steps to her piano. She and Eric both stood, bowed together to the trickle of applause, and then sat down. She made eye contact with him across the expanse of both pianos. He smiled and nodded, and then began. Cassie listened closely to his opening subject—today she heard confidence and determination, and she answered with the same when her entrance arrived.

We're on fire, she thought as the movement continued.

Energy crackled out of both pianos, making the hair on Cassie's arm stand up. She felt completely and utterly alive. Colors seemed brighter, and the notes played themselves. She could feel what Eric was thinking even before he struck a note.

We're one mind, she thought. *Bach, Eric, and me—we're one mind!*

In the second movement, Cassie stopped being aware of any reality beyond the music. The competition, the judges, her hair, her dress—none of it existed. The notes defined her universe. And as she and Eric passed the sensuous lines back and forth, she dissolved into them. She was the piano, and the piano was her. She was Eric, Eric was her. And Bach was what held everything together. There were no mental pictures and no stories. Just the music, and Eric, and the piano, which seemed to grow out of her fingertips.

After the third movement, she heard the applause and bowed automatically. She and Eric exited the stage and accepted compliments from Shanna. Still in the music, she could hardly hear what anyone said, and when she looked at Eric she noticed that he looked a little dazed as well. A thin line of sweat had formed on his forehead, but he didn't seem to be aware. When he made eye contact with her, she felt it Right. Down. There. Her legs shook. Her mouth went dry. And in that moment she knew she would give him anything he asked for.

When Dr. White came and escorted Shanna on stage, Eric took Cassie's hand, led her to the dark second dressing room, and pinned her up against the wall as soon as the door closed behind them. The brute force of his kiss took Cassie's breath away. Everything about him was rock hard. As his tongue entered her mouth, she groaned and wrapped her arms around his neck. Everything was fire. And the fire spread down her body as his lips left her mouth and travel down her neck toward her chest. Gasping for air, knees shaking, she didn't resist as his hands travelled up her legs, under her skirt, and into her underwear.

"Oh my God," he groaned, one hand going farther and farther down until his fingers brushed the silky center of her.

Cassie gasped as his fingers entered her. And she continued to gasp as he started stroking her, each touch winding her up tighter and tighter. With his free hand, he clumsily unbuckled his belt and trousers, grabbed Cassie's hand, and wrapped it around him. She shrank back a moment, stunned by his heat and size. He insisted, taking her hand to it yet again, his other hand stroking her with increasing intensity. This time she grasped it and started stroking it in time to his thrusting hand and groin.

A moment later the world exploded into a wave of energy, followed by a series of pulses that slammed her with so much intensity that she must have cried out, as suddenly Eric's free hand was on her mouth. A second later he exploded.

"Oh, I love you, I love you, I love you," he groaned as Cassie's hand became drenched.

Later, after they had cleaned up and straightened clothing and hair, they slipped back into the hall unnoticed. And while neither of them said it, they both knew this was the way it was going to be whenever and wherever they could arrange it.

Dr. White called a little after eight that evening with the news that Cassie and Eric had won the concerto competition. Cassie—who had been thinking more about Eric than the competition—was stunned.

"Really?" She sat down heavily in a kitchen chair. Maureen gave her a quizzical look. She covered the mouthpiece of the phone and said, "We won!"

Maureen gave her a broad smile and two thumbs up. Dr. White kept talking.

"...will be scheduled for the November concert."

"Pardon?" Cassie asked.

"You and Eric will play the Bach for the November concert," he repeated. "Congratulations, Cassie. You both played more beautifully than I have ever heard you play."

Cassie thought again of that erotic second movement, and then of the follow-up in the dressing room and blushed. She could still feel his fingers. And her lips were slightly bruised from all the kissing.

"Thank you, Sir," she said. "Have you told Eric?"

"I will call him once we hang up. " He paused a second. "One more thing. One of the judges, Dr. Rutan from Linfield College, is interested in speaking to you about transferring there once you finish here."

"Oh." Cassie blinked, feeling equal parts pride and fear. "Does he—or is it she?—want Eric too?"

"I'm sure he would be interested in talking to Eric, but he asked about you. He left me his card and has asked you to consider contacting him."

"OK," Cassie said, trying to sound calm and cool. "What do I say?"

"We can talk about that in your lesson tomorrow," he assured her. "For now, however, discuss this with Maureen. Again, Cassie, congratulations. You should be very proud of the job you did today."

After saying goodbye, Cassie stood and slowly hung up the phone. Maureen looked at her, eyes eager for information.

"So? What did he say?" she asked.

"We won!" She said calmly, and then the excitement grabbed her. "We won! We won! We won!" She grabbed Maureen's hands. "Can you believe it?"

Maureen stood and gave Cassie a big hug. For the first time since moving to Oregon, Cassie returned the hug with no reservation or hesitation.

"We're playing it for a concert in November! With the orchestra!"

Maureen laughed as Cassie jumped out of their hug and twirled around a couple of times like a drunken ballerina.

"Eric is going to flip over this," she added, dropping into a chair. She thought again of the Linfield professor. "Where's Linfield?"

Maureen looked confused at the change of topic. "It's in McMinnville, a little southwest of Portland. Why?"

Cassie absently twirled a bit of hair around her fingers. "I guess one of the judges came from there—a Dr. Rutan. He told Dr. White he wants me to go there after I'm done here."

Maureen looked both pleased and worried. "Oh, congratulations, Cassie. Linfield is a private college, and a good one. Did Dr. White give you the professor's contact information?"

Cassie shook her head. "He'll give it to me at my lesson tomorrow. Apparently this Dr. Rutan wants to talk to me about the college." She shrugged. "He asked about *me*," she said, wonder in her voice.

Maureen grinned. "Well, you are pretty special," she said. "But when you talk to him, be sure to ask him about scholarships, OK?"

Cassie nodded, topic already forgotten. There would be more Bach rehearsals with Eric, a real concert performance with a real orchestra, in front of an auditorium that could seat several thousand. She could already see it: Eric would be in a tuxedo, and she would wear the most gorgeous dress she could find.

"May I get a new dress?" she asked.

"Absolutely!"

"I'm thinking a deep blue," Cassie chattered as she and Maureen walked out of the kitchen. "It will be colder, so maybe something in rich velvet? Eric would love that."

Maureen gave her an appraising look. "You really like him, don't you?"

Cassie ducked her head. "Yeah. He's sorta my boyfriend." She thought again of the dressing room and blushed.

"He seems like a great guy," Maureen told her. "Very polite, and obviously disciplined enough to become an advanced pianist. Just be careful."

Cassie nodded vigorously, mentally kicking herself for mentioning Eric and getting this conversation started. "Oh, I will."

Maureen gave her a serious look. "I mean it. No unprotected sex."

Cassie wanted to die; it would be preferable to the mortification of hearing Maureen say the word "sex."

"We're not, um, well, you know," she mumbled. *Hands didn't count, did they?*

Maureen gave her another serious look. "Well if you do, 'um, well, you know', please insist that he use a condom."

Cassie resisted the urge to put her hands over her ears and go bury herself in the back of her closet. "OK, Maureen. I promise." *Please change the subject,* she begged internally. *Just stop talking about this!*

"If you got pregnant, it could derail your career."

Cassie nodded. *Please stop! Please stop! Please stop!*

Mercifully, Maureen decided she had said enough, and she and Cassie sat down and watched an episode of "Seinfeld" together before going to bed. Once she was in bed, however, Maureen's words came back to Cassie, and she alternated between the embarrassment of the conversation and the tingly reminder of Eric's hands and lips and tongue and that shivery, thrilling surge and release that was like nothing she'd ever felt before.

Chapter 9

October passed in a blur. Between rehearsing for the concerto performance and preparing for a January scholarship audition at Linfield, Cassie spent six days a week in the music building. Despite her earlier fear, she found her college classes easy. She used the daytime breaks between classes to work on her solo audition pieces, and then she and Eric practiced the concerto each evening in the hall. Several times a week Dr. White dropped in and coached them; on the other days they rehearsed on their own, often cutting the rehearsal short and leaving campus early in Eric's car. If they rehearsed quickly, they could have a full hour together parked in a secluded place before their 10 p.m. curfews. It was Cassie's favorite hour of the day—for sixty minutes, her world was touch and taste, anticipation and release, with no room for any other thought. Afterwards, when Cassie cuddled against Eric's warm body, they would talk. And lately the conversation focused more and more on scholarship auditions and college entrance exams.

"Did you talk to your Mom about auditioning for Linfield in January?" she asked drowsily.

He kissed her hair and didn't respond.

"Dr. Rutan sounds really nice on the phone, and his bio is amazing," she continued, her voice bright. For the last few weeks, she had been trying to get Eric excited about Linfield, but he always found a way to change the subject.

"And if you went there, we could still be together," she added. And waited. After half a minute, he responded.

"Well, we'll see."

Cassie felt a cold panic starting in the pit of her stomach. "Don't you want to go to Linfield?"

He sighed. "I want to. I just don't think I'll be allowed to go there."

Cassie pulled out of his arms and looked at him. "Why not?"

He shrugged, not meeting her eyes. "It isn't a Christian college."

The panic spread. "Christian college?" she asked.

He nodded. "There are a bunch in the Midwest and the South," he replied. "There's even one in Waco. Didn't you ever go to any concerts at Baylor?"

Cassie fought a wave of nausea. "Um, yeah. I forgot it was a Christian college."

"The thing is, my parents—especially my Mom—want me to go to a Christian college. In fact, they want me to go to Regent University in Virginia because it is the top school training people to reclaim the seven mountains. The only reason I have been allowed to go to community college is because I can live at home, and Dr. White is an amazing teacher." He paused. "If my Mom had her way, I'd be at Regent right now. Dad convinced her I was too young to go to college across country."

Seven mountains? Cassie gave him a puzzled look. "What do you mean, seven mountains?"

He gave a disgusted snort. "My Mom is crazy religious," he said, bitterness in his voice. "The seven mountains idea is to train Christians to get into positions of power in seven areas like government, business, the arts, and whatnot so that we can reclaim the country from the godless heathens."

For a moment, His voice flooded Cassie's mind. *But when the word is made flesh again, it will come according to the seven seals.* She shivered and cuddled closer to Eric. "Is it sort of like the seven seals?"

"Seven seals?" Eric asked. "Like Navy Seals?"

"Navy Seals?" Cassie asked, confused. Then she laughed. "No. Like the Book of Revelation."

He shot her a surprised look. "You know about the Book of Revelation?"

Cassie's heart started racing, and she had to fight back His voice again. "A little," she said.

He looked like he was going to ask her more questions, so she pulled him toward her and kissed him. Conversation ceased. As His voice tried to enter her mind, she pushed it away by boldly running her hands down Eric's body and into the front of his undone Levi's. Despite recent satiation by her hands, he sprang to life again the moment her fingers curled around him. He groaned and buried his fingers in her hair.

"I have to get home. I'll get in trouble if I'm late," he said as his hands left her hair and cupped her bare breasts.

"Mmmm hmm," Cassie replied as she tugged his jeans back for better access.

"My parents are really strict," he added, looking at his watch. "Oh shit. It's almost eleven!"

He climbed back into the driver's seat, buttoned his jeans, and started the car. Cassie was still buttoning her shirt as he threw the car into gear and gunned the engine.

"Do you think you'll be in real trouble?" she asked as she buckled the seatbelt and then leaned over to tug on her boots.

"If I'm even five minutes late I get interrogated," he said as he shifted gears.

Cassie felt confused. She had met Eric's parents after one of their rehearsals and his mother had been very nice to her. "Your Mom seems to like me," she said. "Tell her you were with me."

He grunted. "That's the problem. She knows I'm with you."

Cassie felt embarrassed. "Oh. Sorry. I thought she liked me."

He shook his head. "It's not you, or rather it's just because you're a girl. I'm not allowed to date girls, I'm supposed to court one when I'm ready to get married. I'm not allowed to have girlfriends."

Cassie looked away. It felt like he had kicked her in the stomach. "Oh. So I'm not your girlfriend?"

He took her hand. "To me you are. But to my Mom you're just my duet partner." He rolled his eyes. "And even that has her freaked out. She keeps asking me if you're Christian, if you attend any church in town, you know, stuff like that." He looked away from her.

"Well." Cassie didn't know what to say. Part of her felt numb. Another part seemed to be yelling, *Danger! Danger! Danger!*

As they drove toward her house, Cassie just stared out the window at the dark, wet trees. She tried to imagine going to Linfield without Eric, and the very thought of it made her fight back tears. She loved him with an intensity she had never thought possible, and she knew they were meant to be together. In her mind their future would be to get married and play concerts together all over the globe.

"Maybe I can go to a Christian college," she said. *How bad can it be?* she thought.

He seemed not to hear her as he drove the rest of the way to the house.

Two weeks later, Cassie went to church with Eric and his parents. After missing curfew, Eric told his mother he had been "witnessing" to Cassie after rehearsal and lost track of time, and Cassie found herself having to attend church to back up Eric's defense.

"Are you sure this is a good idea?" Maureen asked her as they waited for Eric and his family to pick her up.

Cassie, wearing one of the Texas outfits her Grandmother had purchased for her, couldn't sit still. She ran her hands over the floral print skirt and kept trying to adjust the cream angora sweater. At Maureen's advice, she wore very little make-up and just simple pearl earrings for jewelry.

Cassie shrugged with what she hoped was nonchalance. "It will be fine," she said with all the assurance she didn't feel.

She reminded herself that she could be anything she wanted to be. She was pretty and popular and normal. Normal people went to church. She would go to church. She ignored His voice, which kept trying to tell her that all other churches were of Satan and that in the end of ages these mild-mannered, casserole-bearing church members would hunt down the True Disciples and kill them. He was dead; she was here; this was normal; end of story.

This false bravado took her all the way through the short car ride to the church, into the front doors, and to the pew. But everything there felt sinister and foreign—the smiling church people, the band playing soft background music, everyone Eric introduced her to, and even Eric himself. He seemed to have disappeared and was replaced by a clone with perfectly combed hair, a sport jacket and tie, and the same wide-eyed earnest expression she saw on everyone else's face. Even his vocabulary and the cadence of his sentences seemed to change. "God" became "Gawd." He was no longer "fine" when asked, he was "blessed." Cassie felt herself slide back into her Texas drawl and Southern girl manner—it seemed to be what these people wanted to see from her.

The service started when the lights lowered, and the praise band began leading congregational singing. The words, magnified on big screens set up on either side of the main platform, were simple and the tunes easy to pick up. Eric started singing with gusto, and after a few seconds, Cassie tried singing a bit as well. Around her, people held up their hands. Several swayed side to side. She shot a look at Eric and was relieved that he kept his arms down; she didn't know if she could go that far, even if it was what everyone expected.

The first song slid into the second, and a fair amount of earnest strumming came from the guitars. The singers held microphones and swayed side to side with their eyes closed. The bass player and the drummer both looked a bit bored and Cassie fought a giggle knowing that Naomi would label the bass player a stoner. To Cassie, he was the only one who looked sober; the rest of the congregation swayed as if drunk.

When asked about it later, Cassie couldn't remember what happened next. The church disappeared, and Eric and his parents disappeared, and she was on the compound in Texas. The heat of the room, the hypnotic sound of His voice as He sang and played the guitar, it was all real. His eyes bored through her. Mom was there, and Dad, and all the others. He kept looking at her, singing, *I am the Way, I am the Truth, I am the Light.* And behind Him, the walls started burning, and Mom and Dad started burning, and still He kept singing, kept hypnotizing, kept Cassie rooted to the ground.

He started burning, first His legs, then His body and arms and the guitar, then His face, until there was only His voice, telling her she was His forever.

"Cassie! Cassie!"

The voice was female and seemed to come from far away.

"I don't know. She just ran out of the sanctuary and in here"

"Should we call her grandmother?"

"Cassie! Cassie!"

"Mommy?" she asked, opening her eyes.

Eric's mother—Mrs. Jackson--and two strangers looked back at her. She looked down and saw she was on the floor of the women's restroom, tucked as far into the back of one of the stalls as she could get. She had tried to stand but was shaking so hard that she collapsed in a heap, feeling as though she couldn't breathe. She closed her eyes and tried to think of Bach, or Barber, or anything other than the panic, but it did no good.

"Cassie, here, I'll help you."

Cassie heard Mrs. Jackson's voice, but couldn't move. *I'm going to die! I'm going to die! I'm going to die!* The mantra kept playing in her mind as she struggled for air. She felt strong hands on her arm, pulling her up.

"Here, you grab her other arm," Mrs. Jackson's voice said.

A voice boomed out of speakers in the ceiling. "And Lord, we just want to thank You for Your blessings. We just want to praise You!"

Cassie opened her eyes, and instead of Mrs. Jackson, He held her arm, and His mocking eyes glittered down at her. She screamed with everything she had in her, wrenched her arms out of His hands, and covered her ears. When she ran out of air, she took another breath and screamed again.

The women jumped back, and Mrs. Jackson stumbled into the toilet paper dispenser. His voice droned on.

"We just pray for the infidels who flaunt Your rule and refuse to be washed in the Blood of the Lamb. We just pray for the coming of Your kingdom here."

"Make him stop! Make him stop!" Cassie screamed, hands over her ears and eyes closed.

"What's the matter with her?"

"Maybe it's the loudspeaker. Turn it down!"

"Can you get another grip on her arm?"

"I'm calling her grandmother."

His voice stopped as abruptly as it had started. Cassie opened her eyes, removed her hands from her ears, and looked around. The only faces staring down at her were Mrs. Jackson and several other women. On their faces she read both concern and fear. She dropped her face into her hands and started sobbing.

"I'm sorry, I'm sorry, I'm sorry." The words were strangled by sobs.

Hands gently lifted her from the floor, and arms supported her as she was led to a small sofa in the adjoining Mother's Room. A woman Cassie had never met sat beside her, wrapped her arms around her, and gently rocked her from side to side.

"Shh, shh," she said. "You are safe. You are loved."

In that moment Cassie felt the loss of her mother so keenly she wanted to die. Curling herself into a ball, she wailed as the woman continued to hold her and rock her. Never having let Maureen hold and comfort her like this, she poured all her grief onto this stranger and the woman, in turn, wrapped her in love. It was the first time since the Apocalypse that Cassie didn't feel that she had to be strong.

The crying had subsided by the time Maureen came to take her home. When she arrived, the loving woman walked Cassie and Maureen out to the car, tucked Cassie into the seat, and then turned to talk with Maureen for a few minutes. Cassie hadn't seen Eric, and she prayed he wouldn't come out and observe her failure. Mrs. Jackson stood a few feet away from the car, waiting to talk to Maureen. When Cassie tried to catch her eye, she looked away. Cassie looked down at her hands. These hands played Bach, and Barber; they knew how to drive and how to please Eric. But now they lay pale and lifeless on the relentlessly cheerful floral-patterned skirt.

After what seemed an eternity, Maureen got in the car and started the engine. She looked furious. Cassie shrank against the door, full of shame for having embarrassed her so badly. They drove a mile before Maureen pulled off the road and turned the engine back off.

She took a deep breath. "I just had one of the most disturbing conversations of my life," she said after a few seconds of silence. "Loretta Jackson is a clueless old bitch!"

Cassie shrank further into her seat and started shaking again. Maureen reached across and took her hand.

"Sweetie, I am not angry with you. I am so, so sorry this happened to you," she started crying. "I am just so glad Cecilia was there to take care of you."

Cecilia? Oh, that must be the name of the nice lady, Cassie thought as the shaking started to subside.

"I'm so sorry," Cassie whispered.

"You have nothing to be sorry about. No, look at me."

Cassie reluctantly met Maureen's eyes. In them she saw love and pain but not a trace of judgment or accusation. Cassie held Maureen's gaze as she continued to speak.

"If I could make it all go away, I would. If I could go through this for you, I would." Tears were now flowing freely down Maureen's face. "I know we never speak to each other like this, Cassie, but please understand that I love you so much. I would do anything to protect you."

Cassie just nodded and kept listening.

"What happened to you, Cassie, it has a name. Cecilia identified it immediately because she told me she suffers from the same thing. It's called Post Traumatic Stress Disorder, or PTSD. It happens sometimes when someone has gone through something awful like you went through in Waco."

Oh great, Cassie thought. *One more thing that's wrong about me.*

Maureen looked out the window for several seconds. "We're going to have to get you some more counseling," she said.

Cassie shook her head. "I'll get over it," she mumbled. "I'll just stay out of churches."

Maureen's lips twitched at that statement, but she kept her focus. "These sorts of things don't go away, Cassie. You have to get help to know how to get through them. It's for you, so you can have as normal and happy a life as possible."

Her words hung there. When Cassie didn't respond, she reached over and started the car again.

"But for now, we're going to take you home and take care of you."

Chapter 10

It was Monday morning, and Cassie couldn't get out of bed. When Maureen came in to wake her for classes, she just looked at her, mutely shook her head, and closed her eyes. As she drifted back to sleep, she could hear Maureen calling the college to get her excused from class. When she woke again, the house was silent, and all Cassie could hear was the drip of rain running through the drain spout outside her window. The clock said 10:30. She thought of the incident, groaned, and tried to go back to sleep, but her need for the bathroom and for a cup of coffee finally propelled her out of bed.

The answering machine blinked, showing four messages. Maureen's note sat propped against the coffee machine. She read it quickly as she made a fresh pot, vowing to drink at least one cup before she listened to any phone messages.

Cassie, I had to go into town for a few hours. I will be home by noon. Love, Maureen

She sighed and watched the rain hit the window as she waited for the machine to finish brewing. As she poured her first cup, she vaguely wondered why Maureen wasn't at work, but then the thought slid away. She thought briefly of the math assignment she was to have turned in that morning, and the rehearsal time she had missed, but it didn't seem to matter. She was grateful that the coffee burned her mouth; that at least made her feel alive.

The incident came back in disjointed flashes—the feel of the cold bathroom tile under her hands, the look on Maureen's face when she came to get her, and most of all, the frightened look Mrs. Jackson wore every time she looked at her. None of it touched her. Everything was shocked into stillness. Even the fragmented images of Him and of fire didn't touch her.

I failed.

She closed her eyes and took another deep, scalding gulp of coffee.

I failed.

She thought of Eric, and nausea slammed her so hard and fast that she ran to the sink convinced she was going to throw up. Gasping, fighting it back down, she turned on the cold water and splashed it on her face. The nausea subsided, but was replaced by an active, burning, curl-up-in-a-ball-and-die shame.

"I failed," she said out loud. "And now no one will ever love me again."

It would be better if I'd never been born.

She thought of Him, and of Mom and Dad. She thought of all the "aunts" and "uncles" and "brothers" and "sisters."

They're all gone.

She turned off the faucet and leaned on the sink as she looked out the kitchen window. The red and gold of the fall leaves were now a muted mess of brown. Sad little puddles dotted the lawn. Even the evergreen trees wept. In that instant, she knew it: she was alone. When Maureen came home an hour later, she found Cassie still leaning on the sink, staring through unseeing eyes, at a landscape drained of color.

Tuesday morning Cassie refused to get out of bed. Maureen sat down next to her and stroked her hair.

"Cassie, you have to get up," she said.

Cassie shook her head and tried to pull the covers over it.

"You have a piano lesson today."

Cassie ignored her, pretending to be asleep.

"You have to go to your lesson, Cassie. You have a concert in two weeks."

Cassie felt a tug inside. But then she thought of facing Eric, and she knew she couldn't do it.

"I can't do it," she mumbled.

Maureen stroked Cassie's hair back from her face, her touch tentative. "What, Cassie?"

Cassie gave up the pretense of sleep and sat up. "I can't do it. I'll just have to cancel the concert."

Maureen sat very still and held Cassie's gaze, her eyes serious. "You don't mean that."

Cassie shrugged, numb inside. "What does it matter?" She dropped her eyes. "I can't face him." They both knew she was talking about Eric.

"He's called three times," Maureen replied. "He sounded very worried about you."

Cassie's chin wobbled. "He thinks I'm a freak. I _am_ a freak."

Maureen sighed. "I'm sure he's worried, but he has to expect that there might be some rough patches, after what you went through."

Cassie shrugged again. "He doesn't know," she mumbled.

"Oh." Silence. "What have you told him?"

Cassie flushed, unable to meet Maureen's gaze. "I told him my parents were killed in a house fire."

Maureen reached over and squeezed her hand. Then she stood and walked to the door. "I'm going to call Tim," she said, pausing at the doorway.

Cassie's head shot up. "NO!"

Maureen shook her head. "I have to."

Cassie threw back the covers and climbed out of bed. "No. Please, no. I won't talk to him! I promise I'll get better, Maureen. I promise!"

Maureen looked at her. "Why don't you like him?"

"He doesn't get it!" Cassie pulled her hair back and wrapped it into a loose pony tail. "He just sits there and pretends to have answers, but he doesn't know a fucking thing about what I went through!" She stopped, stunned at her own outburst.

Maureen look equally stunned; Cassie had never before used such language in her presence.

"I won't talk to him." Cassie added with finality.

On Wednesday evening, Cassie was startled to see a stranger enter the house with Maureen. The woman's face looked familiar, and as a gentle smile greeted her, Cassie remembered: the woman from the church. She looked smaller somehow, in her blue jeans and black parka; on Sunday she had seemed to be an all-enveloping circle of blue sweater-clad arms and waves of love holding her tight.

"Cassie, you remember Cecilia," Maureen said. "You met her on Sunday at church."

Cassie nodded, her face flaming with embarrassment. "Hi," she mumbled, looking at her feet.

"I invited Cecilia for dinner," Maureen continued, taking off her coat and helping Cecilia out of hers.

Cassie glared at Maureen. *And now I am supposed to make conversation with a stranger?* She crossed her arms and stood very still.

Cecilia smiled at Cassie. "How are you doing?"

Cassie shrugged. "Fine," she lied.

Cecilia and Maureen exchanged a look. "I'm going to get dinner started," Maureen said as she walked into the kitchen.

Cecilia sat down on the sofa next to Cassie. For five minutes she said nothing. Cassie kept sneaking little looks at her as the silence became more and more awkward, but she didn't have the energy to try to make conversation and didn't know what to say if she tried. *I'm sorry? Is that right? I'm really not crazy? No, better not put that word into her head. I was coming down with the flu? No, screaming and crying are usually not flu symptoms. Oh shit. I just want to die. She must think—*

"When I was seventeen, my whole family died in a car crash," Cecilia finally said, not looking at Cassie.

Cassie didn't look at her, but she could feel every bit of herself listening to Cecilia's words.

"It was a cold night, and my father was driving. We hit black ice right as we got to a bridge. The car went out of control, crashed into the river, and everyone died." She paused a second. "Except for me."

Cassie waited, not even aware that she was holding her breath.

"I lived because as soon as the car hit the water, I kicked my sister out of the way, climbed through a broken window, and swam for the surface. My mother and father and sister all drowned. My last memory of my sister is the look of shock she had on her face when I kicked her away from the window. I didn't try to save her and I didn't try to save my parents."

Cassie realized that her hands were shaking and that she felt cold all over. She clenched her hands together both for warmth and to get the tremors to stop.

"When the ambulance arrived, I was in hypothermia and shock. Later, in the hospital, they told me I was brave and strong. Then they told me I was the only one who survived. I wished I'd died."

Cassie felt wetness on her cheeks before she realized she was crying. Something inside seemed to crack open, and the tears just leaked down her face.

Cecilia turned and looked at Cassie, tears in her own eyes. "It took me a year before I could ride in a car without a tranquilizer. It took me three years before I could drive across bridges. Every time I tried, I started shaking and crying. Several times I got so upset I threw up. I still won't go out if the temperature goes below freezing."

"How," Cassie's voice sounded as shaky as her hands felt. "How did you get better?" she asked.

"Prayer, talking to other people who had tragedies in their lives, and time," Cecilia replied. "And I spent a lot of time talking to an older cousin who fought in Vietnam. He's the one who told me I had PTSD—Post Traumatic Stress Disorder. He suffered from the same thing, only in his case he had flashbacks to being attacked by Vietcong soldiers."

Cassie shot a look toward the kitchen before she whispered, "Did you have to go to therapy?"

Cecilia smiled. "In my time it just wasn't done, but about ten years ago I started going to a Christian counselor and he helped me very much. I wish I'd had him to talk to when I was younger."

Cassie shook her head, looking again at her hands. "It doesn't do any good. They don't know what it's like."

Cecilia gave her a gentle smile. "But they are trained to help people process pain."

Cassie crossed her arms and looked away. A minute passed.

"Maureen tells me you love music," Cecilia said, changing the subject.

Cassie shrugged. *Here comes the bit where she tells me to go back to practicing and to lessons and to school.*

Pulling her large handbag onto her lap, Cecilia opened it and removed a portable CD player with headphones and a stack of CDs. She handed the CDs to Cassie and then studied the player a second.

"I can never figure these things out," she muttered, squinting at the buttons. "Mind lending a hand?"

Cassie put the CDs in her lap and took the player. She studied it a second, popped it open, and then opened a jewel case and popped a CD into the machine. She pressed play and the sleek silver player purred to life in her hands. Through the headphones she heard Rachmaninoff's C# Minor Prelude. Cecilia studied her with a small smile.

"I didn't know what composer you liked best, so I got a variety," she said. "Maureen said classical piano, and so that's what I told the guy in the record store. I bought the ones with the best-looking men on the covers."

A quick flip through the CDs showed youthful pictures of Andre Watts and Vladimir Ashkenazy. Cassie giggled for the first time in days. "May I listen to them?" she asked, making eye contact with Cecilia for the first time.

Cecilia reached over and squeezed her hand. "The player and the CDs are for you, Cassie. They're a gift."

"Oh, I can't!" Cassie protested. "It's too much! " She turned off the player and tried to hand it back to Cecilia. She knew, without having priced anything that the player and the CDs had to add up to several hundred dollars.

Cecilia put it firmly back in Cassie's hands. "It's a gift, Cassie." Her eyes met and held hers.

"Oh, thank you," Cassie said, looking at the recordings with the first real longing she had felt for anything since Sunday. "I'll pay you back."

"No, but you can pay me forward," Cecilia promised. "Someday you will be there for someone else just as people were there for me."

With a boldness that she couldn't explain, Cassie hugged her. "Thank you," she whispered while Cecilia just patted her back.

Cecilia left shortly after dinner and Cassie cleared the table and did the dishes in silence. Maureen worked just as silently as she put the leftovers and clean dishes away. Cassie was rinsing the sink before Maureen spoke.

"I'm sorry if your felt ambushed by this," she said.

Cassie refused to look at her, choosing instead to grab the washcloth and start wiping down the kitchen counters.

"Cassie, please, just look at me."

Cassie rinsed the dishcloth and hung it over the faucet. She heard Maureen sit down heavily in one of the kitchen chairs. When she turned around and faced Maureen she was surprised by the look of fear on Maureen's face.

"I didn't know what else to do," Maureen said as she took off her glasses and dropped her head into her hands. "I failed your mother, and now I'm failing you too."

Cassie tried to feel empathy or guilt or even anger, but she was just too numb. She sat in the chair next to Maureen and mumbled, "I'm sorry."

Maureen shook her head. "Before your mother was born, I'd never been a parent; before you showed up in April, I'd never been a grandmother. You are my second chance, and I can't seem to get this right either."

"It's not your fault," Cassie mumbled, a little guilt creeping into her numbness. "I'll try to do better."

Maureen met her gaze. "Cassie, you need to get back into counseling." She held up her hand as Cassie started to protest. "We'll find another counselor if you don't like Tim. I'm sorry, but this is non-negotiable."

Cassie dropped her gaze and held her breath. *Great. Just great.*

"If I had gotten counseling for your mother, maybe things would have been different for her too," Maureen added, her voice nearly a whisper.

Cassie met her gaze. "What do you mean?"

"I didn't know what she was struggling with until after she left home," Maureen said. She took a deep breath. "Cassie, your mother suffered from severe depression. She tried to kill herself two years before you were born."

Cassie felt a wave of shock roll through her. The memory came back in a flash—Mom lying in bed for days at a time while Dad tried to get her to eat something. *Was I six or seven?* She remembered tiptoeing around the house, terrified that her mother would die. *Was she ever depressed after they joined Him?* Cassie never saw her lie in bed like that again; He made everyone get up early in the morning and do hours of exercise. *But was she happy?* She thought of her mother's devout face tilted toward Him in meetings like a flower toward the sun. *Did I ever even know her?*

"If I had found a counselor for her then, maybe things would have been different," Maureen added.

They sat silently for a couple of minutes.

"I'll go to counseling," Cassie mumbled. *But I won't like it.*

Late that night when Maureen had gone to bed, Cassie put on one CD after another and listened while lying in bed. The rain had stopped, and pale moonlight came through the curtains. She loved all the CDs. With the headphones, it felt like being inside the piano. Each note seemed to come from under her skin. But while she relished each piece, two in particular called her to return to them over and over: Rachmaninoff's Prelude in D Major, which allowed her to weep, and Chopin's Barcarolle, which somehow seemed to knit something back together deep inside of her. Somewhere in the middle of her fifth time through the Barcarolle, she fell asleep.

Thursday, after Maureen had gone to work, she pulled on jeans and boots and a big parka and went walking. With the player tucked under her coat and the parka hood pulled up over her head and the headphones, even the rain didn't slow her down. She walked until she reached the edge of the ravine overlooking the Umpqua River, and there, finding a large rock to sit on, she turned off the player and listened to the music of the river. In it she heard all the notes she had ever played, all the Chopin and Rachmaninoff she had just been listening to, and under the notes, a joyful playfulness older than time.

"I miss you," she said.

Neither the river nor the notes needed to ask who it was she missed. And in their sonic circle of music and playfulness, Cassie could feel her father's solid love and her mother's quick wit.

"I love you," she added, eyes closed, breathing in the damp air, rich with the scent of water, moist earth, and soggy vegetation. And as a settled peacefulness filled her, she knew her words had been redundant.

On Friday morning Cassie got out of bed and went back to school.

Chapter 11

From backstage, the audience sounded like a forest of rustling leaves with a chaotic overlay of orchestra members warming up and people moving on and off stage. Cassie stood in the hallway outside the dressing rooms listening, a combination of excitement and nerves making her skin feel super-charged and her breath shallow. She looked down at the black satin heels peeping out from under the skirt of her midnight blue velvet and satin gown and wondered if she should have worked harder to find shoes that matched the gown.

Too late now, she thought, pushing the dress over her shoes.

When she had arrived at the hall thirty minutes earlier, Naomi came back to the dressing room to see her and squealed when she saw the dress.

"Oh my God!" Naomi gushed. "Where did you find it? It is so not Roseburg!"

"My grandmother sent it to me," Cassie admitted, covertly admiring herself in the mirror.

The dress had been a surprise that Maureen and Grandma had collaborated in purchasing. When it showed up in a UPS package, Cassie felt as though she had been transformed into Cinderella. A few last-minute adjustments with the local seamstress, and now the dress hugged her slender frame like a sinuous glove.

"And the hair is stunning," Naomi added, walking around the back to see the mass of curls cascading from the crown of Cassie's head to the middle of her back.

"Thanks," Cassie said, patting the side of the up-do gently. "It took the hairdresser two hours, and I may never get all the hairpins out."

Naomi fussed over her and then wished her luck before leaving and going back to her seat in the auditorium. And now, standing in the hallway thirty minutes later, she wondered if perhaps Naomi might be a true friend.

Eric came out of the men's dressing room wearing a tuxedo and a very controlled facial expression.

He's nervous, Cassie thought, surprised. Somehow she didn't think he would be nervous.

He took her hand and leaned in to kiss her. Cassie turned her head and his lips landed on her cheek.

"Lipstick," she said. "Sorry."

He smiled, and the nervous look left his face. "You look gorgeous," he said. He ran his fingers up her arm—it was the only part of her not covered with fabric or make-up.

He's so gentle, she thought, not for the first time. He had been like this for the past week and a half—ever since she told him about Him, the Apocalypse, and PTSD, or as she mangled it at the time, PSTD, which made him wonder if she had an STD, which then dissolved them both into helpless gallows-humor laughter. At the same time, he hadn't tried to be alone with her since that visit to his church, and he didn't speak at all of college or the future.

Don't think about it, Cassie told herself as she leaned against the wall and closed her eyes. *Think about the Bach.*

In her mind she could hear the opening notes of the concerto and could see the color-coded score—yellow for Eric's moments, blue for hers, pink for the times they were in unison and therefore needed to back out of the dynamics. Cassie had studied the score so much she now heard each section in its designated color. Her mental notes sounded through the audience rustle, the orchestra warm-ups, and Eric's formal shoes on the tile floor as he paced back and forth.

She watched the concert master go through the stage door and listened as the orchestra fell silent, waiting for the tuning pitch, then the clear, bright "A" that sang out over the auditorium, quieting the rustle to a low murmur. Soon the whole orchestra reverberated on A as though it was the first sound ever uttered. Then silence, then applause as the conductor walked through the stage door and out into the lights.

"We're starting," Cassie murmured to Eric.

He shot her a panicked look. "I wish they had put us first. I just want to get this over with," he admitted. "This waiting is killing me."

She walked up to him and wrapped her arms around his waist, careful not to crush the front of her dress. "We're going to be amazing," she said.

"I know," he said, hugging her back, but she could hear the doubt in his voice.

Cassie had heard that there was nothing like the last few minutes before walking out on stage to play a big performance, but nothing could have prepared her for the dizzying slide from excitement to nervousness and back again. She closed her eyes, stood with her hands by her sides, and tried to feel connected with the floor. Energy coursed through her so much that she half-feared that gravity would give way and she would just lift right off the floor like a helium balloon. She tried to listen to the orchestra playing the "Allegro Deciso" from Handel's Water Music, but she couldn't concentrate on it.

Pictures flashed through her mind—sitting at the piano in Waco, practicing late night with Eric, watching the waves at the beach, the first time Eric kissed her, the feel of the keys under her fingers, the way the Bach seemed to play her rather than the other way around. There was no order to the pictures—they just popped into her head, and for a second she was there, then another one appeared, and on and on.

I have to breathe. She drew in a deep breath, counting to four, and let it out, counting to four. As she repeated it—four beats in, four beats out—she could feel her body calming and her mind focusing on nothing more than the breath. *In-two-three-four; out-two-three-four; in-two-three-four; out-two-three-four.*

The Handel ended and the audience answered with a wave of applause. The conductor—a guest from the University of Oregon—came backstage while the stage crew moved both pianos to the stage and re-arranged the orchestra. When they finished, the conductor motioned Cassie and Eric to the stage door, wished them well, and then the long walk to the pianos began.

The audience applauded as they stepped on stage. All Cassie could see was a wall of black behind bright stage lights. The bow was automatic, the conductor shook both their hands, and they sat at the pianos. Cassie sat very still, waiting for Eric's cue that they were ready to start. He adjusted his bench, looked up, and when their eyes met over the expanse of both grand pianos, it was as if someone had supercharged the lights. They stared at each other a second, letting the audience disappear until it was just the two of them, the orchestra, the conductor, and Bach. A slight nod to the conductor and they launched into the first movement. The music washed over and through Cassie, and her fingers found the keys without thought or concern. She couldn't tell where she and her piano ended and where Eric and his piano and the orchestra began, and it was only after the performance that she found a word to describe it: transcendent.

She didn't hear the darkness until the beginning of the second movement when Eric played the first entrance. Where he once had communicated passion, she heard sadness and regret. She answered with her entrance, *why?* His reply gave her nothing beyond an aching sadness, and all the while the strings kept playing pizzicato, each note sounding like the ticking of a clock as time was running out. When the strings made their melodic entrance, they made the intimate sadness a public grief that held a touch of wistfulness at the edges. Eric and Cassie answered the strings, and each line, passed back and forth between the two pianos like sensuous caresses, contained everything they loved about the music and each other, as well as the grief that this was all they would ever have. As they came to the end of the movement, Cassie had tears in her eyes, and a quick glance at Eric told her that he, too, struggled to keep his composure.

A deep breath between movements steadied her enough to start the third movement with all the strength and confidence it demanded. Eric's lines were just as strong, and the orchestra obliged by playing with a meaty, masculine tone that grounded all the pianos' scale passages. She played automatically, focusing on clean and even notes, firm attacks, and balance with Eric and the orchestra. As the movement came to an end, the applause propelled her off the bench and into a bow, a gesture to the conductor and the orchestra, another bow, then offstage, then back on for a second bow. She and Eric had a second to breathe, and then the orchestra came backstage for intermission. Congratulations, hugs, and handshakes followed. The backstage doors opened, and Dr. White and Naomi rushed through. Hugs, praise, congratulations—from an emotional distance Cassie watched herself hug everyone, smile, and accept compliments. It had been a wonderful performance, but inside she knew nothing would ever be the same again.

Maureen arrived, wearing a voluminous silver scarf floating behind her like a shimmering comet trail. She reached for Cassie, wrapping her in an enormous hug and lifting her off her feet.

"You played like an angel!" she gushed, putting Cassie back on her feet.

Cassie laughed and automatically checked her hair with her hand.

"It looks fine," Maureen told her. "I am so proud of you!"

She loves me, Cassie realized, letting the warmth engulf her. That realization, along with the intensity of the performance, brought more tears to her eyes. She gulped and tried to make a joke.

"Don't make me cry," she said. "It will ruin my make-up."

Mr. and Mrs. Jackson, who had been congratulating Eric, came up to Cassie. She hadn't seen them since the incident and in that moment she wished she could disappear. Good Southern manners took over, however, and she accepted their praise with a poise she didn't know she possessed. She could see Mrs. Jackson's appraising eyes studying every inch of her. Mr. Jackson seemed unfazed, and shook hands enthusiastically, his graciousness a balm to Mrs. Jackson's distasteful expression and reluctance to get too close. Maureen threw Cassie a look that was full of admiration and pride, but Cassie was so worried about Mrs. Jackson's reaction that she barely noticed.

The five-minute warning bell sounded and everyone started returning to their seats for the second half. As the orchestra went back on stage, and everyone else went back to their seats, Cassie and Eric stood alone in the hallway. All thoughts of Maureen, Mrs. Jackson, and the performance disappeared, replaced by an ache as she looked at Eric. The orchestra started playing Mozart's *Jupiter* Symphony, but the silence between Cassie and Eric seemed louder than the notes from the stage.

"Do you want to go and listen from the auditorium?" Eric asked.

Cassie shook her head. "So this is it, then."

He didn't pretend to misunderstand her. "Yes."

Cassie drew a sharp breath. "Why?" she whispered.

He appeared to fight tears. "I got accepted into Regent and I'll be starting there in January."

"But I thought you weren't going until next fall." Cassie's voice shook, but she prided herself on not crying.

"Yeah, well, my mother had different ideas," he said bitterly. "She's afraid you and I might get too serious, and she wants me to marry a Believer."

Cassie turned away as his words seemed to cut right through her. She didn't reply.

"I was given a choice—go to Regent, where my parents will pay for my education, or move out and support myself." His voice sounded hollow.

"Why didn't you tell me?" Cassie said, her voice steadier than she felt.

"I was going to, and then everything happened at the church, and we had this performance." His voice trailed off. "I'm so sorry, Cassie."

She just shook her head, counting breaths again to stop the shaking.

"I love you," he added, and his voice broke.

She couldn't reply. Turning away, she walked down the hallway, struggling to keep from crying. After a few seconds, he followed her. When he reached her, he gently touched her arm and turned her toward him. She refused to meet his gaze, choosing to look at his bow tie instead. He continued to promise that they could stay together even if he was back East, and that once he got out of college his mother wouldn't be able to run his life anymore. She barely heard his words. She thought instead of his notes—that poignant and permanent goodbye he had crafted with the phrases of the second movement of the Bach. In those notes she heard the truth: He was leaving, it was over, and he would never be hers again.

She held herself with all the dignity Grandma had taught her. Her perfectly styled hair framed a smudge-free face. The dress and shoes gave her extra stature and grace. In her mind she could see her grandmother's knees, stocking-clad legs, and perfectly polished shoes as she sat on the sofa and watched The Apocalypse on TV. She drew further and further into herself, walling off Eric's words and the touch of his hand on her arm, and by the time he stopped talking, she felt dead inside, and perfectly calm.

Reaching up, she pulled his face to hers and kissed him. Every kiss they'd ever shared was in that kiss, and it went on and on until they ran out of air.

She pulled back, looked him in the eyes, and waited.

"It isn't like I'm going away forever," he said.

"Yes, it is," she replied with stoic finality. "And we both know it. It was in the notes."

He nodded and then turned his head, his chin wobbling. She smoothed her dress, cleaned up her smudged lipstick with the edge of her finger, and tried to maintain her composure. She wanted to cry and try to keep him from leaving. She wanted to drag him around the corner to a dark room and do with him all the things Maureen was afraid she was doing. She wanted to believe all his words, and hold on to the dream of getting back together and maybe even getting married. But the notes got in the way—those notes that once told her how much he wanted her now told her he had already left her, even when his words told her he wanted to stay.

After the concert ended, they attended a reception where both of them laughed and joked with everyone. Cassie could feel him watching her as she greeted friends and accepted praise for the performance. Naomi noticed too.

"What's up with Eric?" she asked Cassie as they stood together, sipping over-sweetened fruit punch. "He looks like his dog died or something."

Cassie took a sip before replying, "We broke up."

Naomi whirled toward her so fast she sloshed punch all over her hand. "Fuck!" she muttered, dabbing at her hand with a paper napkin. "What the hell happened?" Her bright eyes begged for details.

"I'll tell you later," Cassie replied, sotto voce as Shanna joined them. Across the room, Eric stood with his parents. Mrs. Jackson stood close to him, claiming him, with Eric looking more miserable by the moment.

She met his gaze and held it. *I love you too*, she thought.

His face relaxed as he got her message. And then, as if scripted, he turned and left, flanked on both sides by his parents.

Chapter 12

"We hate him."

Cassie and Naomi sat on the floor of Naomi's bedroom listening to Nirvana while they pretended to work on their college application essays. Naomi, full of indignation at what she saw to be Eric's betrayal, preferred to complain about Eric than to write.

"I mean, really! All this whiny bullshit about his mother making him go to that Bible-thumper college." She rolled her eyes. "Whatever!"

Cassie nodded and tried to push away the sick feeling she got inside every time she thought about Eric. She hadn't told Naomi about the incident at Eric's church, and as far as she could tell, he hadn't told anyone either. She knew with dead certainty that she had ruined everything by not being able to keep her composure and that Eric's breaking up with her was the price.

Of course he left, the voice inside her head repeated on what felt like a continuous loop. *You're a freak.*

Naomi stretched across the floor. "You're gorgeous, and he was lucky to get you," she added. "Fuck him. We need to get you someone better."

Cassie grimaced. *So I can be a freak and drive another one away?*

"Smells Like Teen Spirit" pulsated through the room. The volume and the bass were up so high Cassie felt the floor vibrating. Since moving to Oregon, she had gotten a crash course in popular music, and Nirvana was one of Naomi's favorite bands. Cassie wasn't as enthralled, but dutifully learned the words to most of the songs in order to fit in.

"It's OK," Cassie said. "I need to focus on my practicing right now anyway. I don't have time for a boyfriend."

Naomi flipped over on her stomach, kicked her Converse-clad feet back and forth, and scribbled in her notebook. Cassie looked at her own essay, entitled "Why Classical Music Isn't Dead," and sighed. Everything she had written read like a boring section of an Encyclopedia.

"Well, there's nobody interesting in Roseburg, anyway," Naomi conceded, putting down her pen. She rolled over and sat up. The disc came to an end, and the silence was such a contrast the room seemed to ring. "I hate writing," she stated. "I'm writing about the Hispanic employees at my parents' vineyard. It's the sort of multi-cultural bullshit admissions people like so much." She got up and put another CD in the player. "What's your topic?"

"Why classical music isn't dead," Cassie replied. She saw Naomi's disdainful look. "I'm thinking of starting over with something else," she added as she scratched out everything she had written.

The new CD started with the screech of an electric guitar and a pounding bass. Cassie edged as far away from the speakers as she could and tried to concentrate on her writing. It was no use. She couldn't think of anything to say, and the music was beginning to give her a headache. She tried not to think of the near-argument she and Maureen had gotten into over the application essay. Maureen wanted her to write about Texas, Him, and The Apocalypse. Maureen said Linfield wouldn't offer a scholarship to anyone without a high school diploma unless they could see there was a really good reason why she didn't have that diploma.

"Naomi!"

The voice cut through the pulsing music.

Naomi rolled her eyes. "Now what?" she asked Cassie, then yelled, "What?"

The door burst open. "I've told you six times to turn that damn thing down!"

Naomi's mother wore black leggings, a huge hot pink sweater, and a furious expression. Her jet-black curly hair was pulled up in a scrunchie. She barely looked at Cassie, which suited Cassie just fine; when she got mad, Naomi's mother scared her, and all she wanted to do was disappear anyway.

"Sorry," Naomi said nonchalantly, moving with exaggerated slowness to the stereo, where she turned down the volume just a little bit. "I couldn't hear you."

"That's fairly obvious!" her mother snapped. "And it's still too loud."

Naomi rolled her eyes and brought the volume down a little more. Her mother seemed to grow even angrier. Cassie pushed herself against the wall and held her breath.

"Don't you roll your eyes at me, young lady! I am your mother. Show some respect!"

"Sorry," Naomi replied, sarcasm just at the edge of her tone.

"And turn that damn music off! My head is killing me."

"Well, maybe if you didn't drink so much," Naomi muttered, turning back to the stereo.

"What did you say?"

Naomi's mother seemed to have fury sparking out the ends of her hair like electricity. Cassie's breath came in short, panicked gasps. She longed to melt into the carpet, or run from the room. And, irrationally, she felt that it was all her fault.

Naomi turned off the stereo and whirled back around in one quick movement. "I said, maybe you wouldn't have a headache if you didn't drink so much."

The words fell like lead in the suddenly quiet room. Naomi's mother's eyes filled with tears.

"I can't believe you have turned into such a hateful child," she said in a pitiful tone as she turned and left the room crying.

Cassie held her breath again. She couldn't think. She stared at Naomi, who stood angrily pulling at the ties on her bed quilt. The anger she had seen flashes of now seemed to transform Naomi into someone Cassie hardly knew. Naomi, seeing Cassie's white face and round eyes, shrugged and flopped on the bed, her nonchalant mask back in place.

"God, what a bitch," she drawled. "Wait till I tell my therapist about this fucking drama! It's like living in my own goddamn Jerry Springer show."

Cassie drew a deep breath. "She, um, seems really upset," she offered.

"Typical," Naomi spat out. "That's my cue to run after her and make her feel all good about herself. Of course, none of us can talk about the truth—that she drinks all the time and couldn't stop even if she wanted to—because that would upset her. Now she'll go crying to Dad, and he'll try and make me apologize. Fat chance."

Cassie wanted to tell her she was lucky her mother was still alive. She wanted to tell her that her own mother never got to see her play a concerto, and would never see her go to college or get married or have children. Every time something great happened, Cassie wanted to tell Mom; every time something bad happened, she wanted Mom to hold her. But all she could talk to or hold was thin air, and the only grave she could visit was a pile of charred buildings created by the fine employees of the United States government. She wanted to tell Naomi that even if her mom drank too much, acted like a bitch, and dressed like an aging Madonna, she should run to her and hug her, and tell her she loved her.

Instead she said, "Yeah. What a bitch."

"How did that make you feel?" Veronica asked Cassie at her next therapy appointment, after Cassie told her about the fight between Naomi and her mother. Since her promise to Maureen, Cassie had spent every Thursday evening in therapy with Veronica—a chunky middle-aged woman who wore lots of "ethnic" jewelry and had a huge silver streak in her black hair.

Cassie fought the urge to roll her eyes. What difference did her feelings make?

She shrugged. "Scared, I guess."

"In what way?" Veronica urged.

Cassie tried to think of a good answer—the right answer!— but her mind just refused to cooperate. How had she felt? She couldn't remember. All she remembered was the fear that the fight was her fault, and wanting to disappear.

"I just didn't want to be there," she said aloud.

Veronica nodded, "I can imagine so. How have you felt since then?"

Cassie gave her a puzzled look.

"When you were talking about the fight just a few minutes ago," Veronica explained, "how did you feel inside?"

"Um, Ok, I guess."

Veronica waited.

"A little worried, maybe," Cassie added.

Veronica waited.

"I thought that Naomi was so mean to her mom. It was like she didn't love her or anything."

Veronica nodded, and waited.

"I mean, her mother does drink too much, and she runs around dressed like Madonna from the 80's, but at least she has a mom."

As she finished speaking, Cassie could feel bitter jealousy at the back of her throat. In that moment, she would have given anything to change places with Naomi—drunk mother and all—to be normal and be raised in a real house, to have a real family where people fought and drank too much, to have a mother she could fight with rather than one who was so stupid she joined a cult, got herself killed, and ruined Cassie's life in the process.

"What you witnessed wasn't pretty, but fights between teen-age daughters and their mothers are part of the growing-up process," Veronica said. "I'll bet Naomi loves her mother very much; it's just at times she doesn't like her very much. Have you ever been really angry at someone, Cassie? Angry enough to say things you wish you hadn't said?"

Cassie shook her head. "No," she answered, a little primly.

Veronica gave her a searching look. "Anger is a natural emotion, Cassie, and it is a powerful one. We are never given the right to spew it on everyone, but we must also take care that we don't bottle it up inside. Remember, that which we choose to ignore is what comes back to bite us in time."

Cassie nodded; for several weeks they had spoken at length about how Cassie's determination to push Him and the Apocalypse as far out of her mind as possible had led to the severity of her reaction at Eric's church. She still wouldn't talk about it to Maureen or to Naomi, but her embarrassment and the fear of another meltdown prodded her into talking about it with Veronica.

"Were you allowed to be angry when you were little, Cassie?"

Cassie shook her head again and stared at the floor. She remembered the time she had been punished along with two other kids when the adults discovered someone had eaten a bag of chocolate chip cookies without permission. The fact that Cassie hadn't done it was irrelevant. She had been in the same room with the others when they did it and thus was spanked. She protested the unfairness by kicking her heels and yelling, and her defiance led to a beating that left her bottom sore for a day and a half. It was the last time Cassie could remember showing anger.

Veronica smiled at her. "With the authority invested in me as your therapist, I hereby give you permission to be angry. Explore your own anger. Find the anger in the music you play and let it teach you how to release it safely."

Cassie agreed to allow herself anger—mostly to get Veronica to move off the topic and on to anything else—but inside she couldn't imagine letting herself go the way Naomi had. Still, Veronica's comment about the anger in music stayed with her, and as she listened to music or practiced the piano, she listened for that anger. In the safety of her own practice room, she even started letting it out in the Beethoven sonata she was learning, and to her surprise, those passages she had accurately assessed as angry gained the fire and intensity Dr. White had been saying they lacked.

An hour spent at the piano, joining her anger to Beethoven's, gave her the insight she needed to write the college application essay that she had spent days struggling to produce. In the quiet of her bedroom she stopped writing about why classical music was important to everyone else and wrote instead about why it mattered to her. Once she got the first sentence down, the rest of the essay spilled out of her pen so fast she could barely keep up.

"When my parents died and everything I knew changed, classical music was the one constant," she wrote. "People say classical music is dead, but I am a seventeen-year-old pianist who knows differently..."

Cassie wrote until her hand ached, and then she put the pen down and re-read what she had written. She hadn't written about the Apocalypse or Him as Maureen suggested, but instead about the one thing that linked her past to her present. She closed her eyes and remembered a quote by Mendelssohn that Ruby had read to her years ago when they were working on a few "Songs Without Words."

"People often complain that music is too ambiguous, that what they should think when they hear it is so unclear, whereas everyone understands words. With me, it is exactly the opposite."

When she first heard the quote, Cassie had found it confusing. Now she knew the truth of it at a bone-deep level. Maureen once asked her why He allowed her to play classical music, and the only answer she could give her was that He thought it was harmless. *I wouldn't have survived without it*, Cassie realized. Her hands shook. She took a deep breath, stood up, and walked to the window. The rain fell with sloppy monotony. She thought of His face as He led songs with His guitar—three or four chords at most and a lot of lyric repetition. *Asshole*, she thought. *The piano was the only thing about me You couldn't own!*

She didn't realize how angry she was until she looked down and saw she was clenching the window sill so tightly her fingers were white. She uncurled them slowly and deliberately as she took deep, measured breaths. She remembered hearing that when he was dying, Beethoven sat up and shook his fist at God. She narrowed her eyes, extended both middle fingers in the direction of the ceiling and jabbed them at Him, gesturing what she dared not say.

Chapter 13

The audition took place behind closed classroom doors— one scholarship-seeking student after another entering the room, playing her best for the musi... and then facing an interview. Standing in the hall outsi... room, Cassie tried to block out the sound of a flute play... audition and to ignore the nervous chatter of two other girls waiting their turn to play. A black-clad accompanist leaned against the wall, flipping through a piece of music, and somewhere down the hall Cassie could hear a phone ringing.

She was freezing. Yesterday, as Maureen drove north on what seemed like an endless stretch of freeway, she studied the clear, cold sky and worried aloud about a forecast of snow. Cassie had never seen snow and had been disappointed by a soggy, grey Christmas rather than a white one; she looked at the frozen fields and half-prayed for a good storm. This morning she got her wish: sloppy wet flakes draped everything in an inch of white, and her thin dress coat and pumps were no match for it.

The flute playing stopped, and the two other girls stopped talking for a second, looked at the closed door, and then at each other.

"I am so freaked," one of them said.

Cassie blocked them out and walked a few steps down the hall. She already liked the place. The day before, one of the music majors—a sophomore trumpet player named Sam—had given them a tour of the building and campus and talked to Cassie about how great it was to be at Linfield. She loved it all—the oak trees, the old buildings, even the trailer where the music department had to put the extra practice rooms.

Maureen was less enthused, and she was incredulous about the trailer. "They charge this kind of tuition, and you have to practice in a trailer?" she muttered to Cassie as Sam went to get a set of keys to open up the band room.

"Well, Sam said they're building a new music building," Cassie replied, already feeling she needed to defend the school.

Now, as she walked back and forth waiting her turn to audition, she tried to block all of it out—the campus, Sam's more personal invitation of having coffee together after the audition, her own deep fear that she was not good enough to get a music scholarship, and the memory of the conversation she'd had with Maureen about Linfield.

They had sat at the kitchen table, coffee cups steaming in front of them. Cassie kept staring at the catalog, reading about all the music courses.

"How much is the scholarship?"

Cassie told her.

"And tuition is how much per year?" Maureen asked.

Cassie flipped through the pages to find the number.

Maureen sighed and closed her eyes. Deep lines etched around her mouth and between her eyebrows, and her skin looked faded and gray. It was the first time Cassie had ever seen her look old.

"Can I go if I get the scholarship?" Cassie asked, fear dropping her voice to a whisper.

Maureen lifted her hands and dropped them back on the table in a helpless gesture. "I don't know, honey. If you get a full music scholarship, yes you can go. If you don't, well, I don't know…"

In that moment Cassie could see everything: staying one more year at the community college while all her friends went on to other schools, working part time somewhere in Roseburg to save money, seeing everyone else move on while she stayed stuck. She had been accepted at the University of Oregon as well. But after having spent an afternoon on a campus that felt like the size of a city, Cassie shuddered at the idea of going to school there. Besides, Naomi had told her that private schools were the best, and even though Maureen assured Cassie that the U of O music department was excellent, she feared she might be missing something by going to a public college.

Cassie nodded and squared her shoulders. "Then I guess I will have to get that scholarship." That determination led to more hours in the practice room and an almost obsessive attention to the details in every measure of her audition pieces.

Standing in the hall, shivering in her damp pumps and too-thin coat, she repeated the phrase like a mantra. She blocked out the concerns Maureen had voiced the night before about the small department and the lack of national reputation of anyone in it except for Dr. Rutan. She blocked out the trailer practice rooms. She focused instead on the gorgeous oak trees, the old buildings, the way the campus already felt so welcoming, and the way Sam smiled when he asked her to have coffee with him. She refused to accept Maureen's suggestion: that her interest in the place had much to do with lack of exposure to other campuses and a budding interest in their trumpet-player campus escort.

What Cassie really didn't want to think about was the unvoiced worry she sensed under Maureen's spoken concerns: that she just wasn't normal enough to go away to college. The more she sensed Maureen's worry, the more determined she became to get into Linfield, go to Linfield, and be hugely successful at Linfield. From her study of popular magazines and books, Cassie knew that this was what normal girls did, and when she arrived at Linfield and saw that the campus looked exactly like what she thought a normal campus should look like, no other campus would do. Besides, Naomi was going to Reed, and Eric was gone.

She paced the hall and blew on her cold hands while her stomach constricted as she thought of Eric. She had seen him once after the concert, in the mall, while she and Naomi were supposedly Christmas shopping, but were really looking at cute clothes and cute guys. Their eyes locked, and Cassie's mouth went dry. She missed him so much she hurt inside. Naomi, not seeing Eric, grabbed Cassie's arm and pulled her into a clothes shop where Cassie stood, flipping through racks of sweaters, and trying to look normal. She later heard he had left right after the first of the year for his religious college. In Cassie's bag was a video tape of their concerto performance. Dr. Rutan wanted her to show it to the faculty as part of her audition. Now, holding the bag with icy fingers, she wondered how she would be able to watch the tape; the one time she had watched it with Dr. White in a lesson, it had been like re-living the break-up, and every note hurt.

I'll play first, Cassie thought. *Then they can watch the video and I can just tune it out.*

"Cassie?"

She turned at the sound of Dr. Rutan's voice. "Yes? Are you ready for me?"

He smiled and came down the hall to her. "They need a ten-minute break and then they'll be back to hear you play. Would you like to warm up on the piano?"

Cassie nodded and followed him down the hall and into the classroom. It was warmer in there. A seven-foot Steinway sat in the middle of the floor, and a small row of chairs was lined up a few feet away from it. She walked to the piano and played a C Major chord.

"Did you bring the video of your concerto performance?" Dr. Rutan asked, pulling out a cart with a TV and VCR on it.

"Yes," she said as she pulled the tape from her bag and handed it to him. "Would it be OK if I played first, and then let them watch the concerto?"

He reached down and plugged in the power strip. "Sure. Whatever makes you comfortable."

Cassie nodded, sat on the piano bench, and ran through a C minor scale. The piano was tuned and voiced, but the action was stiff and the pedal felt unwieldy. She checked the upper register by playing some arpeggios and then tried not to grimace—the upper register sounded as though all the notes were wrapped in cotton, and that meant she would have to work like mad to bring out the right-hand melodies.

"This piano is used primarily for vocal accompanying," Dr. Rutan said as he positioned the TV and checked that everything was working properly. "The faculty will not expect your melodies to ring out with as much clarity as they would on the Steinway we have in Melrose Hall. "

Cassie smiled, surprised that he had guessed her fear and addressed it without her even having to ask. She ran through several sections of the Barber, the octave section of the Liszt, and checked the opening tempo of the Mozart. Hearing the door open, she stopped playing and dropped her hands in her lap. As several faculty members wandered in, coffee cups in hand, she wondered if she should stay on the bench or move to one of the chairs. Finally, the need to remove her coat and put her bag someplace, propelled her to a chair propped against the back wall, away from the seats the faculty were rapidly filling. The door closed and a short man Sam had introduced to her as the department chair, smiled at her and then addressed the rest of the faculty.

"This is Cassie Carlyle. She's a pianist and studies with Jerry White at Umpqua Community College in Roseburg."

Smiles and nods of recognition from the faculty; Dr. White had told her he had worked as an adjunct professor at Linfield before getting a full-time position at UCC. Cassie felt relieved that they remembered him and, judging from their smiles, seemed to like him.

"Cassie will be performing part of her audition live, and part of it will be presented as a videotape of a concerto performance she gave last November." The faculty shifted and looked surprised and impressed. He smiled and nodded at her. "I will let her tell you what she is going to play for you."

Cassie stood, smiled, walked to the piano, and clasped her hands in front of her before she spoke. "Thank you for being willing to listen to me play today. I will begin by playing the first movement of Samuel Barber's *Excursions*, and will then perform Franz Liszt's *Sposalizio* from his Italian year of pilgrimage." By the time she was halfway through her introduction, she realized she was hearing Grandma's voice coming out of her mouth—soft Texas drawl, Southern manners, and just a little honey at the end of each sentence. She briefly considered forcing herself back into an Oregon accent, then just as quickly decided it would be too difficult to do and just finished her sentence as gracefully as possible.

Face flaming, she stepped to the piano, adjusted the bench, smoothed her skirt, and then started the Barber. The left hand ostinato put her right back on that train and by the time she reached the end of the first page, the room, the faculty, Linfield, and even the coveted scholarship had fallen away. It was just her and the music and that hot, dusty train rocking through a flat Texas landscape. When the last of the notes trailed away, she took her hands from the keys, acknowledged the polite applause from the faculty, and then closed her eyes for a moment to put herself into the Liszt.

When Dr. White had introduced her to the piece, he told her how Liszt wrote it to depict musically Raphael's painting of the marriage of the Virgin Mary to St. Joseph. Then he told her about

Liszt's relationship with Marie d' Agoult and how they were falling apart during the time he wrote the piece. Then he spoke of how the lines of the pieces are full of tenderness but never quite connect to each other—like two people who try to connect and no matter how much they love each other, just can't do it.

She heard all he said about it and tried to connect to the words, but when she learned the notes and got inside them for herself, *Sposalizio* became a thread that connected her—through death—to her parents. Part of her believed the notes could travel through time and that somehow, wherever they were, her parents could hear them, and her practice goal became achieving just the right clarity on each note to be able to cut through the veil of normal life to reach beyond the grave. She told no one, choosing instead to send the notes to her parents with no verbal explanation to the living.

Taking a deep breath, she put her hands on the keys, closed her eyes a second, and then played the opening lines. The muted upper register hampered her attempt to get a bell-like tone in the first right-hand arpeggio section. She tried to play through it, thinking of each note as being wrapped in thick velvet. Perhaps the clarity was there, at the center of all that velvet? What the piano took away from the upper register it gave back in the middle; when Cassie started what she always thought of as the prayer-like section—the one where she sensed she needed to breathe the notes rather than just play them—the velvet tone gave the notes a warmth she had never before been able to achieve on any other piano. The sound matched the one she had been hearing in her mind, and the magic of reality matching the ideal was so strong that she could feel the hair on her arms bristling. Normal life fell away, and for those breathless moments she sensed that the notes were getting through and that somehow, someone was on the other side, hearing all the love and loss she poured into each pitch.

When the piece ended, it was hard to come back. She lingered in the keys until the sound died and only then, reluctantly removed her hands and placed them in her lap. There was a moment of silence and then applause. She stood automatically, bowed, and then walked back to the chair that held her things. Dr. Rutan stopped her.

"Wait, Cassie, come on back. The faculty would like to ask you a few questions."

She turned, walked back to the piano, and then had a moment of indecision. Should she sit? Stand? She stood awkwardly for a second and then took a seat on the edge of the bench, crossed her ankles, and pasted a polite smile on her face. She hoped they couldn't see that her hands were shaking as she clasped them together in her lap.

"How long have you studied the piano?" a middle-aged man asked.

"Ten years, sir. Since I was seven," Cassie answered, and then smiled again.

"You play very well," an older woman said. "Would you be willing to sight-read some music and play us some scales and arpeggios?"

"Yes, ma'am," Cassie replied. "What would you like to hear?"

"F-sharp Major and the parallel minor," she replied. "And play tonic and dominant seventh arpeggios."

Dr. Rutan gave the woman a disgusted look. "We don't usually ask for arpeggios," he said.

"Well, I just wanted to see if she knew them," the woman replied coyly, steel under the sweetness of her tone.

"I am happy to play them," Cassie said, addressing both the woman—for whom she had developed an instant dislike—and Dr.

Rutan. "And would you also like to hear a diminished-seventh arpeggio when I play the minor?"

The woman gave her a strained smile, and Dr. Rutan broke into a wide grin.

"That would be lovely," the woman replied, her tone softening just a little.

Cassie played the requested scales and arpeggios and then turned back to the faculty. Dr. Rutan put some sheet music in front of her, and she sight-read that as well. After she finished, she again faced the faculty.

"Why are you interested in studying at Linfield," Dr. Rutan asked.

"I feel that Linfield will best help me reach my goals of becoming a better musician," Cassie replied, voicing her much-rehearsed answer. "And I love it here," she added spontaneously.

The faculty smiled and nodded. Dr. Rutan moved the TV/VCR stand into place and then introduced the video, while Cassie moved back to her chair in the back of the room. Shivering with nerves, she wrapped her coat around her stocking-clad legs, and sat on her hands as the video started.

As she watched Eric and herself walk onto the stage, it was like watching people she didn't know performing something a long time ago. *Maybe I'm over him*, she thought, waiting for the music to start. Eric's opening line started, her line answered, and the emotions came back with each phrase. In the notes she had to admit the truth: she wanted out of Roseburg because he wasn't there anymore. She wanted out because he had left her. *I have to keep going. I have to pull myself up and just get on with life because that's what people do: they leave.*

She was relieved when Dr. Rutan stopped the video after the first movement. When the music stopped, it became so much easier to put Eric into the back of her mind, put the sick longing away with him, and stand, smile, shake hands with the faculty, take the video from Dr. Rutan's outstretched hand, and leave the room with her head high. And later, after coffee with Sam, dinner with Maureen, and an hour of re-hashing the audition to Naomi over the phone, it was as if her feelings for Eric had never been. She imagined the future: Linfield, Sam, maybe join a sorority. She would be happy, normal, and in charge of her life. She fell asleep wondering how she would get through the rest of the year until fall semester.

Chapter 14

The letter was waiting for Cassie when she returned home after her Tuesday classes. It sat on top of the pile of junk mail and bills addressed to Maureen, and its Linfield return address caught her attention immediately. The school acceptance letter she had received a few months ago had felt encouraging, but she knew this one contained the news about the music scholarship and thus the key to her future.

You won't know until you open it, she thought as she ripped it open. Taking a deep breath, she opened the letter and started to read. When she saw that she had been offered the piano scholarship, she squealed, dropped the letter, and pirouetted around the kitchen a couple of times before rushing to the phone and dialing Maureen's work number.

"I got the scholarship!" she announced as soon as Maureen picked up the phone.

Maureen gasped. "Oh, Cassie, congratulations!"

"They offered me the full piano scholarship," Cassie said, her words coming out so fast she was barely breathing. "Can I go? Can we do it?"

"Well, we'll run the numbers tonight, but if my math was correct, yes, you may go!"

Cassie let out a yelp, and Maureen laughed and said, "We'll talk when I get home."

Cassie hung up and hugged herself as she walked around the room. It didn't seem real. *It's where I belong*. She imagined herself walking across the Linfield campus, holding her books in one arm, her blonde hair glinting in the late afternoon sunshine. *I'll be in the center of things*. She walked back to the phone and looked at it.

Even though she had vowed to forget about him, she longed to call Eric and tell him her news. For a second the pain was sharp. She took a deep breath, pushed him out of her mind, and dialed Naomi's number.

When Naomi answered the phone, it was obvious that she had been crying. Cassie got no further than identifying herself when Naomi announced that Kurt Cobain was dead and then started crying again. Twenty minutes passed as Cassie listened to Naomi and murmured what she hoped were the correct platitudes. *Why don't I care?* she thought as she promised to come over later that evening. As soon as she hung up, she realized she had forgotten to tell Naomi about the scholarship. She picked up the phone to dial Naomi again and then slowly put the receiver back down. *She won't care.* Cassie thought of the other pianists in Dr. White's studio and the other students in her classes at the community college. *No one cares.*

"I have no one to tell." She spoke it aloud to the empty house.

She remembered the time Ruby had helped her learn Mozart's "Rondo alla Turca" and how she played it for her father late one afternoon. She could still see the delighted smile he had worn when she made it all the way through the coda without a stumble. More memories returned. Each time she learned a new piece, one of the adults would compliment her on the accomplishment. Even He told her one time that God had blessed her with a special talent. She remembered the first time He had had her help out with the singing in one of the Friday vesper meetings. Candles were lit, everyone sang, and Cassie knew she was safe and loved and that she belonged right there in the middle of it.

Cassie couldn't breathe. She put her face in her hands as memories flooded through her. It felt as if she was there, in the meetings, and for the first time, she missed them. She missed Friday evening meetings when they heard the word by candlelight. She missed work days when the adults constructed the main house and she and the kids played Bible charades. She missed knowing beyond all doubt that she was part of the Truth and that she was at home, surrounded by family. Most of all she missed being a daughter. *I'll never be anyone's daughter again. I'll never belong to anyone again.*

She remembered singing hymns with her mother as they cleaned the meeting room together. Cassie always harmonized an alto line to her mother's lilting soprano. *People said we blended so well they couldn't tell who was singing what part.*

"I want everyone singing," He always said.

"We've come this far by faith, leaning on the Lord, trusting in His holy word, He hasn't failed us yet," her mother always sang.

Cassie shivered as the realized that outside of sight singing class she had stopped singing since the Apocalypse. *Get a grip. Get a grip.*

She thought of how He would preach about the latter days, being part of the Wave Sheaf and remaining true to the Spirit of Prophecy. He told them to keep the Sabbath holy, take the Elements, and to hold tightly to the hope which burned within their hearts. He promised He would never leave them or forsake them and that everyone who followed Him was part of His family. *And you taught us to die with you,* she thought bitterly.

When the government agents first hit the compound, He told them it was the Fifth Seal, and that this was the cry of the martyrs who were killed for their beliefs.

"We've come this far by faith," her mother always sang.

"Hold fast to the Truth," her father told her as she left the compound. "You are part of the Wave Sheaf."

When did I stop believing it? Was it before the Apocalypse or after?

On March second when she and the other children were led out of the compound, Cassie hadn't turned to look back. Her parents said they would follow her in a few days. She met Grandma, a woman she only knew from pictures, at the Methodist Children's Home, and it hadn't seemed possible it would be the last time she saw her parents, or that the life she knew would soon be burned to the ground.

Why didn't you leave with me? What brought you there in the first place?

It hurt too much to miss her parents. Anger was easier, and soon it began to replace her yearning for the past. She remembered the year before they moved to Mt. Carmel and how her mother spent most of it in bed and her father spent most of it working two jobs to keep the family solvent. *Was it one of Mom's friends who first brought her the tapes?* One day it seemed Mom couldn't get out of bed, the next she played His sermon tapes over and over again. Cassie remembered arguments behind her parents' bedroom door, Mom crying, and then one day Mom was happy, Jesus had healed her, and they were all moving to Mt. Carmel to prepare for the Wave Sheaf. Cassie remembered.

"Was this the only way you could be happy?" Cassie asked out loud. "Were you so selfish that you had to sacrifice your daughter?"

Silence. The kitchen clock ticked. Cassie watched the second hand go round and round until the phone rang again. Somehow thirty minutes had passed, and Cassie couldn't account for a minute of it.

"That bitch Courtney killed him," Naomi stated. "I just can't believe it."

It was 11:45 at night. Cassie and Naomi sat in Naomi's living room, Nirvana pounding out of the stereo, and Naomi drinking one rum and coke after another. Cassie, who hated soda, drank tempranillo from Naomi's family vineyard. She had never had wine before and she was enjoying the way it filled her with warmth and a glowing contentment.

"Uh huh," she replied. She hadn't been listening. Naomi had stopped by just after Cassie and Maureen finished dinner, and Cassie had promised to be home by midnight. The last few hours had been spent listening to Naomi cry about Kurt Cobain and watching her become drunker and drunker.

"We should drive to Seattle for the vigil," Naomi said, her voice breaking. "Listen, I mean just listen."

Cassie dutifully listened to the recording. No matter how many times she heard the songs, they failed to move her. *What am I missing here? Is it me?* She looked at Naomi, who sat curled up in the corner of the sofa with her bare feet tucked under her. She was most decidedly drunk. A new question edged out the old: *How am I going to get home?* She looked at the clock and again at Naomi, who was now resting her cheek on the arm of the sofa. *Maureen will be asleep and Naomi is in no condition to drive.* She looked at the glass of wine in her hand, and had to stifle an irrational giggle. *If He could see me now.* She looked again at Naomi, who now had her eyes closed as she cried and sang with the CD. *I wonder what it's like to have a rock star's death be the most tragic event in your life.*

As soon as the thought formed, Cassie felt guilty. *She's the normal one, I'm not.* For a second she felt bitterly jealous. She thought again of the letter from Linfield, and it soothed her. *I will be normal. I will have a regular life.* She drained her wineglass and stood to go and refill it. When the room swayed, Cassie realized that she, too, was decidedly drunk. She sat down slowly.

"I got the piano scholarship to Linfield," she said to Naomi.

Naomi didn't reply. When Cassie looked more closely, she saw that Naomi had fallen asleep.

"Shit," she muttered.

She weighed all the options: It was too far to walk, and Maureen would be angry to be awakened at midnight to come and get her. *Would she even hear the phone?* Cassie thought. The past year's observation had taught Cassie that once Maureen went to sleep it took a lot of noise to wake her. Maureen hadn't ever admitted to being hard of hearing, but Cassie had learned early to speak loudly and distinctly to Maureen if she didn't want to have to repeat herself. She looked again at Naomi. The clock struck midnight. A few minutes later the CD ended and the house settled into silence.

The living room was dark except for one table lamp, and Cassie heard nothing but the ticking of the grandfather clock. *It sounds like the house's heartbeat.* It was a big room, and darkness seemed to pool in all the corners. Cassie shivered as the memory came back.

It had been a hot July night, and Cassie had been unable to sleep in the sticky heat. She put on a light cotton dress and crept downstairs to the main living space of the big house. Her bare feet allowed her to walk soundlessly through what she thought was a deserted room until a gasp from one of the chairs made her jump. A light switched on, and she saw her mother curled up, feet tucked under her. It was obvious that she had been crying.

"What's wrong, Mommy?" Cassie had asked as she walked over to her, knelt on the floor by the chair, and leaned her head into her mother's lap.

"Nothing that Jesus can't fix," her mother had replied.

The memory faded, but the guilt she had felt at not being able to fix her mother stayed with her. She looked at Naomi; without all the bravado, she looked like a little girl. *I can't fix anyone.* She heard a car stop outside the house, and a few seconds later, the front door opened. Joel stepped into the room and shrugged out of his coat.

"Hi," Cassie said.

He jumped. "Oh, I didn't see you there. You're Cassie, right?"

Cassie nodded. She pointed to Naomi. "She fell asleep."

Joel looked at the remains of Naomi's rum and coke and the nearly empty bottle of wine and smirked. "Passed out is more like it."

Cassie blushed. "She was, um, pretty upset about Kurt's death and everything."

"Kurt?"

"Cobain."

He rolled his eyes. "Were they personal friends or something? She can be really dramatic sometimes."

Cassie grinned. *So it's not just me!* "Unfortunately she was my ride home," she said.

He looked at his sister and shook his head. "She'll be out awhile. Don't worry, I'll take you."

He put his coat back on and picked up his car keys. Cassie stood carefully and tried to walk a straight line to the coat rack. She heard him start laughing as she struggled to get her arms into her coat.

"I guess she's not the only one," he said, as he held door open for her.

The cool night air steadied her. As Joel backed out of the driveway, she covertly studied his profile. Where Naomi was skinny, he was lean. *He's a college guy,* she reminded herself. *He sees you as one of his kid sister's friends.* She wondered what he was doing home in the middle of the semester but wasn't brave enough to ask.

"Where do you live?" Joel asked as they left the driveway.

Cassie told him and then fell silent. *Say something! Anything!*

"Do you enjoy playing the clarinet?" she blurted. *Why did you say something so stupid!*

"I used to play," he replied. "I gave it up when I went to college."

"Oh." *That was a real conversation starter.*

He made a right turn. "How about you? Are you musical?"

"I play the piano," she replied. "Like Naomi."

"Are you good at it?" he asked.

"Some days," Cassie replied and then blushed. *Some days? Another stupid comment!*

He laughed. "That's an honest answer."

They drove the few miles in silence. Cassie thought again of her mother. *I never got to talk to her about boys.* The picture of her mother curled up in that chair came back to her and with it, the guilt. *If I had been able to cheer her up, maybe they would have gotten out in time.* She knew it was irrational, but she still blinked back tears.

Joel parked in front of Cassie's driveway and waited while she undid the seatbelt and climbed out of the car.

"Thanks for the ride," she said as she started to close the car door.

"Drink a couple of glasses of water and take some aspirin before you go to sleep," he advised just before the door shut.

She waved and walked to the front door while he drove away. *It wouldn't matter if he did notice me,* she thought as she opened the front door and walked into the house. *I'm such a freak he wouldn't want to be with me anyway. Nobody would.*

The house was silent. Cassie walked to the kitchen and took two aspirin with a couple of glasses of water. The warmth the wine had given her earlier had faded and she felt empty and terribly alone. She gripped the edge of the kitchen sink and stared out the window. *I've got to make this stop. The only way I am going to be normal is to make this stop.* She thought of Maureen and of Grandma and tried to convince herself that she belonged to both of them, but she knew better. Neither had been part of her life before she left the compound, and pretending that blood made them family did nothing to make her feel less alone. She thought of the Bach Prelude and Fugue she was working on and closed her eyes as she let herself be swept into the clear lines. The empty loneliness dissipated. *That's home,* Cassie thought as she left the kitchen and prepared for bed.

Chapter 15

On Tuesday, April 19, Cassie and Maureen called in sick and took a trip to the beach. In the two weeks after getting notice about her Linfield scholarship, Cassie's attention was on homework, practicing, and rehearsing with vocalists she was accompanying for spring music juries. She knew it was the anniversary of the Apocalypse, but felt a clinical detachment from that knowledge as though she was remembering that the Baroque era was approximately 1600-1750, or that Chopin was a Romantic composer. Whenever Maureen or Veronica tried to get her to talk about the anniversary, she dutifully responded to questions, nothing more.

Cassie woke early that morning and was already running through her mental list of tasks for the day before she got out of bed. It was clear, and early morning sunlight shimmered off the damp grass and leaves. Cassie opened her bedroom window and stood shivering as she breathed in the scent of damp earth, vegetation, and fresh air until the cold forced her to close the window. Stretching, she decided she would wear her jean mini-skirt, black tights, and little black turtleneck with lots of silver jewelry. The skirt was new—a look she had seen in *Glamour* and had vowed to copy as soon as she could afford it.

She walked barefoot to the kitchen, where she made a pot of coffee. She loved this time of the day—the quiet thirty minutes or so before Maureen got up. The house felt so peaceful, and Cassie sank into the silence while she sat sipping coffee and feeling her brain wake up. She remembered that she was scheduled to meet Naomi to study for a pre-calc test, and that she was supposed to help Megan—the stupidest soprano Cassie had ever met—learn her notes for her solo in an upcoming choir concert.

She heard Maureen's alarm clock go off, and then a few minutes later, listened as Maureen left her bedroom and then shut the bathroom door. She stood, refilled her coffee cup, and walked to the living room where she turned on the TV.

His face filled the screen, and it frightened Cassie so badly that she yelped and dropped the coffee down her front. She couldn't feel the scalding liquid, which drenched her pajamas and spread in a rapidly cooling damp spot on the carpet. She couldn't feel anything, just a shaking so intense that she sank to the floor, where she curled up into a little ball and wrapped her arms around herself.

His eyes looked right through her. He knew where she was. He knew how she'd strayed from His teachings. He knew about Eric. He knew she drank wine and that she watched TV and read magazines. He had done what He predicted: He was resurrected, just as He said He would be.

The scene changed, this time shots of the Apocalypse— flames, and smoke shooting up, the sound of gunfire, and a reporter with windblown hair and a grave facial expression. Cassie watched her mouth move but couldn't hear anything but rushing white noise.

Maureen rushed out of the bathroom, ran to Cassie, and then stood frozen as she, too, watched the screen. Cassie stared at her, wild-eyed.

"He's back," she croaked. "He's back."

Maureen grabbed the remote and turned off the TV. She was breathing heavily and her face had a slight green tinge to it. She grabbed Cassie and shook her. Cassie couldn't move. She stared at the blank TV screen until Maureen gave her face a gentle slap.

"I'm sorry," Maureen said, sinking to the floor next to Cassie.

"He's alive," Cassie whispered, her jaw shaking.

"No, Cassie, He's not," Maureen replied, wrapping her arms around Cassie. "Not one of them is alive."

Maureen started crying, and in that moment Cassie realized Maureen wasn't holding her to give her comfort but because she missed her daughter and she needed comfort. Cassie unclenched her hands from around her legs, wrapped herself around Maureen, and just sat there shaking as Maureen cried. As Maureen's crying and Cassie's shaking subsided, the panic receded, and she knew He was just a news clip, not the resurrected Messiah. That was quickly followed by a wave of hate so strong that she wished He had come back from the dead just so she could hack Him to death with a steak knife.

"I fucking hate that guy," Cassie said, with a steadiness only achievable from pure rage.

"So do I," Maureen said, her voice breaking.

Neither of them could eat breakfast. They drank coffee, took showers, got dressed, and then sat in the living room. Cassie thought of all the practicing she wanted to do, and of her appointment with Naomi, and her rehearsals and classes, but even as she tried to get up and get out the door, she couldn't make herself do it. Maureen, sitting across the room, the paper unread on her lap, didn't move either—even though she was already late for work.

"We're going to the beach," Maureen announced.

Cassie nodded, relief allowing her to release a breath she hadn't known she was holding. She waited until Maureen had called in sick and then called Naomi and the music department and made her excuses. Cassie changed out of her new outfit into comfortably worn jeans, waterproof boots, a chunky sweater, and a rainproof parka. A year in Oregon had taught her that just because the day started sunny was no guarantee it would stay that way— particularly in April.

Maureen brought her old Stones and Beatles CDs for the trip. As the miles slid by, Cassie marveled how even though the songs were so new to her, they now felt like old friends. Somehow the voices from an earlier—and what Cassie suspected was easier— time pushed the horror of this day outside the car. She kept time with her fingers, and that also kept her from falling into the black, icy void of terror that kept pulling at the edges of her mind. As she listened to Maureen sing, she wondered if she, too, was feeling the same fear.

It's like being on an island surrounded by black nothingness, she thought. *Every time I look, the black gets closer and closer.* She had the sense that if she could keep diving into music, the music would shield her.

They drove to Bandon, where they parked on the Beach Loop road and then got out and started walking. The beach was deserted except for several sea gulls and some dramatic chunks of driftwood. Maureen was taller than Cassie, but Cassie's long legs matched Maureen's, so they walked nearly in step with each other. After walking south about a mile, they stopped, sat on a piece of driftwood, and stared at the water.

"No mother ever plans to outlive her kids," Maureen said.

Cassie looked at her, but Maureen kept her eyes on the horizon, and her chin was steady. Cassie waited.

"I had your mother when I was just twenty-three-years old," Maureen continued. "Your grandfather and I got married right after we graduated from college, and I got pregnant shortly after that. Your mother was the most beautiful baby—" she stopped and drew a deep breath. "Anyway, your grandfather and I were good Christians so she went to church school—Roseburg Junior Academy and then Milo Academy. She converted to Adventism and wanted to go to Walla Walla College." She turned and looked at Cassie. "She had a degree in nursing. Did you know that?"

Cassie shook her head. "She never talked about her life before she and Dad met Him. It was like it didn't matter." Cassie didn't add that she didn't even know that Maureen existed, that although she had been told that her grandfather was dead, she had never heard of Maureen and had assumed she had died as well.

"Well, she met your Dad, married him in the Roseburg Seventh-day Adventist Church, and after the honeymoon, he took her back to Texas. She got pregnant with you, and had just given birth when your grandfather died. She and your Dad flew up here for the funeral. She tried to talk to me back then about the Branch Davidians—she and your Dad were already part of the group, although David Koresh had not yet pulled them into his collective." Her mouth tightened. "I wish I'd listened. A couple of years after that your Mom and Dad met Koresh. Your grandfather's funeral was the last time I saw her."

She thought again of her mother and felt another flash of anger. "Why was she so selfish?" she asked.

Maureen blinked. "What do you mean?"

Cassie bit her lip and started picking lint off her sweater. "The rest of us have to get out of bed every day and function like grown-ups. She gets depressed, stays in bed for a year while my father has to work two jobs to keep food on the table, and then she decides the way to be happy is to drag all of our asses off to join a fucking cult!"

Maureen's jaw dropped open. She took a deep breath, started to speak, and then closed her mouth for a minute. "I don't know why, Cassie," she finally said. "I wish I did. If I understood her maybe..."

She left the sentence unfinished. Cassie clenched her jaw and folded her arms across her chest. "Sometimes I hate her," she said.

Maureen's eyes filled. "I know," she replied.

Cassie watched as Maureen tried to control her emotions. Her face remained still, but her chin shook, and silent tears ran down her cheeks.

"Today I hate her too for what she did—to herself, to me, to your Dad, and most of all to you," Maureen added, her voice breaking. "On a day when I should mourn, I feel rage. She robbed all of us and for what? What did I do wrong? Should I have sent her to public school? None of our friends' kids went off and joined a cult, even though they went to Christian schools..." She buried her face in her hands and sobbed.

Cassie edged closer to her, wrapped an arm around her shoulders, and leaned her head on Maureen's shoulder. She was stunned; it was the first time she realized how much Maureen had suffered too. She thought of all the times she had pushed Maureen away when Maureen tried to comfort her or to get her to talk. She remembered all the times Maureen tried to hug her and how she stiffened and tried to back away. And she wondered whether Maureen thought she had rejected her just as her Mom rejected her.

Cassie's throat closed up, and the tears erupted. She cried for Maureen, for her Mom, for her Dad, and for a nameless loss that ached so deeply she couldn't give it words. Maureen's arm wrapped around her waist and they held each other until both of them cried themselves dry. Then they sat without talking, just leaning on each other and watching the waves.

"Where did they go, when they died?" Cassie asked. She thought of all the times she felt as though she was almost able to brush their fingertips with the notes she played; it didn't seem possible that Naomi was right, that when you're dead, you're dead.

Maureen shook her head. "I don't know. There was a time I would have believed the standard Christian line that they are in heaven, but now?" Her voice trailed off.

"I think they're still around somehow," Cassie stated with a surprising amount of conviction. "I don't know why, but I just do."

Maureen gave her a squeeze. "I sure hope you're right." But she still looked skeptical.

Later, after they walked back to the car and drove to a fish and chips restaurant for a late lunch/early supper, Cassie sat across the booth from Maureen and watched Maureen add cream and sugar to her coffee. Her grey hair fell across her forehead in wind-and-rain-styled disarray, and her glasses steamed as she picked up the coffee for a sip. Cassie looked at both her hands and noticed, for the first time, that Maureen had the same hands Mom had, or rather that Mom had Maureen's hands. They were lovely—long fingers, oval fingernails, and perfectly proportioned. Maureen wore a heavy silver ring on the middle finger of her right hand; as far back as Cassie could remember, Mom had never worn a ring.

"What?" Maureen asked, putting down the coffee.

"Nothing," Cassie replied. "I like your ring."

Maureen studied it with a gentle smile. "A gift from your Grandfather for our ten-year anniversary," she said. "Or rather, this is the one I picked out. He planned to buy me a huge gold ring with both our birthstones, but it was what he wanted me to wear, not what I preferred."

Cassie looked at the silver ring again. "I think this was a better choice for you."

The waitress arrived with their orders of fish and chips and placed the steaming plates in front of them. After bringing them ketchup and vinegar, she re-filled their coffee cups and then left them to eat. Cassie took a chip and bit into it, savoring the perfect combination of hot greasy potato and salt. They ate in silence for a few minutes. The restaurant was nearly empty except for an old man seated at the counter and a family with two small kids eating in the back booth. Country music played lightly in the background, and the waitress bustled by in her brown uniform, carrying a pot of coffee. Cassie drank in the normalcy of it. She studied the family and felt jealous of the kids. They looked so ordinary. She dropped her gaze to her plate as she thought of Him.

"I'll never understand why my parents were so stupid," she said.

Maureen stopped eating. "They weren't stupid," she said gently. "They were just misled."

Cassie shook her head. "Stupid or misled, what's the difference? They still got pulled into a cult."

She remembered the day they arrived at Mt. Carmel. It had been sunny, and the windows were down. The wind had whipped Cassie's long blonde hair across her face, but she hadn't cared. It was a beautiful day, everyone was happy, and God had called them to follow Him. Dad had his elbow resting out the window, and he smiled as he drove. Mom's face shone, and she sang, "We're marching to Zion, beautiful, beautiful Zion, we're marching upward to Zion, that beautiful city of God."

The memory faded, leaving a dull ache in Cassie's gut. She looked at the remains of her fish and chips and thought of how

Veronica always wanted her to bring up the memories so they could be healed. *I can't keep dredging this stuff up. I've got to move on.*

Maureen sighed. "I don't know if anyone will ever know why they did what they did. But they loved you, Cassie. I'm sure of it."

Cassie clenched her jaw. "If you say so." She felt both grief and anger. *They're dead. I have to bury them. They're dead.*

"I say so," Maureen replied with conviction.

How would you know? Cassie thought. *You never got to see them with me.* She thought of Him and of all the preaching and all the singing. She thought of the work days and the daily calisthenics. She thought of the Apocalypse and of the pictures of burned buildings and smoldering ashes. *You're dead*, she mentally told all the memories, and then she slowly pushed them back in her mind until it felt as if she had closed a door between the memories and herself. *I'm done thinking about you, and I'm done crying for you. It's over.*

Maureen dropped her fork on the table and gave Cassie a horrified look.

"What?" Cassie asked. "What's wrong?"

"We forgot to call your Grandmother!"

"Oh, shit," Cassie whispered. She could see her Grandmother sitting in her perfectly pressed suit, waiting by the phone in that pristine kitchen. She knew, without even thinking about it, that Grandma would want to avoid friends that day, and that Cassie would be the only person she would want to talk to.

"We have to find a phone," Maureen announced, standing up and walking to the register.

Cassie sat and watched her ask about a phone. The woman shook her head. Maureen asked again, this time a pleading expression on her face. The woman relented and disappeared into the back. A few minutes later she came back out, a smile on her face. Maureen motioned for Cassie to join her.

"We can use a phone back in the office," she told Cassie.

Cassie and Maureen followed the woman through the loud and steamy kitchen to a closet in the back, where someone had crammed in a desk and chair.

"Thank you," Maureen told the woman. She rummaged in her wallet and produced a calling card. Handing it to Cassie she said, "I hope you remember the number."

Cassie nodded, read the directions on the card, and then started dialing. As the phone rang, she saw herself back in that kitchen, sitting next to Grandma, not knowing what to say. Grandma was so strong it was hard to imagine her ever needing anyone. *It was her strength I drew on this year,* Cassie realized as she heard her grandmother's greeting. *It was because of her I got this new life.* She looked at Maureen with her short gray hair and windbreaker and visualized Grandma with her perfect helmet of white hair, wearing one of her many flowered dresses.

They are my family now, she thought as she said hello. *I've got to make this work.* She reached out and squeezed Maureen's hand. "I love you," she said to both of them.

Part II

"But for all their lyricism and tragic passion and exuberance, the Aria and the Variations seem of a divine substance entirely refined and purified of anything personal or ignoble, so that in playing them one seems only the unworthy mouthpiece of a higher voice. And even beyond the scope of the emotions that have been aroused, the effect of the whole is one of boundless peace, in which one returns cleansed, renewed, matured to the starting point, which seen a second time seems so transfigured in the light of this traversed spiritual journey.

But how Bach himself in pious humility would ridicule these high-sounding words of ours with a wry face and with god-like laughter."

--Ralph Kirkpatrick (1934)

Chapter 16

When the World Trade Center towers came down, Cassie watched it on TV in the Omaha, Nebraska airport. The waiting area fell silent as news footage flashed incomprehensible images, interspersed with the pale, frightened faces of New York newscasters. Cassie's bag slid off her lap unnoticed as the old white noise she hadn't heard in years blanketed her mind. The newscaster's voices disappeared, along with the sounds of the falling buildings, and only the images remained.

"Oh shit!"

Gabe's voice seemed to come from far away, even though he sat beside her. Cassie ignored him, unable to tear her attention from the TV screens. An airline attendant crossed in front of them, her face a frozen mask. Cassie could feel Gabe shifting beside her, pulling out his cell phone and punching in numbers.

"I can't get through," he said.

Cassie forced herself to look away from the TV. "What?"

He closed his phone with a gesture of frustration. "The lines must be overloaded."

Cassie nodded, looking around the waiting area. No one but airline attendants moved. Behind the counter she could see one of them talking on the phone, and two others talking quietly to each other. She studied the faces of their fellow travelers, and in them she saw her own feelings: shock, disbelief, fear, and horror.

"This can't be happening," Gabe said, staring once again at the TV coverage.

Cassie nodded but said nothing. A woman sitting across from them started crying. An announcement came over the airport loudspeaker, telling everyone that all flights were grounded for an indefinite length of time. She followed Gabe and the rest of the passengers to the Delta desk to get hotel reservations. Gabe stood in line for both of them, while Cassie stood to the side holding Gabe's violin and their bags. No one seemed to know what to do. People stood in the middle of the floor, bags around them, looking as if they didn't know where to go. When they finally got to the front of the line, Gabe looked exhausted.

"They've got us a room in the Super 8," he said, taking his violin from her. He looked around the airport, a helpless expression on his face. "I guess we should go there?"

As they walked through the airport, Cassie noticed that no one seemed to move with purpose. Everyone had the frozen expressions of the walking dead.

"Apparently another plane hit the Pentagon," Cassie told him, relaying what she had overheard while waiting for him.

"Oh, shit," Gabe said again.

She looked at his hand; it was clutching his violin case so tightly his knuckles were white. A lifelong nervous flier, Gabe had to take beta blockers to even get on a plane. Cassie wondered if, when the planes started flying again, they would have to take a train back to Oregon. All around her, people moved slowly. Cassie remembered a scene in a movie of war refugees clutching small children and belongings as they stumbled across a frozen landscape—their faces etched with exhaustion and loss. As she looked at her fellow travelers streaming out of the airport, she saw the same expressions again on the faces of well-fed Americans.

There was a line at the shuttle stop, and Cassie and Gabe had to wait for another hour to get a shuttle to the motel. All the seats were taken, so they stood, clutching straps hanging from the ceiling, through the fifteen-minute ride. Gabe didn't even complain. Cassie wondered if it was the first time he had met an inconvenience without throwing some sort of fit.

When they arrived at the motel, they were among the first to the desk. They got their room keys, took the elevator to the second floor, and dragged their bags into the room. Gabe turned on the TV and then sat on the end of the bed and pulled out his cell again.

Cassie walked over to the window and opened the curtains. The skies were a stunning shade of blue, and the horizon seemed to stretch forever. She could hardly remember a time when no jet contrails streaked the sky. *This must have been what the skies looked like a century ago,* Cassie thought as she turned away from the window.

Gabe sat hunched over, staring at the TV. His cell lay silent beside him. For the first time, Cassie noticed bits of gray shining through his dark hair and deep crevices on each side of his mouth. *He looks old*, she thought.

She had never thought of him as old. Gabe said age was a state of mind, and it didn't matter that he was forty and she was twenty-five—all that mattered was that they loved each other. Gabe also said it didn't matter that he was married, and that he and his wife had a ten-year-old son and a six-year-old daughter. What was narrow Puritanical thinking in the face of true passion? Now, as Cassie watched him pick up the phone again and hit re-dial with a look of desperation, she knew things that didn't matter yesterday mattered a great deal today and that nothing would ever be the same again.

She crossed the room and sat on the bed next to Gabe. He turned his back to her as he waited for the call to go through. When it did, he got up and walked into the bathroom and shut the door. She dug out her own phone, called Maureen, and left a message, telling her to let everyone know she was OK and would be home in a few days. When she hung up, Gabe was still in the bathroom. She turned back to the TV and watched footage repeat and repeat. Survivors and panicked family members wept openly.

Now you know, Cassie thought as she watched reporters struggle to maintain their professional images. *Now you understand.* She tried not to feel bitter that no one seemed to care that at Mt. Carmel the U.S. government had burned many of its own citizens to death. She tried not to care that it took an attack by other religious extremists to get her fat, materialistic fellow citizens to understand pain. And more than anything she tried not to care that instead of sitting with her, comforting her, Gabe was in the bathroom, talking to his wife and pretending that she—Cassie—was just his accompanist, not his lover.

The footage continued to play, Gabe stayed in the bathroom, and Cassie tried not to care—and failed.

Later that evening, after an indifferent dinner at a local chain restaurant, Cassie and Gabe lay in bed as chaste as brother and sister. The air-conditioner hummed, blocking out all street noise and the sound of the neighbor's TV. Cassie could tell that Gabe was pretending to be asleep, and she knew beyond doubt that once he got back to his wife and kids he would have worked out in his mind that it was his moral and patriotic duty to stay with his family. She thought he might even get the religion he pretended to have when performing for Republican fundraisers. She felt a bitter twisting in her stomach and rolled over on her side, clutching a pillow.

It isn't like you weren't warned, Cassie thought as she fought tears.

When Cassie had first introduced Gabe to Maureen, Maureen disliked him on sight. Cassie was just his accompanist at that point, but Maureen saw his intentions before Cassie even considered it a possibility.

"You watch yourself with this guy," Maureen had told her. "He will never leave his wife."

Now, two years later, Cassie wished she had listened to her. Gabe played the violin with the same finesse and passion that Cassie soon learned he showed in bed. After several fumbling relationships with college-age lovers, Gabe's sure, smooth hands and knowing tongue sent Cassie to a world she didn't even know existed. And in the beginning, that was enough; somehow over the last six months, however, she had found his self-absorption and self-satisfaction more and more difficult to stomach. Musically, he was always right, even if he was wrong; personally, he acted the same. She thought of all the press about him: "Gabriel plays like an angel!" and Gabe's personal favorite, "the Archangel of the violin." He used both of those quotes on all his promotional material, and Cassie was tired to the point of sarcasm of how much he referred to them.

"Fallen angel," Naomi had snorted when she first saw Gabe's press packet. She, too, had warned Cassie not to get involved.

Gabe shifted beside her. Cassie became very still and pretended to be asleep. *Is this the point when he wants to make love to me or break up with me?* She had no interest in the first option and knew that she had to propose the second option herself, just to save face. She felt shame and disgust—what had felt so romantic and exotic for the past two years now felt tawdry.

"Cass?"

She ignored him. He reached over and gently shook her shoulder. She tried to send out non-verbal leave-me-alone vibes. He shook her again.

"Cass?"

She gave up and opened her eyes. "What?"

"I don't know what I'm going to do," he said brokenly. "If we get home, things are so different now."

Cassie felt her earlier sadness evaporate into a cloud of irritation. "What do you mean, if we get home? I think it's more like when we get home." *Oh my God, he wants me to comfort him?*

"You never know," his voice trailed off ominously.

Cassie shook her head, now fully irritated. "We'll be fine." *Hell will freeze over before I coddle your ego yet again.*

"You just never know. Life is so fragile." His voice had taken on the pseudo-emotive tone he liked to use onstage when talking to an audience and offstage when chatting up attractive women at post-performance receptions.

"You'll get over it," Cassie said coldly.

"Fine. Whatever. Sorry I bothered you." He rolled over, his back to her, every bit of him radiating righteous indignation.

Cassie seethed a few minutes then sat up and addressed his back. "I don't want to be involved with you anymore," she said, her voice clear and steady. She could feel the cold, steely resolve she always got when she made up her mind about things. *Like a door slamming shut*, she thought, remembering Naomi's long-ago description of Cassie's response to being pushed too far.

He got very still. Cassie waited.

"Well? Don't you have anything to say?" she asked.

He sniffed. "What's to say? Obviously you've made up your mind."

Cassie waited, but he said nothing more. "I'll get my own room tomorrow," she added.

"Do what you want," he said.

Neither of them spoke for a couple of minutes. Cassie lay back against the pillows and breathed evenly to calm the shakiness she felt.

"I just can't believe how selfish you are," he added, his voice aggrieved. "You have no idea how deeply today has affected me, and frankly I can't understand why you are so cold about it."

She didn't reply. *You fucking narcissist,* she thought. And she wished she had the nerve to voice it.

"Maybe because you're so young you don't understand tragedy," he continued, his tone becoming more self-righteous with every word. "I remember when my cousin had to fight in Vietnam. I've been to Auschwitz. You have no idea how something like that affects someone."

Cassie thought of the Apocalypse with the flames and the gunfire and the end of her world—stories she had never shared with Gabe. She thought of Grandma, who had died alone several years ago, not wanting to leave the city of her only son's death, yet unable to let her friends and fellow church members do anything to make her less lonely. She thought of Maureen losing a daughter and gaining an unexpected dependent granddaughter. She thought of how her parents never saw her play a piano concerto, never watched her graduate from college or graduate school, and would never be there to walk her down the aisle someday or hold any future grandchildren.

"I'm sure you're right," she said quietly.

Three days later, Cassie flew home alone. She sat in a window seat and ate airline peanuts while staring out the window. It had taken her two hours to get through the new airport security measures, and everyone seemed jumpy as they boarded the plane. Now flight attendants did their best to pretend that everything was normal and that flying was the same as it had been a week earlier.

She had a Brahms Intermezzo stuck in her head—one of his simpler ones, in A Major. Its repeating theme followed her into sleep as she leaned against the window and dreamed of finding herself completely alone on a dusty unpaved road in Texas. The Brahms seemed to amplify the pathos of the dust and sun, and it fueled the sobbing she did in the dream—great, heaving gasps that shook her entire body but never made the crushing ache in her chest go away.

She woke with a start as the captain announced their imminent arrival at Portland International Airport. Her cheeks were wet, and she sneaked a look at the woman sitting next to her, fearful that she had been sobbing in her sleep. The woman smiled and held out her hand to take Cassie's peanut wrapper to hand to the flight attendant.

"Did you have a nice nap?" she asked.

Cassie nodded and gave her a polite smile. "Yes, thank you."

The landing was smooth, and Cassie noticed that people exited the plane with more courtesy than she had ever before witnessed. *It's as if we're all being more gentle with each other*, she thought as she stood and pulled her bag from the overhead compartment. The line moved slowly up the aisle and off the plane. Naomi met her at the newly erected security station and gave her a wordless hug. Cassie waited for the "I told you so" she knew was coming, but Naomi didn't say it. Instead, she released Cassie and gave her a searching look.

"Now what are you going to do?" she asked with real care and concern on her face.

The caring got her. Cassie's eyes filled, and she shook her head to keep from crying. "I don't know," she choked out. For the first time since she had moved to Oregon, there was no clear next step, no approved career or life path mapped out for her.

"Well, first of all, I'm going to buy you dinner and we're going to split a really good bottle of wine," Naomi said.

Cassie nodded, sniffed, and gave her a shaky smile. They turned and walked to the parking garage, Naomi chattering the whole way about a shoe sale at Nordstrom's, her asshole landlord who wouldn't let her have a cat, and how much she hated her job working as an office intern for a local ballet company. She followed that with a list of all the things she hated about her current boyfriend—a bass player by the name of Steve who (as far as Cassie could tell) spent every waking hour smoking pot—and she ended it with the thing she always said when she got furious with guys.

"God, I wish I were a lesbian!" she said as she opened the hatchback on her Acura.

"Me too," Cassie agreed, for the first time.

Naomi stopped and stared at her. "OK. First food, then wine, then we will tear that motherfucking fallen angel of a violinist to pieces."

She's always been here for me, Cassie thought, feeling warm for the first time in several days. She could feel herself wanting to tear up again, but she fought it with a dash of mean-spiritedness.

"And then we could have the dick-less wonder killed," she added.

Chapter 17

The first two weeks after Cassie got home, she floated around her studio apartment and did little more than sleep late every day and then go out and walk the streets of downtown Portland for exercise and to convince herself that she was still part of life. She was surprised that she missed rehearsals with Gabe more than she missed Gabe himself. Without rehearsals to organize her days and weekend performances to anticipate, one day flowed into another in a murky cocoon of time. She woke each morning with a nagging fear that she would never get a piano job again and that when her money ran out, she would have to go to work selling shoes in a high-end department store.

"Well, have you contacted your network of friends and your former professors?" Maureen asked her when Cassie confessed her fear to her during what was turning into daily phone calls.

"No," Cassie admitted. It was evening, and out the bank of windows that faced the city and the river, Cassie watched the lights coming on all over Portland. Her neighbor across the hall had his stereo booming, and upstairs she could hear her landlady banging around the kitchen and calling to her cats.

"Why not?" Maureen's usual patient tone had a hint of frustration behind it.

"I don't know," she mumbled. *Because maybe I'm not that good, and they won't want to give me any work.* She glanced at her upright piano pressed against the wall. It was covered with sheet music and now a thin layer of dust.

"You're a great pianist, and they'll want to help you out," Maureen said, almost as if Cassie had spoken her fears out loud.

"Yeah, I guess," Cassie replied. But inside she didn't really believe it.

She waited two days after that conversation to bolster herself with a double espresso, sit down at her computer, and email all her music contacts. It took an honest look at her finances and a growing fear that if she didn't do something she would soon be insane as well as broke. She kept the email lighthearted—mentioned that she had resigned from being Gabe's accompanist, but said nothing about the personal relationship. Most of her friends knew nothing of it anyway. As she hit the send button, she hoped Gabe would give her a good reference if anyone contacted him to ask about her work. He called once after she got home, but when she told him—again—that it was over, he didn't try again. Once she had made the decision to leave him, it was as if any feelings she ever had for him were replaced with mild disgust at his duplicity and a sickening sense of shame at her own behavior.

"You were just in it for the sex," Naomi told her when Cassie confessed her feeling to her.

"Well, I thought I loved him," Cassie replied, but even to her ears it sounded insincere.

The first gig came in a few hours after she sent the email: Dr. White was organizing a commemorative concert for the terrorist attacks, and he wondered if she might be willing to play a piano solo on the program. She emailed him and said yes. Even though it didn't pay, she was relieved to see that she had something on her calendar—even one appointment made her feel a little less invisible to the rest of the world.

Several other people responded, asked her if she was still living in Portland, and then offered to keep their ears open for any gigs. Others suggested that she join the Oregon Music Teacher's Association and start giving piano lessons. Maureen offered to let her move back in with her, but once Cassie had her independence, the last thing she wanted to do was live with people again.

That evening she sat and watched the city while drinking a glass of syrah. She left the lights off in the apartment and didn't turn on any music. Her neighbor's stereo was quiet, and she suspected the landlord was out for the evening. The stillness was broken only by the sound of city traffic. She tried to think of career options, and her mind kept going blank. With a growing sense of horror, she realized she had no idea what she wanted to be when she grew up.

As she sipped her wine, she tried to think if she had ever known what she wanted. When she first came to Oregon, all she wanted to do was play the piano and be normal. Then the competitions and scholarships and college and graduate school, and right after graduate school, Gabe. She couldn't even think of life before Oregon—it was as if her life began with the Apocalypse and that everything before that day happened to someone else. After so many years of practice, her lies about her past now rolled off her tongue with such sincerity that she nearly believed them herself.

Now life stretched in front of her, a blank canvas that seemed to roll forever into a dark future. She tried to imagine getting her doctorate and felt exhausted at the prospect. She considered starting a piano teaching studio, but feared she would never be able to attract students and, even if she did, would not be a good teacher. She knew she didn't want to be a soloist; graduate school had brought her to her true love—chamber music—and the prospect of working alone all the time left her cold. Finances were a definite concern. She had enough money to pay expenses through December, but had no idea what she would do about January. She thought again of her grandmother's estate and wished for the first time that the entire estate was not tied up in a trust until her thirtieth birthday. Every quarter Cassie got a statement telling her how the half-million-dollar trust was being invested, and now, when she really needed the money, it irked her that she could do nothing to get it.

Cassie finished her glass of wine and was rinsing out the glass when her phone rang. She picked it up and smiled as Mark's voice jumped out of the receiver at her.

"Cass! Oh my God! Really? I mean, I just got your email. Is this for real?"

Cassie laughed. A very beautiful, very flamboyant, very gay, very talented violinist she'd been friends with in graduate school, Mark made every conversation a party.

"Hi sweetie," she said. "Yes, it's true."

"Thank God!" He replied dramatically. "I couldn't stand your making sweet music with that old dinosaur!"

"Yeah, well, that dino is now extinct in my book," Cassie replied.

"Well, good. You were too good for him. And we need you," Mark replied.

"Who's we?" Cassie asked.

"Oh, Greg—you remember, gorgeous, plays the cello so well he makes me cum just to listen to him."

Cassie remembered: tall, sandy-haired, broad-chested, with a sensitive tone and impressive technique. She and half the other women in graduate school had a crush on him, but it soon became apparent that he preferred men.

"He and I have been in a piano trio with Margaret since we graduated."

Cassie thought of Margaret and almost laughed. Passionate, attracted to gay men she thought she could turn, Margaret played with fire and brilliance—as long as she stayed on her meds. When un-medicated, she would swing from delirious enthusiasm to suicidal depression.

"And she has gotten even crazier, if you can believe it." He paused.

"What do you mean?" Cassie asked. She tried to imagine Margaret crazier than she was in graduate school, and her imagination failed her.

"Well, it really became unbearable when we were trying to record our first CD, and she got into this weird sexual thing with our producer. Halfway through the recording she decided to pull the plug on the whole thing. Greg is so pissed at her he isn't even speaking to her," he added. "After all, it was his father who gave us the money for the project, and so his ass was on the line there."

Cassie shook her head. It didn't surprise her.

"So we tried to make it work because we've got a cruise gig coming up, and we figured we could ditch her after the gig, but now, since the attacks, she's in a panic—she won't leave her house, and she absolutely refuses to set foot on a plane ever again."

"Damn!" Cassie said, stunned. "She really is far gone this time."

"Totally looney-tunes, cupcake," Mark replied. "So Greg and I were shitting ourselves trying to think of what to do: do we try to get her pulled together enough to do this gig or do we try to replace her? But as you know, we only like certain pianists, and since you said no to us and ran off with that god-awful dino-with-a-vio, we were stuck with her. But now you're free and you have to come back to us, honey!"

Cassie laughed. "I'd be on the next plane if I had the money. You know I love playing with you."

"That's the point, sweetie! There is money involved! And a trip around the world. Honey, we have a world cruise gig on Sterling Cruises!"

"I've never heard of them," Cassie said.

"Neither had I, but Greg comes from money, as you know, and he says it's the top cruise line in the world—the one richy-rich people cruise on if they aren't rich enough to have their own yachts."

"But," Cassie stammered, sitting down and clutching the receiver. "But, but, why? Why would they want a trio? I don't get it." What she knew of cruise ships came from watching old re-runs of *The Love Boat*, and she couldn't see a piano trio fitting into a world of sun decks and umbrella drinks.

Mark laughed. "Yeah, I know. Apparently they're bringing on a jazz trio, a classical trio—that's us, cupcake--and they have a ship band, lounge pianists, and guest entertainers. It's a floating luxury resort, and the guests get what they want. We'll be playing at various times in the schedule, and each segment we will play a small mini-concert. The rest of the time is ours. And," he paused for dramatic effect, "we are being given guest quarters! We won't even have to live below deck with the crew! Fiji, darling, the South Pacific. Australia. Asia. Sweetie, the whole fucking Pacific Rim!"

Cassie blinked and tried to steady her racing pulse. She didn't even ask how much it would pay, when they would sail, or how long the cruise would be. She just took a breath and blurted out, "When do we leave?"

The next month flew by in a maelstrom of activity. Cassie applied for her passport, filled out all the background information forms and country visas for the cruise line, gave notice on her apartment and started packing boxes. Maureen was adamant that she should not waste money on rent when she would be out of the country for four months and offered to let her move in with her. Cassie thought of the little house and tried to imagine where she would put her piano, her futon, her computer, and all her books, and decided to put all but her clothes, the piano, her music, and her computer in long-term storage in Roseburg.

Mark mailed her copies of the music they would be playing. Cassie had played most of the standard trios in the repertoire and so expected to know most of what they would be rehearsing in a few weeks. The collection of Broadway tunes, Strauss waltzes, and easy classics Mark sent caught her completely by surprise.

"You're joking," Cassie said, cradling the phone against her shoulder as she looked at a *Phantom of the Opera* medley some sicko had arranged for piano trio.

"No, sweetie. Our agent said this is what the guests like to hear. Greg hired an arranger."

Cassie put the medley aside and continued looking through the stack of music, her dismay growing. *"Oklahoma!?"* she asked, her voice rising.

"Oh, don't be a snob," Mark cajoled. "It's so boring."

"Mark. 'Surry with a Fringe on Top.' What the fuck?"

He sighed. "Cassie, you are such a classical snob. Get over it. Think of it as what you have to play in order to live in luxury for four months and see the world."

Cassie looked at the *Phantom* medley and shuddered. She thought of the scene in *The Blues Brothers* when the band had to play *Rawhide* behind a chicken wire because that's what the crowd demanded and understood their predicament for the first time.

"We will get to program a real concert each segment," Mark added, his voice chipper and upbeat.

Cassie closed her eyes and sighed. "You're right. How bad can it be?"

A day later, as she practiced the arrangements, she tried to adopt some of Mark's optimism. *It's sharing music*, she told herself firmly. *Don't be a bitchy snob*. Still, when Naomi came over later in the day to help her pack, she couldn't help complaining. Her complaints landed on deaf ears; Naomi was too envious of Cassie's opportunity to spare any sympathy for schlocky musical arrangements.

"You are one lucky bitch," Naomi told her as she helped her move a box.

She had brought over a bag of croissants, a carton of orange juice, and a bottle of Veuve Cliquot, saying that no one should pack without sustenance. They made mimosas and blew through half the bottle of champagne within an hour, and now Cassie felt as though her head had been filled with helium.

She leaned back on the floor. "Yes, I know." She thought of long, lazy days at sea, of blue South Pacific waters, and smiled. It would be worth it.

Naomi threw the champagne cork at her. "Get up, lazy ass! I am not your Sherpa!"

Cassie laughed, sat up, and added more books to the box. "I've never been on a cruise ship," she admitted. "I've never even been out of the country." She pushed down a twinge of fear. Mark and Greg would be there; she'd be OK.

Naomi stretched packing tape across the box as Cassie held it shut. "Nothing to it. Just eat some Meclizine."

"What's that? Is it legal?" Cassie asked warily. Naomi had once tricked her into eating several large pot brownies that made Cassie so sick that she went for six months without being able to eat chocolate.

Naomi rolled her eyes. "It's like Dramamine—it's for sea-sickness. Of course it's legal."

Cassie shrugged. "Mark says these ships are so big, and they have stabilizers, so you can't even feel them move."

Naomi laughed. "Only if they're in the harbor. Trust me; you'll feel them move."

Cassie made a mental note to purchase some Meclizine and then changed the subject. "Are you playing for Dr. White's 9/11 commemorative concert?" she asked.

Naomi took a sip of her mimosa and nodded. "Yeah. My brother"—she made a face—"and I are playing the second movement of the Brahms First Clarinet Sonata."

"Your brother is playing again?" Cassie asked, surprised. "He told me years ago that he gave it up." She remembered the night he had driven her home and she blushed. *Could I have been any more awkward?*

"He did for a while," Naomi said, making another face. "He was supposed to be the talented one. He won all sorts of competitions when he was in high school, and then once he graduated he refused to play for two years. God, my Mom was pissed."

"What else is he doing now?" Cassie said, trying to sound nonchalant.

"Now he makes wine, and I guess he has started playing again." She stood up and walked to the window. "Did I tell you about Zack?"

Cassie nodded, following the abrupt change in conversational direction. "Poet. Works at Powell's, amazing in bed, right?"

Naomi flashed a wicked grin. "You don't know the half of it."

She continued talking, and Cassie leaned back and let the words wash over her. Outside it had started to rain, and Portland looked like a watercolor painting. She would miss this apartment.

She would miss Naomi. *It's only four months*, she reminded herself. But deep inside it felt as though nothing would be the same when she returned.

Chapter 18

Cassie drove to Roseburg the day before the 9/11 commemorative concert. Cold November rain made for poor visibility as she followed the U-Haul down I-5. Her little Honda hydro-planed a couple of times as she hit pools of water, causing her hands to cramp due to her death grip of the steering wheel. Naomi's poet boyfriend proved more worthwhile than Cassie expected when he agreed to drive her U-Haul to Roseburg for $100. Naomi traveled with him, leaving Cassie alone with the weather and her thoughts.

It didn't seem possible that she would be leaving the country in six weeks. Her emotions ran between excitement and blind panic. She spent hours searching the cruise line's website, trying to learn as much as she could about the ship and the on-board experience. She fretted over her wardrobe, worried that her clothes were not expensive enough and that she would never be able to pack for both the South Pacific and Alaska in two suitcases and a carry-on bag. Mark shared her wardrobe fears; Greg flew to L.A. and went shopping.

Part of the job description included mingling with the guests, and this frightened Cassie more than anything. Always the listener, never the talker, Cassie wondered how she could have anything to say to people who had seen the world.

She mentally ran through the clothes Mark and Greg had helped her purchase when she was in San Francisco a few weeks earlier for rehearsals with them. They also took her to a top-end salon and talked her into getting a wildly expensive haircut and make-over. Now her blonde hair hung in a smooth, shoulder-length cut that Mark assured her was very sophisticated and not at all "Oregon." She had expensive cosmetics and rudimentary training on how to apply them. That, too, earned Mark and Greg's approval, and they told her she looked very European and not at all "Oregon." For Mark and Greg, one of the biggest insults they could give another person was to say they looked like they came from Oregon.

It was dark by the time they reached Maureen's home. Maureen had several community college students waiting to help unload the truck, including the piano. They set it up against the wall in the hallway, pulled Cassie's computer and clothes and music off the truck, and then they drove to the self-storage place a few miles away to unload the rest of her belongings. Everything got done in just forty-five minutes, and after dropping the truck off at the rental office, Cassie drove Naomi and Zack to Naomi's parents' home and drove back to Maureen's.

As she followed the familiar streets, she had a sense of déjà vu. Would all roads always bring her back to Roseburg? When she was away from the town, she rarely thought about it, other than thinking about Maureen. When she was here, it was as if the memories she tucked away waited until she drove back into range and then drenched her with thoughts of the past.

She hadn't asked Dr. White if Eric would be playing in tomorrow night's concert, probably because she didn't want to seem too interested. Naomi had told her that Eric had gotten married right after college and was living in Bend, where he and his wife owned a small music academy. Apparently they had a child, although Naomi wasn't sure if it was a boy or a girl.

It's none of your business, she told herself. Still, she wondered, and she decided to wear one of her new sexy evening gowns for the performance the next day.

Cassie parked behind Maureen's Subaru, picked up her purse and coat, and ran through the rain to the front door. Maureen greeted her with a hug and a kiss as she walked into the living room, spatula in hand.

"I made fettuccini," she said. "It'll be ready in just a few minutes."

Cassie disentangled herself from her coat and followed Maureen into the kitchen. The room was just as warm and delicious smelling as she always remembered. *It's home*, she thought.

"How was the drive?" Maureen asked as she set the table.

Cassie grabbed the silverware and napkins and started placing them on the table. "Dreadful," she said. "It was raining buckets all the way down, and visibility was really poor."

Maureen placed wine glasses on the table and opened a bottle of local pinot noir. She showed the label to Cassie. "Did Dr. White contact you about the winemakers' dinner this winery is hosting right after Thanksgiving?"

Cassie shook her head. "I haven't checked my email for the last couple of days."

"Ask him about it tomorrow," Maureen said, pouring the wine. "Apparently they're looking for a pianist for the event and Dr. White recommended you for the job."

"That was nice of him," Cassie said. "I'll send him an email later and thank him."

Maureen lit candles for dinner, and Cassie put on a CD of the Goldberg Variations. As Cassie listened to Glen Gould's pianistic wizardry and watched the candlelight caress the face of the person she loved best in the world, she felt overwhelmed with gratitude.

"I'm going to miss you," she said quietly.

Maureen swatted her arm. "What do you mean? You will be living the high life on the high seas and won't have time to worry about an old bat back here in Roseburg."

"Good point," Cassie conceded with a laugh.

But as her eyes met Maureen's she knew they both felt the same way and that somehow, although she had lived away from home since leaving for Linfield, this was different. They sat at the table until the wine was gone and the candles burned low in their holders.

Cassie arrived at Jacoby Auditorium an hour before the concert in hopes of getting a little time to reacquaint herself with the piano. The hall was dark except for the stage lights and the sound booth in the back, and the concert grand sat in the middle of the stage still unopened. She opened the lid to full stick, adjusted the bench, and ran a couple of scales. The action was still as she remembered. She closed her eyes and played the opening of the Liszt, relishing the way the simple, noble theme filled every corner of the hall.

When she had accepted Dr. White's offer to play in the concert, he told her she could play whatever she wished. She spent a day going through the music she had played during her graduate school years, and despite all their pyrotechnics and dizzying technical demands, none of them seemed right for the event. In the end she chose Liszt's *Sposalizio* because it was one of her favorite pieces that she had learned while studying with Dr. White, and it seemed to be the only piece that addressed the shocked silence she felt in her friends since the towers came down.

She stopped at the end of the opening section and then skipped to the left-hand octave passage toward the end of the piece. Her hand moved sluggishly over the keys, and she had to remind herself to stop digging in so deeply; the déjà vu returned: every time she played this piece on this piano, she had to remind herself of the same thing.

She played the Liszt to the end and then let the last notes fade longer than she would in concert, just enjoying the warmth of the piano and the ring of the notes in the empty hall. Finally she released the notes and the pedal, and then jumped as someone started applauding behind her. She whirled around on the bench as Eric stepped on stage from the wings.

"That sounds beautiful, Cassie," he said, smiling.

"Thanks," she replied, and felt her face flush. He looked different; time had filled him out, and he carried himself with an adult dignity and confidence.

He walked up to the piano as Cassie stood. "It's good to see you," he said, and gave her a quick hug. "You look as beautiful as ever."

Cassie, who had not yet put on her gown, looked down at her sweater and jeans and shrugged. "Thanks. You look good too."

Her eyes met his, and for a second neither of them said anything. The stage door banged shut and footsteps walked in their direction. A child wailed. Cassie broke eye contact a second before Eric did and turned toward the sound. The woman walking toward them was a plump twenty-something with shoulder-length permed blonde hair, slouchy jeans, an "I heart New York" sweatshirt, and white tennis shoes: she was carrying a squirming toddler.

"He needs to eat," she said to Eric. The child squirmed in her arms, his face red and indignant. She turned to Cassie, gave Cassie's slender frame and designer haircut a cold assessment, and then turned back to Eric. "Are there any dressing rooms back here?"

"Julie, this is Cassie," he said, the tight muscle in his jaw telling Cassie he was trying to be polite even though Julie had irritated him. "Cassie and I played the Bach Double together my last year in Roseburg."

Julie turned and gave Cassie a fake smile. "Pleased to meet you."

"Cassie, this is my wife, Julie, and my son, Nate."

In the space of just a couple of minutes, Cassie had gone from the aching glow of remembered passion to the bracing cold of real life. She forced a smile on her face and extended her hand to Julie.

"It is wonderful to meet you too," she said, practicing her best Sterling Cruises hostess voice. "And what a darling little boy!"

The darling little boy let loose with another wail, his face scrunched up like one of Satan's minions. Julie pushed frizzed bangs out of her eyes, and Cassie bent over and picked up her purse. She couldn't believe a child that small could make that much noise.

"I'll leave you with the piano then," she said to Eric. "Nice to meet you," she said to Julie. Then she turned and walked as quickly and as politely as possible to the women's dressing room. As the door shut behind her, she had a flashback to the many hours she and Eric had spent making out in that very dressing room. Flushed, she felt embarrassed at the romantic streak she had never been able to rid herself of.

Her dress hung in a garment bag, and the strappy evening shoes, still in their box, sat on the floor under the dress. She unzipped the bag and looked at the dress—a stunning black satin slip dress, it was embellished with strategically placed black beading and a figure-flattering cut that Cassie knew made her look even more slender than usual. It was the perfect dress for a high-end cruise ship and all wrong for Roseburg.

Laughing, she shook her head at her own vanity as she stripped off her sweater and jeans and slid the dress over her head. *What were you thinking?* she asked herself as she adjusted the hang of the dress. *That you could make him wish he hadn't broken up with you?* She took off her boots and socks and stepped into the evening shoes. A pair of sparkly chandelier earrings completed the look.

She thought again of the wife and the baby. It felt incomprehensible that someone her age could be married and be a parent. She tried to imagine late-night feedings and diaper changes and the dull monotony of domestic routine as a positive thing, but all she could conjure up was a feeling of being trapped in some inner circle of Hell.

She smoothed on some red lipstick, combed through her hair, and then shrugged back into her long dress coat—the slip dress offered little protection against the dressing room cold. She was putting her street clothes into the garment bag when the door opened and Julie's voice reached her.

"Well, I don't care what you think about it. I don't like her!"

Cassie froze. From where she stood, she knew Julie couldn't see her, and she didn't know whether to announce her presence or duck around the corner into the shower stall and hide.

"You just met her," she heard Eric reply as he followed Julie into the dressing room. "You don't know anything about her."

That decided it. Cassie grabbed her garment bag and purse and hid in the shower, all the while hoping they wouldn't discover her. Her face burned. Of course they were talking about her. She pressed herself into the corner and tried to make herself disappear.

Julie gave a snort of laughter. "I know what I need to know. Your mother told me how she is demon-possessed, and everyone at U of O is still talking about how she was messing around with Gabriel. She's got a taste for married men, and I am not going to let her get her fangs into you."

Cassie felt hot all over as she leaned against the shower stall, shaking with shame. *Demon-possessed?* She remembered the awful visit to Eric's church, that dreadful PTSD experience, but didn't remember Eric or his mother ever telling her they thought she was demon-possessed. *And how does she know about Gabe? Does everyone know about Gabe?*

"Julie, that's not true, and it's not fair, and you know it," Eric replied, his voice even and deadly calm.

"I know what I know," Julie replied. "Here. He needs changing. It's your turn."

Cassie waited, barely breathing as she listened to rustling and the baby's contented gurgling. Would they ever leave? She wanted to run from the place and never return. She knew she would be a professional and do her job, but more than anything she just wanted to disappear. *You sail in six weeks*, she told herself. *You just have to hang on until then.*

Footsteps came toward the trash can, which was located just outside the shower. Cassie held her breath as Eric appeared. He wore the fatigued expression of one who knew he was trapped, and in that instant she felt sorry for him. He didn't see her; after tossing the dirty diaper, he turned, washed his hands in the sink, and left with his wife and child. Cassie waited a few seconds before emerging from the shower stall. Her legs were shaking so badly she feared she would twist an ankle in her high heels. She sank into one of the two chairs in the room and practiced the four-part breathing exercise she had learned in a college yoga class.

The door flung open again and Naomi burst into the room. She rushed at Cassie as soon as she spotted her.

"Oh. My. God!" She grabbed Cassie's hands in her own. "Did you see Eric? Did you see his wife?"

Cassie nodded, but Naomi didn't notice as she unbuttoned her coat and revealed one of the sexiest red dresses Cassie had ever seen. *It's a Cher dress*, she thought. It showed more skin than fabric. The days of braces and skinniness all gone, Naomi was now a fiery beauty who made much of her slender frame and spectacular ass.

Naomi checked her lipstick in the mirror, her eyes glittering wickedly. "She's a fucking cow," she announced. "Total mumsy-type—all chubby and dressed like shit. She even has a perm, for God's sake!" She smoothed her dress and checked her profile. "Can you believe he can fuck her? Ewww!"

Cassie thought of all the reasons why it wasn't nice of her to think badly of Julie. She thought of how Julie must feel, trapped with a toddler and nothing to look forward to but more dirty diapers and more drudgery. Still, she laughed.

"Yeah. Can you imagine?" She added, her eyes wide. The horror of Julie's words receded just a little bit with every bit of nastiness Naomi uttered.

"I am never having kids," Naomi announced. She looked at her watch. "I have to dash—my brother and I need to do a sound check before they open the house."

She left the room as quickly as she'd entered it. Cassie took off her coat, checked her reflection one last time, and followed her out the door. She stood in the wings and listened to Naomi and her brother play the opening of the Brahms. The clarinet line was so beautiful it made her throat ache. *If Naomi doesn't want to work with him, I'm going to see if he wants to play with me when I get back from the cruise.* She closed her eyes and let the sound wash through her, dissolving her anger at Julie, her nervousness about playing, and her fear of the future. She felt rather than heard Eric behind her.

"It's beautiful," he said, standing close enough that if she leaned back even an inch she would have brushed against him.

"Yes, it is," she replied, the hair on her arms standing up. She kept her eyes closed and her face immobile.

He said nothing for a few minutes, but she could feel his breath on the back of her neck. "I'm sorry," he said, finally.

She turned. "Why?"

"I should have stood up to her, to my Mom," he answered. "I never should have left."

Cassie went very still. "We were young," she finally replied.

He lifted her chin with his hand, and for a brief second she thought he was going to kiss her. She wanted him to. At the same time she thought of Gabe, of how that started and where it went, and she knew it would be the same story, different guy, with Eric. Stepping back, she took his hand in her hands and gently pushed it away. His shoulders slumped and he looked at his shoes. Cassie turned back to the stage as Naomi and her brother stopped playing and walked in her direction.

"Sounds great," Cassie told them as they reached her.

Naomi grinned, "Yeah, he still plays well even though he makes wine instead of music. You remember my brother, Joel? Joel, this is my friend Cassie."

"I remember you," he said as he grinned and extended his hand.

Gone was the lean college kid she remembered. He was now a six-foot-tall, dark-haired Adonis who looked born to wear a tux. Cassie shook his hand and tried not to stare. She could feel herself blushing and was glad for the dark backstage lighting.

She turned to introduce Joel to Eric, but he had gone.

Chapter 19

The ship sailed from the Port of Los Angeles in San Pedro on a sunny January day. Cassie flew to LA on an early morning flight and was picked up by the ship's representative as soon as she had claimed her luggage. She shared the ride to the ship with several other cruise passengers and also one of the ship's ambassador hosts. She quickly learned that the passengers sitting next to her were not signed on for the entire world cruise; those were picked up in limousines rather than vans. It was her first contact with the passengers who she knew would be rating her, and already her face ached from sustaining a sweet smile. She was, in a word, terrified.

Flat, dusty-looking sunlight illuminated the freeways and mile after mile of shopping centers, business complexes, and housing developments. She had never been to LA before, and the sheer sprawl of the city felt dizzying.

Oh I wish Mark and Greg were here, she thought as she pulled nervously at the sleeve of her coat. Logic told her that they would be on the ship when she arrived, but the panic still threatened to surface. *I can't do this, I can't do this, I don't belong here, I'll never fit in, I never should have agreed to do this, I should have stayed in Oregon.* She closed her eyes to try to quiet her thoughts and quell the panic that threatened to engulf her. She tried to think of the music she and Mark and Greg would be playing, but thinking of those maudlin arrangements of classic's and show tunes didn't work. She thought of Maureen and wondered if she was home yet. She had driven her to Portland the night before, taken her all the way to the security checkpoint to say goodbye, and then stood waving as Cassie turned and walked down the causeway. Both of them were holding back tears.

She'll be OK, Cassie told herself. *And it's not like I'm going away forever.*

She thought of Joel. After the concert, they had chatted together at the reception, and the attraction between them had been palpable enough for Naomi to roll her eyes and tell them to "get a room." It was advice they took several weeks later after Cassie played for the winemaker dinner, which Joel attended. Good food and great wine led to spectacular making out against the wall of Joel's winery and earth-shattering (or so Cassie felt) sex at Joel's small house shortly after that. She noticed that he sampled her with the same intensity and pleasure that he tasted the food and the wine. Nothing prepared her for lovemaking with a man who believed that three things should never be rushed: a fine wine, a good meal, or an evening of love.

Afterward, as Cassie lay naked, tangled in the sheets, she reminded him about the cruise.

"You know I'm leaving next week, and that I'll be gone for four months," she said, running a finger down his arm. She resisted the temptation to follow that finger with her tongue. The last man she had been with had been Gabe; it was amazing to be with a firm-bodied man her own age.

He kissed the top of her head. "Yeah. Bad timing."

She nodded, regretting the upcoming cruise, but knowing this was just one night, and her career was forever. Neither of them said anything about waiting for the other. After a few minutes, Joel rolled her over on her back and kissed her, hard.

"I guess we'll just have to make the most of the time we have then," he said, a wicked grin on his face. He followed his words with a trail of kisses down the length of her, and by the time he reached her inner thighs, she forgot about anything but his mouth and his hands.

He didn't come to Portland to say goodbye. Instead, they spent her last night in Roseburg in his house where he made her a dinner of smoked salmon, home-made pasta, green salad, and plenty of his own wine. He said she was dessert. The next day, they had coffee together, and then he went to work and she went to Maureen's to prepare to leave.

Will he even remember me when I get back? she wondered. It surprised her that she cared. With most of her other boyfriends—even Gabe—once it was over she had walked away with very little emotional reaction. Naomi once told her she was like a guy that way, that she was one of the few women who really could have one-night stands and not think she was in love with the guy the next day. Cassie supposed it was an asset, but sometimes she worried.

The Sterling *Paradiso* was one of the smaller ships docked at the pier, but even with that perspective, Cassie felt overwhelmed by the sheer mass of it. It seemed inconceivable that the thing could even float. *It's a floating city*, she thought, staring up at deck after deck. The van rolled to a stop, and the driver stepped out and opened the side door. Cassie started to rise when the ambassador host put a hand on her arm to stop her.

"Wait for the guests to get off first, or they'll rip you to shreds in the ratings," he whispered to her.

Cassie flushed hotly and sat back down. "Thank you," she whispered back. *I'm not on the ship, and already I could have messed up!*

The guests were greeted by porters pushing large luggage carts, and a ship's representative wearing a Sterling-logo scarf and a bright, lipstick-heavy smile. As the guests followed her to the cruise center entrance, Cassie and the ambassador host got off the van and followed the group.

"Lance," the host said, extending his hand.

"Cassie," she replied.

"First time on board?" he asked. He was a courtly man who looked to be in his early sixties, and Cassie noticed that his suit was immaculate.

She nodded. "I'm one of the on-board musicians," she said, trying to sound calm and confident.

He smiled. "You'll do fine."

Red carpet spilled out of the cruise-center entrance, and stretch limousines deposited well-heeled elderly guests onto it like Hollywood stars. A jazz trio played just inside the front doors. Cassie stifled a giggle as she realized it looked like a geriatric version of a blockbuster movie premiere. She and Lance stepped into a short line, and after presenting her passport and visas, her cruise ticket, stateroom assignment information, and proof of health insurance, she had her picture taken for her on-board identity key card and went up a staircase to another station where another photographer took a welcome aboard picture. She left terra firma in a covered causeway, and stepped into a floating fantasy.

A line of uniformed staff greeted everyone as they came through security. A luxurious three-story silver sculpture fountain rose from marble floors, and somewhere in the background, Cassie could hear cocktail piano music. She felt as though she was sinking to her ankles in the plush royal blue carpet. One of the uniformed staff greeted her, asked about her stateroom number, and then whisked her to a bank of elevators. When they reached her floor, he led her down a long hallway of doors, opened her stateroom with a flourish, asked her if he could assist her in anything more, and when she replied in the negative, he wished her bon voyage and withdrew.

Cassie sank slowly on the down-comforter-covered bed and just looked around her. Her room was decorated in shades of plum with silver accents, and every detail spoke of a luxury she didn't even know existed before today. It seemed incomprehensible to think that she had been given one of the least expensive staterooms and that the others were even more opulent.

Light streamed through the large picture window, which looked out on the promenade deck and, beyond the deck, the bay. Her room held a queen-sized bed, a small loveseat and coffee table, a cabinet that looked to be a combination of dresser, mini-bar, entertainment center, and desk, and a small refrigerator. To her left she noted a large closet, where the open doors showed a plush white robe and terry-cloth slippers. She shrugged out of her coat and walked a few feet to the bathroom and then nearly tripped as she stepped up into it, catching her foot on the threshold. She turned on the light and was greeted by a wall of mirrors, marble, chrome fixtures, and a small bathtub/shower. Luxury soaps and shampoos were lined up as if to welcome her. The toilet was a bit of a surprise; the flush was a loud sucking sound that bounced off the marble walls and caused Cassie to jump.

Cassie had just finished washing her hands with a little jasmine-scented soap when someone knocked at the door. She opened it to the porter who greeted her and carried her luggage into the room for her. On the way out he handed her the mail that had already accumulated for her on the clip outside her door. As the door shut behind him, Cassie thumbed through the papers. Dinner seating assignment, second seating, a welcome letter from the cruise director, and instructions to join an Entertainment Staff meeting the next day, a ship newsletter, and a note from Mark, telling her he was in room 7001 and to call as soon as she arrived.

She dialed from the bedside phone, and Mark picked up after the second ring.

"I'm here," she said, in response to his greeting.

"Oh my God, Cass!" he gushed. "What room are you in? "

"7007, I think" She looked at her stateroom assignment. "Yes, 7007."

"Oh, good. You're just a few doors down from me," Mark said. "Can you fucking believe this place? It's unreal!"

Cassie laughed, his voice relaxing her so she took her first deep breath in hours. "It's overwhelming," she replied.

"I just spoke with Greg," Mark continued. "He's in 10007. The Penthouse deck. Bitch got a balcony! Don't know how he pulled that one off, but I suspect it had something to do with a dishy assistant cruise director he's known for years."

Cassie laughed harder, the last of her tension melting away. "Would you expect Greg to settle for anything less than the penthouse deck?" She thought of his custom-made tuxedos and sporty BMW and shook her head. Just once she wanted to see him slum it and drink cheap beer out of a can.

"We're all meeting on deck for drinks and the sail-away party in an hour. Be there, sweetie, and wear something smashing."

Cassie agreed and then hung up. She pulled her cell phone out of her purse and dialed Maureen's number. She got the answering machine and she left her a long bon voyage message. She thought about calling Naomi, but then remembered that Naomi wanted her to call from the deck of the ship, as it sailed, with champagne glass in her hand.

She unpacked quickly, hanging her dresses and blouses with care. Her new shoes lined up neatly on the chrome shoe rail. Silky underwear and stockings and scarves filled the closet drawers, and after both suitcases were empty, she pushed them under the bed and went about personalizing the room with little touches she had brought from home. She put a picture of Maureen on the desk, and a picture of Naomi next to it. She wished she had a picture of Joel. She put her music and several novels on the bookshelves above the mini-bar, and stacked her CDs in one of the drawers under the TV. This was home—at least for the next four months.

Picking up the miniature map of the ship, she studied it, floor by floor, carefully trying to memorize where everything was and how to get there. In the paperwork Sterling had sent her a month earlier, she learned that as a representative of the cruise line she was expected to wear a nametag when outside her stateroom and to assist any guest who asked. She found the nametag in the big envelope of paperwork she had received as she came on board, and placed it on the desk. She changed into a pair of cotton slacks, white blouse, and breezy scarf and then combed her hair until it looked like a silky curtain. Lip gloss and a pair of obscenely expensive high-heeled sandals completed the look. She pinned the nametag on her blouse, put her key card, lip gloss, and cell phone in a little purse, took a deep breath, and left her stateroom.

A large group of guests waited at the elevators. Cassie chose to take the stairs rather than wait, and by the time she reached the pool deck she was out of breath. She walked out on deck to see two pools, waiters carrying trays of glasses of champagne, and the University of Southern California marching band—in full regalia—setting up for a sail-away performance. Shading her eyes, she searched for Mark and Greg. One floor up, on the sun deck, she could see Mark waving at her and she wove her way through guests and waiters to one more flight of stairs.

"Sweetie!" Greg greeted her with a hug and a kiss, and then Mark followed.

"You need champagne!" Mark announced, and then turned and took a glass from a passing waiter and handed it to her. "Cheers!"

Cassie took a sip. "Oh wow! It's the good stuff."

Mark grinned. "It's Fantasy Island, Sweetie. A ship of free-flowing Veuve!"

They turned to Greg. He smiled and then gestured to his cell phone, which had just started ringing. After he answered it, he turned his back to them and walked over to the ship's rail.

"It's his boyfriend," Mark confided. "Greg is all, like, 'Oh, sure we'll stay together.'" He rolled his eyes. "But you know what a little slut he is. He'll be chatting up some hot young waiter before we've even hit open sea!"

Cassie laughed and took another sip of champagne. A light breeze ruffled her hair. It was perfect—this ship, the champagne, being here with Mark and Greg—all of it. She hadn't seen the sun in two months of miserable Oregon rain; now she closed her eyes and tilted her face to the sky, determined to soak up as much of it as she could.

Her phone rang, and she fumbled in her little purse to get it out before it went to voice mail. It was Joel's phone number, and she nearly dropped her champagne in her haste to answer it. Mark caught her purse before it hit the ground.

"Hello?" She turned away from Mark and walked over to the railing for some privacy.

"Are you on the ship yet?" Joel asked. In the background Cassie could hear noise, and she knew he was calling from the winery.

She hugged the phone tighter, more thrilled than she dared admit that he had called. "Yes. I'm on deck with Mark and Greg and a whole lot of Veuve."

She looked at her champagne glass; it was empty. A Philippino waiter appeared, whisked away her empty glass and handed her a full one.

"And I'll bet it's sunny too," Joel added with a laugh.

"Yes, I'd guess seventy-eight degrees. It's stunning."

"It's raining here," he replied. "But you probably could have guessed that."

Cassie laughed and turned to look at the ship. The party had picked up, and guests now wandered the pool and the sun decks, champagne in hand. The marching band kicked up its first song and Cassie laughed again.

"What is that god-awful sound?" Joel asked.

"USC marching band," Cassie replied, still giggling. "It's part of the bon voyage party."

"Sterling brought an entire marching band on board for a sail-away party?"

"I know," Cassie agreed. "This whole place is surreal. I feel like Alice in Wonderland."

"Well, have a drink on me," he said.

"I will." She paused and then just blurted out her thoughts. "I wish you were here."

He hesitated a moment. "So do I."

For a moment neither of them spoke. Finally Joel broke the silence.

"I'll be here when you come home," he said quietly.

"And I will come home," Cassie replied, just as quietly.

Chapter 20

After a one-day stop in Cabo San Lucas, Cassie didn't see land for over a week. Cabo proved to be a disappointment. Eager to make her first out-of- country visit, Cassie was on one of the first tenders to shore. Once there, she found herself surrounded by American chain restaurants, cheap bars, and street hawkers who followed her like a swarm of mosquitoes. She walked the length of the pier, then, dripping with sweat from the unaccustomed heat, she walked back to the tender pier and went back to the ship. Once back aboard, she showered, changed into her bikini, put on a sundress and sandals, and then went to the pool deck with sunscreen, a big hat, and a stack of magazines and spent the day lounging and gossiping with Mark and Greg.

They sailed from Cabo shortly before sunset, and the sail-away party featured margaritas, mariachi music, and a dance show from the ship's band, and singers and dancers, plus decks full of well-dressed and tipsy guests. Cassie found a spot on the upper deck where she could watch the entire party and enjoy the sunset and the warm sea air. She held her drink and pretended to sip it—it was easier than turning down drink offers every time another waiter walked by. She wondered if she would ever learn to like any alcohol other than wine or champagne.

As the ship headed to open waters, Cassie turned and looked toward the darkness on the horizon. The shoreline receded behind them, and the emptiness beckoned. Behind her the party continued; in front of her lay a vastness she had only sensed when she was in the desert in Texas. A chill ran through her, and she turned back to the warmth of the party, the band, and the well-dressed, tipsy guests.

Sea days settled into a predictable routine. Cassie got up early, went to yoga class, and then had coffee and yogurt in the bistro café. At 9, she rehearsed with Mark and Greg in the

Performance Lounge, and at 10, she went to the sun deck for an hour. Their performance schedule required them to play for high tea every afternoon, and to play a concert every two weeks. Every once in a while they had an Entertainment Staff meeting, and they were—of course—required to dine with guests in the evening as part of the cruise enhancement perks offered by the cruise line.

"They stick us with the most obnoxious guests," Mark grumbled several days into the cruise. "I think they do it so the rest of the passengers won't have their cruise ruined by these assholes."

In Cassie's first segment, she found herself placed at a table with Mark, Greg, an octogenarian widow from Denver (who had an obvious crush on Mark), and a plastic surgeon and his girlfriend from Manhattan (both of whom looked as if they had been under the knife multiple times). The widow and the surgeon hated each other on sight. Mark had to keep the widow happy without upsetting the surgeon. Cassie just tried to be quiet, keep a pleasant smile on her face, and try not to offend anyone. Her jaw ached by the end of every dinner from the effort to keep her smile intact.

"We'll get shuffled around next segment," Greg promised, when Mark complained about their table companions.

Despite those annoying guests, Cassie was amazed to be in a place where the most difficult decision she faced each day was what to order at dinner and what to wear. She loved the cocktail parties with all the tuxedos and sparkly gowns and glasses of champagne. She adored the hot tub and the sun deck, and for the first time since moving to Oregon, she was getting a slight tan. Her world became the ship, and everything else seemed a lifetime away. Her mind seemed numbed into a pleasant coma, and she had been onboard for over a week before she realized she hadn't even thought of practicing anything other than the music she performed with Mark and Greg.

"It's not real," Greg reminded Mark and Cassie one morning after their rehearsal. "Enjoy it, but don't forget, it's a make-believe world."

Mark just rolled his eyes. Cassie nodded in agreement, but inside wondered if perhaps she might be able to get some kind of job with the cruise line after this cruise ended just so she could live on board forever. Each day, after finishing their high-tea performance and before she had to get dressed for dinner, Cassie walked several miles around the deck; after her walk, she sat at the stern and watched the ship's wake as the sun went down. In those moments there was no past, no future, just the gentle rocking of the boat, the sound of the water and the engines, and that warm sea air. Cassie sank into those moments, and everything inside seemed to melt into a stillness she that hadn't even known existed. Those moments at the stern got her through the dinners.

They had sunshine and calm seas the day they crossed the Equator. After their morning rehearsal, Cassie and Mark went to the upper decks for the crossing party; Greg disappeared to his stateroom, promising to join them in a bit.

"He's absolutely no fun anymore," Mark complained as they climbed stairs. "He told me the other day that his boyfriend Sean will be flying to Auckland to sail a couple of segments with us."

"He's in love," Cassie replied as they reached the top of the stairs and walked out into the damp tropical heat of the open air.

Mark rolled his eyes. "Yeah. Whatever."

Cassie watched him scan the crowd, obviously looking for the Italian dancer he hadn't stopped talking about since the first night of the cruise. A waiter walked by and handed both of them mimosas. Cassie drank half of hers before she forced herself to slow down.

"Excuse me," Mark said, as he crossed the deck to talk to his dancer, who was dressed like some kind of Mer-man in honor of the crossing.

Cassie studied the crowd for a moment and then walked up the outside stairs to the sun deck. It was windier up there, but from that vantage point she could see the entire party. She leaned on the railing, watched, and sipped her drink. She finished it quickly, and a waiter handed her another almost immediately. She watched Mark and his dancer, wishing again that she could remember his name. In less than a week he seemed to be living in Mark's stateroom.

At least Mark has a karaoke buddy, she thought. She and Greg resolutely refused to go to karaoke, or to stay up drinking and dancing every night, and Mark always complained that they were old and boring.

The sea stretched endlessly in every direction. From the deck it seemed as if she could feel the curvature of the earth. *Chaos, chaos, everywhere.* It made her dizzy to think of it. The ship was a floating pleasure palace, and Cassie noticed that most of the passengers never really looked at the water, preferring to look inward at their little floating world. *A make-believe world sailing on chaos.* She remembered a short story she had read in an English literature course—something about a party where everyone pretended that a plague, which was stalking the country, would never get them. It frustrated her that she couldn't remember the name of the story or the author, but she did remember that the plague—death—was one of the masked guests.

Rob, the golf pro, walked up and joined her at the railing. He was a New Yorker, born and bred, and Cassie guessed that he was about thirty years old. He had been flirting with her since the first entertainment staff meeting.

"They're going to throw new sailors into the pool," he told her, leaning against the railing, his arm lightly grazing hers.

"Whatever for?" Cassie looked at him, suspicious.

He shrugged. "Tradition. Something about appeasing King Neptune." He studied the party for a second. "But, of course, it won't be any of the guests, just entertainment staff like us."

She threw him a horrified glance. "No!"

He nodded. "Yes. But if you're up here, I doubt you'll be one of the victims." He pointed his glass at one of the more flamboyant guests—a septuagenarian wearing a Speedo and sporting a huge belly, lots of gray chest hair, and bonhomie only achievable from lots of champagne and hot tropical sunshine. He leaned closed to her and said in a conspiratorial tone, "The other night one of the old lady guests told me that having to see that guy sitting around the pool in his Speedo every day has made her completely unable to eat hot dogs."

Cassie snorted, choked on her mimosa, and nearly spit it on the deck below. It took her nearly a minute to quit coughing. "You are evil," she stated, still laughing, her eyes watering.

He gave her an innocent look. "Just saying what I heard." He pointed at another of the guests, a fit forty-something woman in a bikini, standing next to a sixty-something man. "Apparently that one likes to shower naked in the pool deck showers."

Cassie laughed again. "The open air showers?"

He nodded. "They forget there are security cameras all over the place. The guys in IT told me about it. They're all wondering if she might be interested in a little bit on the side some evening when her sugar daddy isn't around."

Cassie shook her head. "How do you hear all this?"

"Crew bar. You've got to come down there sometime."

In her mind Cassie could already see the scene. Crew bar—or "screw bar," as Mark told her it was called—was the place for cheap booze, thick cigarette smoke, loud music, and casual hook-ups. It sounded revolting.

"I'm not much of a drinker," she said out loud.

On the deck below, King Neptune—a large, hairy man—made an appearance and Cassie and Rob watched as he roared at people, pointed out "offenders," and had his "court" throw the offenders into the pool. Cassie laughed out loud as Mark was grabbed and dragged to his dunking.

"He totally loves the attention," she said to Rob. "And at least they let him take off his Gucci loafers before they threw him in." Mark came out of the water sputtering promises of revenge. The guests loved it, and several of them applauded. *That'll help our ratings*, she thought.

"How long have you been a trio?" Rob asked.

"Just this trip," Cassie replied, looking at him.

His jade green eyes seemed to pull her toward him. *I could drown in those eyes.* Half the ship was in love with him, and Cassie had heard that he and the assistant cruise director had something going. *Pull yourself together!*

"But we played together in graduate school," she said out loud.

"I heard the set you played yesterday during tea. You guys are really good."

And he even sounds sincere! Cassie gave him a wry smile. "Yeah, we can really knock out musical medleys."

He laughed and edged just a little closer. "Well, you play them really well."

Cassie edged away just a little bit. "How can they all drink so much at their ages?" she asked, changing the subject. She gestured at the guests.

"Practice makes perfect?" He shook his head. "One last hurrah? Hell, I'd love to go out that way." He gave her a sidelong look. "You know we already lost two of them."

She nodded. The first had died of a heart attack their first day at sea, and his body had been flown home from Cabo. The second was just two days ago; she was being stored in the two-berth morgue somewhere in the belly of the ship. Cassie didn't want to think of what the crew would do with a third body if they had two more deaths before reaching port.

"I was just thinking of a short story I read in college, by Edgar Alan Poe, I think." The name had just come to her, and she hoped it made her sound literary. "Anyway, it was about a group of people trying to keep death out by barring the doors and partying, but of course he gets in anyway and is in the middle of the dance floor when everyone unmasks at midnight."

"'The Mask of the Red Death'," Rob said. At Cassie's surprised glance, he continued. "I was an English major in college." He looked at the guests. "I can see the similarities."

Cassie looked at the horizon—impossibly vast and so impossibly blue and bright—and felt a creeping uneasiness. "I know there's a good medical staff on board and everything, but I doubt we have a surgeon. What happens if I get—oh, I don't know—appendicitis or something?"

He gave her a serious look. "You die."

She shuddered and emptied her glass again. Rob's was already empty. He grabbed two full glasses from a passing waiter and handed one to her.

"To long life," he said, clinking his glass against hers.

"Long life," Cassie echoed, then turned her back to the water and let the champagne, the sunshine, and the party lull her into forgetting the water and the nothingness of the horizon.

Rangiroa, French Polynesia, was their first stop at the bottom of the world. Cassie tendered ashore with Mark, Pasqual (the Italian dancer), Greg, and Rob, and the jazz trio—Derek the pianist, Jack, the bass player (and his stewardess girlfriend, Anita), and Marcel, the drummer. Pasqual, who had been there several times before, promised to take them to the best resort on the island, where they could swim, get some great food, and drink local beer.

As the tender plowed through the waves, Cassie couldn't stop looking at the different shades of blue of the water. She had seen pictures of the South Pacific, but assumed the blues were color-enhanced. Now, seeing them in person, Cassie realized that most pictures didn't do the blues justice.

"Are there any phones or internet on this island?" Cassie asked Pasqual.

"I think there are a few phones, but they're very expensive. I doubt there is any internet," he replied.

Maureen had made Cassie promise she would call and email as soon as she could, but Cassie figured that could wait until she got somewhere a little more commercialized. From the sea, the island looked like a movie set, with nothing visible but palm trees, some reefs, and several chains of grass-covered huts strung together like pearls over the blue-blue water. She thought, briefly, of Joel, and for a moment wished he could see what she was seeing, then Rob pointed to a sting ray in the water, and she forgot all about home.

She wore her bikini, a sundress over it, and sandals. Her hair had become nearly white-blonde from all the time she spent on the sundeck, and her long legs and arms were toasted a light caramel color. She had coral polish on her toes, and a drippy silver anklet; coral drop earrings completed the look. She didn't need a mirror to know she looked good.

The tender docked, and cruise attendants helped everyone out of the boat. Pasqual led them around several makeshift shops where cruisers were already shopping and down a road graveled with crushed sea shells. Groves of palm trees lined the street, and every once in a while small shack-like houses could be seen. Cassie wanted to stop and take a picture of everything, but the rest of the group didn't seem to see the charm in what they passed, so she kept walking. They had gone what Cassie estimated to be a quarter of a mile when the complaining started.

"Where the fuck is this place?" Mark muttered. "The South Pole?"

"Just a little farther," Pasqual promised, and started walking faster.

The road stretched on, eventually curving to the left. Cassie began to regret wearing her dress sandals with the kitten heels; every time she took a step it seemed some of the crushed up shells ended up under her toes, and she was getting tired of having to kick it all back out. A brief glance confirmed it: everyone else had had the sense to wear flip-flops.

"I don't think there's a resort," Anita muttered. "I think he's just dragging us around the entire island for kicks and giggles."

They came to the end of the long left turn and found themselves at the edge of the water; beautiful, but still no resort in sight. The road now headed back parallel to the direction they had just walked.

"There wasn't a more direct route?" Mark asked. "As in, maybe we could have turned left right off the pier?"

Pasqual gave him a look that bordered on impatient. "This is the only road," he replied.

"Mark had better watch it," Greg said sotto voce to Cassie. "He's going to push him away with all his whining."

Cassie nodded, but inwardly agreed with Mark. They walked. They saw more palm trees and more unidentified shrubs. Her left big toe was beginning to get a blister on it. Still, they walked. She started wondering if it might be easier to just risk walking barefoot.

"Finally! Like Moses spotting the Promised Land," Rob said to Cassie.

She looked up and—as if by magic—the resort had appeared in front of them. There were huts placed on shore, connected by attractively groomed trails, hammocks strung between palm trees, and a long pier that led out to a main building and a chain of small bungalows—all of which sat over the water. This time she didn't care what the others thought. She stopped, pulled her camera out of her straw bag, and started taking pictures. They moved on without her, each of them seemingly intent to get inside the bar, where cold beer and fruity drinks awaited.

As they entered the building, silence descended. Cassie stood very still, closed her eyes, and listened to the waves and the sound of wind in the palm trees. She breathed deeply, taking in the warmth, the silence, and the momentary solitude. She realized it was the first time she had been alone—other than in her stateroom—since she came on board, and she opened to it the way a parched plant welcomes rain.

"Cassie, are you coming?" Mark's voice shattered the quiet.

She sighed, opened her eyes, and felt a sense of loss as she waved, put her camera back in her bag, and then walked to the pier to join them.

Chapter 21

"It's official; I'm never leaving," Cassie announced as she stretched her legs on the lounge chair and closed her eyes.

"You seem to think we're on Fantasy Island," Greg said lightly, but Cassie could hear the sarcasm under his joking tone.

They sat on the deck of a private over-the-water bungalow on Tahiti. One of the disembarking guests had rented it for a week after his cruise ended there, and he invited several production show dancers, his butler, Cassie's trio, and one of the bartenders to spend the day drinking champagne, eating caviar, and jumping off the private deck into the turquoise water.

Cassie murmured agreement, but felt the oh-too-familiar disorientation that came every time someone made a pop culture reference to anything before The Apocalypse. Most of the time she pretended to be too high-minded to know Sesame Street songs or discuss favorite '80s TV shows, but she always wondered what it would be like to have a shared history.

Jackson—their host—sat at the bottom of Greg's lounge chair and filled Cassie's champagne flute. She smiled and thanked him, even though she really didn't want to drink any more for a few hours; two days earlier, after a boozy catamaran ride off Moorea, she realized she had been drinking every day since the ship left Los Angeles. It was just too easy to say yes and to take one more sip.

"You gonna do any swimming?" Jackson asked.

Cassie turned to answer him and then realized he was talking to Greg. When they had first met Jackson, Cassie feared he was interested in her. But after a few minutes she realized he was only interested in trying to teach her to swing dance. Greg was his target of choice. The fact that he was nearing seventy and that Greg was twenty-eight years old and partnered did not deter him.

Greg had spent much of the last week trying to find polite ways to say no.

"He made a pass at me in the sauna," Greg had told Cassie and Mark during their last rehearsal. "No one does that!"

Cassie's response was two-fold: an open jaw, followed quickly by an inarticulate "Euuuuwwwww!"

Mark's response had been a bark of laughter, followed by "I will never sit naked in that sauna again!"

Greg glared at both of them and said, "Thanks for your support!"

At that, they both laughed.

When Jackson had approached the trio after their last performance and invited them to his bungalow, Mark had accepted for all of them. Greg was still angry, Mark stayed in the water with the rest of the guests, and Cassie tried to avoid the appearance of taking sides. Secretly, however, she agreed with Mark: this bungalow, the champagne, the caviar, the water, the sunshine—wasn't it worth a few hours of Greg's having to ward off advances? They were sailing at sunset, and Jackson was staying in Tahiti, so how bad could it be?

She closed her eyes and listened to the murmur of conversation, the splash of the waves and the swimmers, and turned her face into the warm caress of the tropical breeze. The swimming, champagne, sunshine, and lounge chair made her content and groggy, and within minutes she gave up the fight to stay awake.

In the dream she sat at the piano in Jacoby auditorium playing the Brahms Second Clarinet Sonata with Joel. The hall was empty of people but full of music. The lines of both instruments entwined around each other like an aural expression of Klimt's *The Kiss*. Each note held a honeyed, golden tone; each phrase whispered across her body like silk. She and Joel were married, and the music with its separate but equal lines held all the tenderness, passion, and playfulness of their partnership.

A splash of water across her legs woke her. Mark was treading water right by the deck and flashing a wicked grin. "Get up, Grandma!"

She waved a hand at him. "Go away."

He splashed her again, and she gave up trying to nap. The dream still haunted her and the notes of the Brahms had followed her into the waking world. She stretched, sat up, and walked barefoot through the spacious bungalow to the luxurious bathroom. As she splashed cool water on her face, the dream receded, and along with it the ache she felt inside from missing Joel.

You have no claim on him, she told herself firmly. *There were no promises. Don't be a fool and hang your dreams on a mirage.*

As she washed her hands, she checked her reflection in the wall of mirrors. Cassie blamed the champagne and the diffused lighting when at first glance she didn't recognize herself. A slim, tanned bikini-clad woman with wavy blonde hair and blue eyes stared back at her. She shivered, gasped, and touched her fingertips to her face. The shy, pale Cassie she always saw had been replaced by the ideal Cassie she always wanted to be. The woman in the mirror looked like Malibu Barbie, minus the astounding curves. This woman traveled the world and knew how to order champagne. She wore formal gowns and danced with multi-millionaires.

She tried to imagine being this person in Oregon. She thought of Maureen and Naomi, but they seemed to belong to the old Cassie—the one who played classical piano, was serious and quiet, and was always afraid. She didn't allow herself to think of a pre-Oregon Cassie. Only Joel seemed real and immediate, and

Cassie knew that he only felt that way because of her dream. And she knew that in this moment, with the sound of South Pacific waves lapping up under the bungalow, she had no idea who she was. Somehow, the person she used to be had disappeared into day after day of sunshine and water and elegant clothes and rich passengers in this place where there was no past and no future, only this perfect, magical present.

She studied her own eyes in the mirror. *It's OK; it's a good thing.* With that, she went back to the deck, where she hoped the tropical sunshine would dispel the chill that had come over her.

"Fantasy Island," Cassie said hours later as she and Greg stood together on the upper deck of the ship and watched Tahiti disappear behind them. She leaned against the railing and closed her eyes. She was warm again, and comfortably mellow from a day of champagne and sun. The air smelled of the sea and flowers. The sunset splashed pinks and reds and oranges across the sky, and the water had become deep navy blue. "It's like I've been living in black and white all my life, and now I'm living in a box of crayons."

Greg smiled at her description. He took a sip of his sparkling water and then gave her a serious look. "Just don't forget that it is a fantasy," he warned. "Even on Fantasy Island, guests had to go home."

She gave him a disgusted look. "Ruin my mood, why don't you? Why don't you love this as much as Mark and I do?"

He looked back at the receding island instead of at her. "Because I've traveled a lot, and I know that if you believe this is reality, you will be a wreck when you get back to Los Angeles and are standing on the dock with nothing but your suitcases and four months of memories." He turned and looked at her. "Be careful, Cass. Things move really quickly on ships, and it feels like the real thing, but it's just proximity and opportunity. Gossip travels faster than the speed of light on a ship."

Cassie looked at him blankly. "Pardon?"

"Be careful what you do and with whom, Cassie," he added. "Everyone notices everything and everyone talks."

Cassie felt hot and then cold. "But, but, I haven't done anything!"

"I'm not judging you, Cass, just warning."

"You think I've been sleeping with Rob," she said flatly.

"I didn't say that," he replied. "I just said, be careful." He looked at her. "Last week's rumor had him sleeping with the assistant cruise director and the world cruise hostess on the same day."

Cassie's eyes widened. "The same day? I thought those two women were friends!"

"They are. They compared notes that evening."

Cassie's jaw dropped open. "Holy shit!"

Greg laughed. "See what I mean?"

Cassie felt her face flush. Rob had been trying to maneuver her into his bed, but something about him made her feel she couldn't trust him. Other than a few kisses on deck one evening, she had kept her distance. She thought of her earlier assessment of herself as a sophisticated woman and knew that, despite appearances, she was still pretty naïve.

"I'll watch myself," she told Greg. "Thanks for the warning." She looked at him. "You're speaking from experience, aren't you?"

He gave her a slight grin and replied, "A stunning head waiter on one of my first cruises."

"Ah!" She waited, but he didn't continue. "That bad?"

"He was, in a word, amazing, but only for the three weeks of the cruise. When we tried to meet up again in Vegas, it was such a disaster that I ended up leaving town before the weekend was over."

"Have you spoken with Mark about this?" Cassie asked. Mark was convinced that he and his dancer were in love.

"Do you think he'd hear me?" Greg asked with a shrug.

"Good point," Cassie replied.

She turned from the railing and looked at the groups of guests wandering around the pool, listening to the ship's band play Beach Boys songs. She thought of Rob and shook her head in disgust. He now joined Gabe in her mind as part of a small but growing group of untrustworthy assholes to be avoided. She thought of Joel—now so far away both geographically and emotionally—and wondered if she would ever get to spend enough time with him to know if he was one of the good guys or not. In this tropical world of luxury and comfort, everything and everyone off the ship now seemed as ephemeral as a mirage.

At their next on-board performance, Cassie was asked to play several selections from Bach's French Suite in G Major as a piano solo. One of the guests had requested Bach—much to the delight of the trio—but Cassie was the only one who had brought any Bach sheet music on the cruise. In preparation, she got up an hour earlier every morning for several days in order to have practice time on the piano. After several weeks of her playing nothing but show tunes and light classics, the Bach felt like getting a steak after a steady diet of cotton candy. She had forgotten how much she enjoyed playing the pieces, and by the second day of rehearsal, she began bringing the rest of her solo sheet music to the piano each morning as well. She was just wrapping up her work on the Bach one morning when the walk-on classical entertainer—an English concert pianist named Jessica Donogal—came into the hall. A tall, rangy woman with silver hair, she had the long-legged gait of a horsewoman.

"Don't stop," she said when Cassie spotted her and immediately pulled her hands off the keys. "It's lovely!"

"Thank you," Cassie replied. She had seen Jessica at the Entertainment Staff meeting, but hadn't been introduced.

"I'm Jessica," the other pianist offered. Cassie couldn't help but notice that Jessica—despite her hair color—seemed to have the complexion of a thirty-year-old.

"Cassie," Cassie replied. "Do you need time on the piano?" She closed her music and placed it on the stack on the chair by the piano.

"Only if you're done," Jessica replied. She studied Cassie a moment. "You have a real affinity for Bach."

Cassie smiled and felt herself blush. "I love it." She stood and picked up her music.

"Are you playing that suite sometime this segment?"

Cassie stepped off the small stage as she answered. "I'll be playing it for part of the high-tea entertainment tomorrow afternoon."

She watched Jessica sit at the piano bench and pull her own music out of a long-handled leather tote bag. Jessica was scheduled to play a solo concert that evening, and the on-board newsletter advertised that the selections would include Chopin, Debussy, Liszt, and Rachmaninoff. *Not a single show tune*, Cassie thought, surprised by the stab of pure envy she felt in that moment.

"I'll be there to hear it," Jessica promised, just before Cassie left the room. A cascade of notes—Chopin's "Ocean" etude—washed through the door and followed Cassie down the corridor.

I want to do that, Cassie thought as she walked to the Bistro for a cup of coffee. She tried and failed to imagine how she might make that happen. *I need a manager. How do people find managers?* She ordered a cappuccino and drank it very slowly as she looked through her music collection.

Each page was both diary and time-capsule. She looked at the Schubert *Impromptus* and was transported to Linfield and one of the dusty practice rooms in the trailer. She was nineteen, dating a tenor (her first and final attempt to forge a relationship with a singer), and learning Opus post. 142, No. 4 in F minor for a scholarship competition. It had been an unseasonably warm day, and she had the window of her practice room open. The lawn was being mowed, and the smell of freshly cut grass became permanently linked to the notes of the Impromptu. Years later, sitting in the Bistro with her coffee, she could still smell that grass as she read through the score.

She opened Morton Gould's *Boogie Woogie Etude* and found herself back in graduate school, defiantly programming the piece for her senior recital as a not-so-subtle swipe at an incredibly snobbish and stuffy piano faculty. She played it for her encore—replacing the Bach-Busoni piece they expected to hear in that slot—and got a standing ovation for her efforts. Had it not been for the strength of the rest of her program, Cassie wondered if they would have flunked her recital and required her to play another one. She shuddered again at the memory of graduate school. Occasionally she still had nightmares about it.

The Bach *Goldberg Variations* sat in the stack, its pristine cover unopened. It had been a thank-you gift from Dr. White for

Cassie's participation in the 9/11 memorial concert, and she wasn't even sure how it got included with all the other scores she had brought on board. She opened the cover and a disc fell out. She grabbed it before it hit the floor and was surprised to see that it was a recording of the 9/11 concert. She put the disc aside and turned back to the title page of the Variations, where she found Dr. White had inscribed a note to her in his instantly recognizable scrawling handwriting:

"To Cassie, who brings both heart and head to everything she plays. With affection and appreciation."

He had signed it, but the signature was little more than a scribble of black ink. Looking at his words, she felt her first pang of homesickness. *I'd give anything for a practice room*, she thought, the need to play feeling like an ache inside. Passengers and officers moved around the Bistro. Sunshine shimmered on the waves splashing against the window. An abyss of loneliness threatened, and she fought back from the edge by drinking more coffee and returning the head sommelier's flirtatious smile.

Chapter 22

I think I'm nervous! Cassie thought as she, Mark, and Greg sat down to play for high tea the next day. The room was full of the regular guests, but over in the far corner, she could see Jessica sitting with one of the guest lecturers. She played the tuning pitches, opened to the first piece in their set, and at Greg's nod, started playing the *Hello, Dolly!* medley.

Oh God, I'm sorry, she thought, wishing she had warned Jessica that much of the tea music was less substantive than the clotted cream. Greg played with his usual professional face—she never failed to be impressed with how he could look interested and engaged when he was bored—but Mark looked hung over. She wondered if there had been yet another crew party the night before. She could hear it in his playing—his intonation was shaky and his melody lines limp. Greg flashed him a look as Mark slid into another sharp note and Cassie noticed a muscle tighten at the corner of his mouth. Mark didn't notice. He just sawed at his violin, his face pale and sweating and his eyes glassy. They staggered through the rest of the medley with Cassie and Greg playing with more vigor than usual in an attempt to drag Mark along with them. When they ended the last note, Cassie released a breath she hadn't known she was holding.

"Pull yourself together," Greg hissed as they set up for their next piece. It was the Larghetto from Mozart's Piano Trio in B-flat Major and one of Cassie's favorite selections in their tea set.

Cassie played the piano solo opening with as much grace and beauty as the piano was capable of producing. Several measures in, she could hear that conversations in the room had dropped to a low murmur and could feel people listening. Mark came in beautifully, his tone clear and sweet, and Cassie thought she heard relief in Greg's tone as he made his entrance. She relaxed, and her next piano solo sang with a freedom she had been too nervous to create in the first entrance.

Then Mark missed his second entrance. She panicked, met Greg's panicked eyes, and then improvised a way back into the beginning of her second solo section. Greg reached over and stabbed Mark's leg with the tip of his bow. He jumped, sat up, and made his entrance on the second go-around. After that, Cassie couldn't relax. Greg kept his professional face intact but the muscle on the side of his mouth was twitching repeatedly, and he gripped his bow with more force than usual.

She tried to connect with both of them in the music, but all she got from Mark was unfocused chaos covered by rote playing, and Greg emoted rage. Finally, she blocked them out and tried to create the most gorgeous piano lines that she could and just hoped they would hear it and join her there. They didn't. Rather than being an intimate exchange among three friends, the tension that had been brewing between Mark and Greg erupted in the Mozart, with Cassie's piano providing background noise to the musical argument. Somewhere, she was certain that Mozart was swearing a German blue streak at the carnage.

"Time for the Bach, I think," Greg hissed, seconds after they finished the Mozart. He put down his cello, leaned over and whispered in Mark's ear, and then both of them got up and left the room.

Cassie nodded, her face flaming. She didn't even look at Jessica; she couldn't remember the last time she had been so embarrassed by a performance. They had sounded like a trio of mismatched high school players, and she knew it.

She opened the French Suites to the Allemande of Suite V in G Major, and then closed her eyes and took two deep breaths before she felt calm enough to start playing. *Get in the sound*, she reminded herself. *Just breathe the lines*. But the tension refused to let go. She breathed deeply, thought about the clean lines of the

Allemande, and felt herself relax inside. She started the first measure tentatively, but by the first repeat, she felt the notes stop being wooden sticks under her fingers and become malleable conveyers of color, emotion, and sound.

At the end of the Allemande, Greg and Mark still hadn't returned, so she turned to the Courante and started playing it. She paused at the end of each dance, but they still didn't return. *I've missed this*, Cassie realized as the Bach danced out of her fingers. This suite was an old friend, and playing it felt like an intimate conversation where she and the music understood each other so well that the real communication was wordless.

She got applause for the Gigue. She knew she had taken it a little fast but it just felt so good to play it—even if it was for a tea-swilling audience on a white, dead-toned baby grand that had been tarted up to look as though it had once belonged to Liberace. She looked around—still no Greg or Mark. *I should have brought the rest of my solo stuff*, she thought as she flipped through the pages to the Suite in B minor. *Is it too dark for high tea?* Still no Greg or Mark. The silence felt oppressive, and Cassie started the suite just to fill in with something.

Dark, intimate, and introspective, the B minor French Suite was one Cassie played frequently in the privacy of her practice room but had never performed. Until this moment, she never asked herself why. Now, sitting on a cruise ship in the South Pacific, she knew she'd never played it for audiences because it was too personal, the lines too exposed and raw, but Mark and Greg were gone and she had to play something so she kept going.

She had learned it during her first year at Linfield—a little side project she started outside of her required lesson repertoire because she had heard another student play the Sarabande, and she knew she wouldn't sleep that night until she sat down and played it herself. From there she had learned the rest of the suite, one bit at a time, and practiced it late at night when the practice rooms were nearly deserted. The lines were now colored with the memory of rain and dark and loneliness. The very key of B minor seemed to take her down dark, foggy roads and blanket her with cold isolation. It was burned-out cinders, husks of what used to be, ghosts. Now, in the color-drenched South Pacific, Cassie saw it all clearly for the first time: it had been about the nothingness after The Apocalypse, when only charred buildings and ghosts remained. It was about abandonment. Loss.

There, in the middle of high tea, on a luxury liner, Cassie played the B minor suite with all the abandonment and loss she didn't know she still felt. She had no other choice—it poured into and out of her with each note, and even when her mind felt in control, she still heard it in the sound. She tried to pull it back a couple of times, but it was stronger than she was, so finally she simply let go and let the Bach play itself the way it wanted to be played. When she got to the end of the suite, she felt as if tension had drained from every part of her body. She barely noticed the applause, and just nodded to Greg as he and Mark returned and picked up their instruments.

"The Andrew Lloyd Weber Medley?" Greg asked.

Cassie nodded, opened the music, and at Greg's nod, started playing. But after the Bach, even the lines of the Broadway tunes seemed to be draped in darker colors. She could hear Greg and Mark's light tone, but couldn't match it. Somehow Bach had walked her out of the world of high tea and luxury cruise ships into a place she didn't recognize, but she knew it had been there all along. After their set, she left the tea room and walked straight to her stateroom, choosing not to talk to anyone or to wait for Mark and Greg to pack up their instruments.

The hum of the air conditioner was a near-perfect mimic to the white noise Cassie knew so intimately, but it still could not drown out the Bach, which now seemed to have become part of her breath. The spacious room felt claustrophobic. Stripping off her black performance dress, she put on her exercise clothes and went outside to walk the deck. The seas were moderate, and each time she turned portside, she found herself walking into a strong head wind. It took a mile and a half of vigorous walking before she pulled herself out of the darkness Bach had thrust her into.

The lounge buzzed with champagne, dance music, and the conversations of formally dressed guests. Cassie, wearing her favorite midnight blue sheath dress, accepted a glass of champagne, pasted on a professional smile, and followed Greg into the reception. They slipped in the side door, preferring to avoid the long line waiting to meet the captain and several of the senior officers.

"Is Mark going to be joining us?" Cassie asked, scanning the room as she spoke.

"No," Greg replied, sotto voce. "I ordered him room service and told him to pull himself together by rehearsal tomorrow."

"Hung over?"

"Massively." He sighed. "He was in crew bar most of the night."

Cassie shook her head. "Idiot."

Greg nodded. "I'm worried about him. Oh, shit, it's her."

The guest crossed the room, dress and scarf floating behind her. A seventy-nine-year-old widow, Dee spent half of her year chasing widowers around Florida and the other half of her year on Sterling ships, looking for younger men. She fluttered up to Greg.

"Now, where's that dance you promised me?" she asked, batting her eyes at him.

He smiled so graciously one could barely see the annoyance in his eyes. "It would be an honor." He led Dee to the dance floor and into a foxtrot. *How does he do it?* Cassie wondered, watching him dance and smile at Dee. *I never know what to say to any of them*. The foxtrot ended, and the band started playing a waltz. As Greg and Dee kept dancing, Cassie sighed, knowing it would be a while before he came back off the floor. Jessica came in, wearing a beautiful red gown, and crossed the room to greet Cassie with a quick hug as if they had been friends forever.

"You were stunning this afternoon!" she said as she released Cassie. "What a treat it was to hear those suites played so well."

"Thank you," Cassie replied, wishing they didn't need to discuss the Bach. She feared that talking about it would bring back the bleakness that had struck her earlier in the day.

"Do you play much Bach?" Jessica asked.

"Not as much as I would like," Cassie replied. "I learned many of the Inventions, of course, and many Preludes and Fugues from both books of the Well-Tempered Clavier. A partita, a couple of the English Suites," she thought a moment, "and when I was a teenager I played the Bach Double in C Minor."

"Ten sixty?" Jessica asked.

Cassie nodded. It seemed as though she had played that a lifetime ago.

"I played that myself, when I was twelve," Jessica said. "Which part?"

"Piano 1," Cassie replied.

"I played piano 2," Jessica said. She smiled. "I haven't thought about that concerto in years. It was—is—fantastic. I still think the second movement is one of the most sensuous ever written."

Greg returned, having escorted Dee off the dance floor, and greeted Jessica. "Lovely concert the other night," he said. "I was particularly taken with the Schubert."

She smiled. "Thank you. I was just complimenting Cassie on her Bach."

"I'm afraid I missed it," Greg replied. "But I have had the privilege of hearing Cassie play for several years. We went to graduate school together."

"Oh, how lovely! Where?"

"University of Washington, in Seattle. Lots of rain, but great coffee and beer. Where are you from?"

He's flirting with her! Cassie thought, hiding her amusement behind her champagne glass as she took another sip.

"London," she replied. "Born and raised. Do you live in Washington?" she smiled at Cassie. "I was there, just once in 1989. I never once saw the sky. Felt right at home, too, with all that rain. Lovely city."

"No, I'm from Northern California, Marin County. I've been living in San Francisco since finishing school. Cassie lives in Oregon."

Jessica smiled and gave Cassie a quizzical look. "I must be slipping. I thought I heard a little bit of Texas in your accent.

Cassie's mouth dropped open. "You can hear that?"

Jessica wore a smug look. "Yes, but it's very faint."

"I was born in Texas," Cassie replied. *How the hell did she hear that?* "But I've lived most of my life in Oregon." *Or at least the last eight years of it.*

"Texas?" Greg asked. "I never knew you lived in Texas? Where?"

"Waco," Cassie replied. It just came out; it had to be the champagne. She had intended to say Dallas.

"Wasn't there something in Waco? Some cult thing back in the nineties?" Jessica asked.

Cassie felt her heart starting to pound and she clenched her champagne glass a little tighter. "Yes," she said very calmly and quietly.

Greg flashed Cassie a quick glance, and then picked up his champagne glass. "I think I need some more bubbly before they shut the open bar and herd us all off to dinner."

They drank more champagne, and by the time they left for the dining room, Cassie was pleasantly drunk.

"We should play the Bach Double sometime," she said to Jessica. *Oh shit,* she thought. *Just shut up until you sober up!*

"Great idea," Jessica agreed, stumbling a bit as the ship pitched starboard. "I think the seas are getting rough," she added.

Greg grimaced, looking at the long line of people waiting for the elevators. "Should we take the stairs?"

"I'll be back on board for the final segment," Jessica continued, grasping the hand rail to steady herself as the ship rolled again. "Maybe Radick would program it."

Cassie shook her head, "We'd need two pianos."

She looked at the stairs, then down at her stiletto-clad feet. She could see it in a flash: a plunging fall to the first landing, where she'd end up an undignified mess with a broken ankle. Holding on to the wall, she slipped out of her shoes and navigated the stairs in her bare feet. Jessica noticed, started laughing, and then took off her own shoes. They walked down six stories of moving staircases in their bare feet while Greg shook his head and laughed at them. At the bottom of the last stair, they put on their shoes and walked to the dining room with as much dignity and sophistication as the champagne and the moving ship allowed them.

That night, after dinner and the late show, the seas continued to be rough, and the pitching of the ship seemed to mirror the chaos that seeped into the corners of Cassie's mind. It came in on the lines of the B Minor French Suite, defeating her usual ability to escape into music. She tried watching TV, but when she got sleepy and turned it off, the music and the darkness returned. Finally, the music followed her into a fitful sleep from which she woke every fifteen minutes before exhaustion finally won sometime after 3:15, and she stayed asleep until her alarm woke her at 7:00.

Chapter 23

It was only after visiting the infirmary with the worst cramps and bleeding of her life that Cassie learned she had been pregnant. The sharp, tearing pain woke her in the middle of the night, and she spent the rest of the night on the floor of the bathroom, moaning, and trying to staunch the blood that seemed to gush out of her. At one point she passed out, but was luckily lying down. She came to several hours later when the phone rang. Too shaky to stand, she crawled to it and answered it, grateful for the first time for the phone the cruise line installed in the bathroom.

Mark's voice greeted her: "Cassie, where the hell are you? We've been waiting for ten minutes, and you know how Greg gets."

"Sick," she croaked. "I can't rehearse."

Mark started laughing. "What did you do? Party too much last night?"

"No." She paused as another bad cramp hit her. "It's, um, well, female trouble."

Mark's laughter stopped immediately. "Oh, Cass, are you OK?"

"I don't know," she admitted. "I've lost a lot of blood and I'm in a lot of pain." She tried to stand, but her legs were still too shaky. Finally, she maneuvered herself onto the toilet, holding the phone between her ear and shoulder.

"How long have you been like this?" Mark asked.

"I don't know." Cassie leaned against the wall of the bathroom and closed her eyes. Another cramp hit, and then more blood. She started crying.

"I'm coming up there and taking you down to the infirmary," Mark stated.

"No, don't," she sniffled, but he had already hung up.

Cassie hung up the phone, tried to clean up as best she could, and then crawled out of the bathroom to put on some clothes before Mark arrived. *Fresh underwear, a maxi pad, clothes.* She kept repeating her thought like a mantra, and by the time Mark knocked on the door, she was dressed in a sundress. She made it to the door by hanging onto the walls as she walked.

"Do you have your key card?" Mark asked as she opened the door.

She shook her head, closing her eyes and leaning against the wall as he hurried past her, grabbed her card from the nightstand, and then rummaged around in her closet for a pair of shoes.

"Here, put these on," he said. "Sorry they don't match the dress."

Cassie tried to smile, but her lips were so dry and cracked she managed only a grimace. He wrapped his arm around her waist and half carried her to the elevator. Several guests waited at the elevator banks and they stared at Cassie with undisguised curiosity.

"Is she OK?" one of them asked.

"She's not well," Mark replied, pulling Cassie closer.

Where the fuck is that fucking elevator? Cassie thought and closed her eyes. *I should have just stayed in my room and died there.*

"It's not contagious is it?" the other guest asked.

"Yes," Mark snapped. "It's a twenty-four-hour brain tumor that has been complicated by a particularly virulent strain of the Ebola virus."

The elevator arrived. They stared at Mark and Cassie, and finally one of them pointed to the open elevator door. "We'll get the next one," she said.

"Fucking dinosaurs!" Mark muttered as the door closed.

The infirmary was empty of guests when they arrived, and the doctor was in his office. A bald, portly German who Cassie thought looked a bit like a Nazi and avoided when she saw him at guest cocktail parties. Now she thought he looked more kindly than Santa Claus.

The initial questions seemed to last forever: name, age, symptoms, health history—Cassie sat on the edge of the examination table and answered automatically, her mind running with what she was truly thinking. *This is humiliating. It's probably just a bad period. I should have lied to Mark. Can I go now? I am so tired. Can't you just give me some painkiller and let me go back to bed?*

"When was your last menstrual period?" he asked, his voice cutting through her mental chatter.

She stopped, thought a moment, and then said, "I don't know. Um…" she tried to remember. Was it the week before she moved her things to Roseburg? How long ago was that? "Two months ago?"

"You're not certain?"

Cassie thought his voice held disdain, and she ducked her head, embarrassed. "I've always been a little irregular, and with the cruise and everything I just didn't think about it."

He gave her a searching look. "It's possible you may be having a miscarriage. Did you know you were pregnant?"

His words hit her like ice water. She stared at him and didn't speak. Finally, slowly, she shook her head. "No," she whispered.

"Well, I cannot be certain without an examination, but it is a strong possibility." He handed her a hospital gown. "Please remove all your clothes and put this on."

Cassie took the gown, stared at the pristine examination table, then stared at him. "Do you have, um, something, I'm well."

He handed her an absorbent pad. "Put this underneath you. I will return in a few minutes." He seemed to see her panic, and his manner softened. "You're young. Chances are you're undamaged. Please relax."

He left the room, and Cassie pulled off her shoes and her sundress with shaking hands. *Relax?* She put on the gown, hesitated a moment, then pulled off her underwear and sat down on the pad. *Just get through this. Don't think. Just get through this.*

It took less than two minutes of examination to confirm the diagnosis.

"You had a miscarriage, Cassie. It appears you were nearly two months along, and."

She lay on her back, a blanket over her legs with her feet in the examination table stirrups, and she started to cry. No sobbing, just fat tears that drenched the pillow under her head. *Joel*, she thought. *It was Joel's.* She wondered if it was a boy or a girl. She knew she wasn't ready for children, but somehow she felt she had betrayed the unborn little one. She thought of Naomi and the abortion she had had while in college. *How had she gotten through it? She acted like it was no big deal.*

"But what concerns me is that you're still bleeding. How long has this been going on?"

"Since three this morning," she said, and then cringed as her voice broke. *Suck it up, Cass. Pull yourself together.*

"You seem to have expelled all fetal tissue, but I will need to perform a dilation and curettage—a D&C--to stop the bleeding."

Cassie nodded, then, knowing he couldn't see her nod, replied, "OK."

Five hours later, Cassie returned to her stateroom with the help of Mark, who had sat in the doctor's waiting area during the entire procedure. He helped her take off her shoes, pulled off her sundress, and put a nightshirt over her head. Her eyes filled, and she blamed it on the anesthesia.

"You don't have to do this," she said.

He kissed her cheek, pulled back the covers, and helped her into bed. "Call me when you wake. We'll order dinner from room service."

She pulled the covers over the shoulder. "How come you're so good at this?"

He smiled, walked across the room, and shut the stateroom curtains. "My mother is a nurse. Now rest."

Cassie didn't hear him leave. When she woke, the room was dark and the ship was rocking side to side like a giant cradle. She turned on the light and looked at the clock, surprised to see that it was already 8:30 in the evening. A message light blinked on her phone but she ignored it. Everything felt numb—her mind, her body, and her thoughts. Somehow she knew she had been pregnant, but it didn't seem real. The only thing that felt real was the numbness.

She got out of bed, walked gingerly to the bathroom, and stepped into the shower. She couldn't get it hot enough; even when her skin turned lobster red the warmth couldn't reach her. Finally she turned off the water and toweled dry in steam thick as fog. She looked down at her naked body—same breasts, same belly, same legs, same feet, but now so unfamiliar. She shuddered and wrapped herself in her bathrobe and walked back to bed.

The phone rang as she sat combing her hair. She stared at it a second, debated if she would answer, and then reached over and picked it up.

"Hello?" Her voice sounded strange, even to her.

"Oh, thank God," Mark's voice replied. "I've left two messages."

"Oh." She couldn't think of anything else to say. "Sorry," she added a moment later.

"Its fine, Cass, I just wanted to check on you," Mark assured her. "Have you eaten?"

"I'm not hungry," Cassie replied. Her stomach clenched at the thought of food. "I'll just eat some crackers and fruit," she added.

"I'll be by in a bit to check on you," Mark told her. "And if you're hungry by then, we can order room service."

"No, Mark, I just want to eat a little something and go back to sleep." Her stomach clenched even tighter at the thought of making conversation.

He sighed. "Are you sure? I'm really worried about you."

She felt herself flush. *Why did I even tell him I was sick?* "I'm sure," she said, trying to give her voice all the cheerfulness she couldn't feel. "Thank you," she added. She didn't notice that the Texas drawl had crept back into her voice.

"OK." Mark sounded anything but convinced.

"Really, Mark, I'm fine," she added, with a little more convincing brightness.

"I'll call you in the morning," Mark promised.

"Ok," Cassie replied.

She hung up the phone and sagged against the pillows. The numbness remained, but the tears had returned. She hugged a pillow and stared at the wall as fat tears ran unchecked down her face. They brought no relief and melted none of the numbness. Sometime before ten o'clock, she turned off the light and went back to sleep.

"We didn't need to rehearse today," Greg told Cassie when she showed up the next morning for their scheduled rehearsal.

"I'm fine," Cassie said firmly. A couple of painkillers, taken with her morning coffee, had knocked any residual pain down to a manageable level.

Mark and Greg exchanged a look. Cassie tightened her lips, opened the gig book, and hit the tuning pitches. "Ready?" she asked, her voice bright and brittle.

The rehearsal started, and Cassie played the notes automatically. The sound seemed to come from far away, as if she was playing in another room. She kept going blank and forgetting which song she was playing and what key she was in, but sheer determination and her familiarity with the music pulled her through.

Focus, she thought. *Focus and pay attention. This is a B-flat chord, now it's an E-flat chord, remember the key change, it's the Gershwin medley, right?*

They finished the first set, and both Mark and Greg had apprehensive looks on their faces. "We don't have to rehearse today," Greg said again.

"What?" Cassie asked. Her heart started pounding and she could feel her face flush. "Was I dropping notes?"

"No, Cassie, not at all," Greg assured her. "You just seem a little, um, distracted—completely understandable and all."

A cold stillness settled in Cassie's stomach. She just stared at him, dead-eyed. Mark looked at Cassie's face and opened the next medley.

"Let's play the Sondheim," he suggested.

They continued with the rehearsal, and Cassie dutifully played every note. Her hands seemed to belong to someone else; she felt nothing. Rather than dispelling the numbness, the music seemed to make it worse. *Just be normal*, she told herself. *Just act normal.*

"Join me for coffee?" Mark asked after he packed up his viola.

"Sure," Cassie replied, a stiff smile on her face.

They went to the pool deck café, where they both got iced coffees and then settled on a couple of shaded chaise lounges. The sea stretched around the ship, a deep, seemingly endless and fathomless world of blue. It was a calm sea day, and the waves were so mild they were nearly indiscernible.

"Everyone tells me this is really weird for the Tasman Sea," Mark said, sipping his coffee and looking at the water. "I guess it's usually super rough."

"It looks like a lake," Cassie agreed. She stretched her legs out and tried to give the impression of calm interest. A guest walked by and said hello to both of them. She smiled sweetly and returned the greeting.

"How are you doing, Cass?" Mark asked. He didn't make eye contact, and for that Cassie silently thanked him.

She took a sip of coffee. "I'm fine. Not too much pain today."

He put out his hand and placed it on her arm. "Stop, Cass. Just stop."

She froze. Then she took a deep breath and held her eyes wide open to keep her tears from spilling over. She thought of favorite *Saturday Night Live* skits and *Seinfeld* episodes. *Anywhere and anything but here.*

"I'm fine," she said, this time less convincingly.

He just squeezed her arm. Finally, she turned and met his gaze. The concern in his eyes caused her tears to spill over. *He knows I lost a baby. Did the doctor tell him, or did I when I was half drugged?*

"I can't talk about it," she whispered. "I'm sorry."

He squeezed her arm again. "I'll listen when you want to talk."

She nodded and ducked her head. Her thoughts went from Joel to Maureen to music, to TV programs, to what she would wear for dinner, to the scheduled dawn arrival in Sydney—anything to avoid thinking of the child she hadn't known existed and now would never meet.

"You still want to tour with us tomorrow?" he asked as he released his hand and his gaze.

"I don't think so," Cassie replied. "I think I just want to be alone tomorrow if that's OK with you."

"OK, but I'll call you in the morning just in case you change your mind," he promised.

Despite herself, she smiled a little. "Thanks, Mark."

He nodded, and they sat in silence for a couple of minutes. Finally he nudged her arm and nodded toward two bikini-clad septuagenarian guests, as nut brown and tough as leather.

"What do you think?" he whispered. "They're auditioning to be Gucci handbags in the next life?"

It was so petty, so bitchy, and so inappropriate that Cassie had to laugh. "In their dreams," she whispered back.

They sat quietly, gossiping about guests as the ship moved so noiselessly and smoothly across the still sea that everything felt suspended in time. For that moment, there was no past, no future, no direction, no movement—just stillness and quiet, warm air and the smell of salt and suntan lotion. Someone splashed in the pool and the deck sound system played one of the rotating pop song playlists. Cassie hardly dared breathe—one breath could break the spell; one breath could make things start moving again, and then the past and the future would crash in on her like a tidal wave. She sipped her coffee slowly, breathed lightly, and tried to ignore the darkness she sensed lurking just at the edges of paradise.

Chapter 24

The hot Australian sun bleached Sydney with a directness Cassie hadn't seen since leaving Texas. Everything looked overexposed, and despite being armed with sunglasses and a hat, she started getting a headache from all the squinting she was doing. The ship docked between the Sydney Opera House and Harbor Bridge—two iconic landmarks that had looked like fairytale props when they sailed into the harbor at dawn that morning, but now looked as stark and overexposed as the rest of the city.

Just like the desert, Cassie thought as she left the cruise terminal and began walking across the wharf. Tourists, street musicians, and vendors swarmed the area. She dodged several people on roller blades, a didgeridoo player, and a blanket offering homemade jewelry and barely noticed them. She had just two missions: to get away from any ship people for a few hours and to find an internet café and a pay phone so she could contact home.

A few blocks from the wharf the congestion thinned, and she soon found herself walking one street so quiet it appeared to be deserted. *Like a ghost town*, she thought, turning a corner back onto a busier street. She seemed to remember visiting a ghost town sometime when she was a kid, but had some suspicion that she might be remembering a movie scene.

She had left the ship as early as possible. She knew that Mark would keep his word and call, and she feared he would talk her into spending the day with him and his dancer. *I just need to be alone*, she thought as she kept walking. It felt good to move. It felt even better to be anonymous. Hidden behind sunglasses, a hat, and a cool, loose, long-sleeved cotton shirt and gauzy skirt, Cassie also felt invisible.

A ghost in a ghost town. She kept walking. She noticed that the bars were plentiful and looked well-maintained, and that the churches were few and many were boarded up. *The opposite of Texas*, she thought.

She had dreamed of Texas the night before—that old dream she used to have of being out in the middle of the desert, alone, and trying to drive a pickup truck and not knowing how to drive. Somehow in the dream, she knew she had to find her father but she couldn't get the truck going and knew she wouldn't know how to drive it if she could. When she woke early to be on deck for the dawn sail into Sydney Harbor, the sheer beauty of seeing the Opera House floating like a sailing ship at the edge of the water drove all thoughts of the dream from her mind. Now, in the sun-baked streets of Sydney, the dream, and Texas, seemed to be everywhere.

She found an ATM and withdrew fifty Australian dollars. As she looked at her transaction receipt, she wondered if the bank calculated her balance in American or Australian dollars. She stuffed the bills into her straw bag, and turned down a street of shops. She knew from her experience at all the ports in New Zealand, that the best place to find an internet café was usually someplace close to shopping centers.

Halfway up the street, she found a coffee shop that offered computer and internet time in addition to coffee, tea, and some enormous pastries. She purchased a cup of coffee and an hour of internet time, and sat down at the only free terminal. She logged into her AOL account, deleted all the spam unopened, and then just stared at the list of personal messages.

What can I possibly say? Everything felt so far away, so far from her life. *Like I've already died and moved on. How can I possibly tell them what's going on?* The question came to her, unbidden: *And what is going on?*

She froze, her mind blank, and white noise beginning to creep in. Shaking her head, she looked at the timer on the computer and saw she had wasted five minutes of her hour. She took a deep breath and opened one of Maureen's emails

Maureen chatted about her spring flowers, about the addition she was considering putting on the house, and about her upcoming retirement. Cassie smiled, picturing Maureen sitting at her computer in the corner of the living room, reading glasses perched on her nose, and squinting at the screen. She hated computers; she worked with them grudgingly while on her job, but Cassie knew what a sacrifice it was for her to use email, and she surmised it was only the fact that it was the best way to stay in touch with Cassie that she had opened an account at all.

Cassie responded with a chatty letter about the weather, the beauty of seeing Sydney from the deck of the ship at sunrise, and about the cruise itinerary for the next couple of days. She wrote about the meals she had eaten and about the eerie stillness in the Tasman Sea. *Just be normal*, she told herself.

She worked her way through most of the other emails using a similar approach. *The less said the better*, she noted, typing fast to make the most of her rented hour. She responded to the easy ones first: Maureen, Dr. White, several friends from graduate school. She had just opened an email from Naomi when her time ran out and she had to buy more time. Logging back into her email, she took a deep breath and read Naomi's message.

"Cass, you slut! It's fucking raining here and you are living like a Diva on a luxury cruise liner. Tell me all about the men, doll. I'm a single girl again, and it is slim pickings around here right now. I think it's raining so much that no good ones are out due to excessive fear of drowning. "

Cassie started laughing. It was vintage Naomi, and she heard her voice in every word.

"Anyway, on to the question in your last email. No, as far as I know, Joel isn't seeing anyone. The winery has him flying all over the country to meet with distributors and promote the wine. He says he hates it, but I think he gets a little too much satisfaction in coming back from SoCal with a tan when I am stuck here working on my dissertation and going stir-crazy from a lack of sex. If he were a better older brother, he'd at least bring me some free wine..."

Cassie read the entire message and then responded with a spicy version of the chatty email she sent to everyone else. She made a special effort to describe how Rob was going from woman to woman on the ship and what an asshole he'd been to her since she brushed him off. When Naomi was between relationships, she thrived on man-hating stories. Cassie sent the email, and then opened the note from Joel.

She always saved Joel's for last; it was like getting dessert after a meal. Most of them were affectionate and chatty. He signed them "Love," but didn't everyone? This one was longer than usual.

"Dear Cassie,

I am sitting in my hotel room in Dallas in the middle of yet another long road trip. In the past week I have been to Phoenix, Flagstaff, Albuquerque, and now Dallas. I hate the desert—it's the world's graveyard with all that dust and bleached tree corpses. Sorry about that last sentence. I'm sampling my own creation tonight and should know better than to email while tipsy--it makes me think I have undiscovered literary talent.

Where are you today? I'll bet you're in Sydney. Land Down Under and all that. I'm guessing it is a lot more interesting than Dallas, and I hope you are out enjoying it and not spending all your time looking at email in some skanky internet café.

Maybe it's all the road trips or maybe I am just tipsy, but I really miss you tonight. I attended a wine and food pairing dinner at one of our distributors' locations this evening, and it reminded me of how much I enjoyed cooking for you. I've never seen a woman enjoy her food like you do—it's insanely sexy.

Oops, sorry about that. It's the wine talking. At least I think it is. Write me back and make me jealous of all the fun you're having, OK?

Love, Joel."

First, came the memory of the last night they spent had together—the wine by the fire, the fantastic food, the hours of long, delicious sex. Everything felt tinged with a slight bit of sadness and loss, making even the most mundane actions appear important. Then came the memory of lying on the examination bed in the ship's infirmary, tears rolling down her cheeks, as the doctor told her she'd had a miscarriage. The second memory robbed her of breath as she knew, in a blinding instant, that somehow, with Joel, she'd started to believe she could be happy and could have a normal life, and the miscarriage was the cold-cosmic reminder that happily-ever-after stories were for other people, not for her.

She stared at the email, hands resting on the keyboard, until her time ran out. She gathered her bag and sunglasses and left the coffee shop with no destination or plan. The streets of Sydney opened before her, but all she could see was coldness, desolation, and emptiness. She could be anyone in any city on the planet. She spotted a bank of international pay phones and sheer determination brought her to picking one up, dialing through the series of long distance codes, and hearing Maureen's phone ring.

No one was home. Maureen's chipper outgoing message greeted her—the same one she had had on the machine since purchasing it years ago—and Cassie took a deep breath. She launched into a happy greeting, in a happy tone, and even tried out a mangled Aussie accent. She hung up after several minutes and walked off in a daze. Logic told her she had been out in the sun for hours and needed to get something to drink.

I've got to keep the animal body going, she thought as she stepped into a small shop and purchased a bottle of water. She walked to the Royal Botanic Garden, found a bench in the shade, and sipped her water.

What would happen if I just didn't go home? Would it matter if at one of these ports I simply didn't return to the ship? She tried to imagine what she would do to survive in Sydney—find a piano bar gig? Teach piano? But while the idea of starting over where no one knew her felt tempting, she knew that if she was too afraid to eat in restaurants by herself, she would never survive walking out of her life and starting all over.

I'm weak, she thought. Little birds pecked around the immaculate grounds, and a light breeze blew. Somewhere behind her she could hear kids playing. She barely noticed any of it. She tried to remember if she'd always been alone. The memories flashed through her mind like slides in an old-fashioned carousel. *Always with people, but always alone.*

The red ball landed at her feet and startled her. A little blonde girl, maybe five or six years old, ran up to retrieve it. She was followed by a tall man—Cassie guessed the girl's father—dressed in jeans, a denim shirt, and a cowboy hat.

"Sorry about that," he said, as he bent down to retrieve the ball and hand it to the girl.

"It's OK," Cassie replied, her smile automatic, and her Texas accent a surprise.

He tipped his hat to her, took the girl's free hand, and then walked down the hill toward the sidewalk, where a thin blonde woman stood waiting. The little girl pulled her hand from her father's and started running toward the woman. She got just a few steps before she tripped and fell face down, the red ball bouncing down the hill.

Her wail was instantaneous. Both the man and the woman ran to her. The man got there first, picked her up, and held her against his chest. The woman joined them a second later and a brief inspection seemed to show the girl unharmed. Within a minute, the wails were replaced with laughter, the woman retrieved the red ball, and the three of them walked hand in hand down the sidewalk and out of sight.

Something snapped inside Cassie. She didn't cry—couldn't cry—but she could feel things giving way inside like one piano wire after another breaking free. She tried to distract herself with music, but even her trusty Bach refuge sounded like a crazed calliope. She waited for the white noise, but it didn't come. Everything was suddenly, terrifyingly present and real. Even the sounds of the birds seemed to grate. She felt possessed by restlessness. Leaving the garden, she prowled the streets of Sydney, no longer a ghost but a predator. Everyone seemed to be walking too slowly, and the lights took a lifetime to change. The noise of the city drilled against her head, and she fought the urge to put her hands over her ears.

A record store beckoned—air conditioning and jazz pouring out every time someone opened the door. Cassie went in and stood in front of a bin of classical CDs, her heart racing, and tried to calm down.

"Looking for something in particular?"

The attendant's voice seemed to come out of nowhere, and Cassie jumped. Her barked, "No!" was harsher than she intended, but she couldn't seem to pull herself together enough to give the attendant an apologetic smile. She pawed through the CD bins blindly, pulling out recordings and pretending to read the back covers while focusing on even, deep breathing. Finally, after several minutes, her heart stopped racing, and she was able to pay attention to the recordings in front of her.

She was familiar with most of them. In the violin section she noticed Gabe's one and only internationally distributed CD, and she gave a snort of disgust. He had made it right after his Carnegie Hall debut in the early '80's and had been trading on the success of it ever since. She hoped that his newly found devotion to being a husband and father had made him fat and miserable. The picture on the front was taken when Gabe was in his early twenties, and it showed a trim, dashing man with no hint of the excesses and compromises to come. Cassie had been four years old when the CD was released.

She returned the CD to its bin and moved down the aisle to a section featuring Bach. She did a half-hearted search of the keyboard music and was pleased to find Murray Perahia's recording of the *Goldberg Variations*. She hadn't heard it yet, but all her pianist friends were talking about it and saying it was the perfect blend of heart and head. She turned it over, looked for the price and then calculated the exchange rate.

"That's a lovely recording, although he uses too much rubato and pedal," the attendant's voice, with its now-grating Australian accent, startled Cassie again. She gritted her teeth and turned to face the woman. "But, of course, it's better on the harpsichord," the woman added.

Mousy brown hair, heavy glasses, a regrettable tie-dye t-shirt—the attendant was a walking dictionary definition of music geek. *Probably plays the oboe*, Cassie thought, forcing a smile on her face. She thrust the Perahia recording at the attendant. "I'll take this one," she said.

The girl shrugged, pushed up her glasses with her free hand, and walked Cassie to the register. "It has received some good reviews," she sniffed, condescension just at the edge of her tone. She gave Cassie a slightly frosty smile. "American, eh? What brings you to Australia?"

Bitch! Cassie thought behind a professional smile. She handed the attendant her credit card. "Work," she replied, then added bitchily, "I'm a musician. I get paid to play the piano." *And you're hawking CDs in a dark little record store,* she added mentally.

The attendant rang up the sale. "Oh, that's lovely. I perform a bit locally and would love to travel, but there aren't too many opportunities. I play the oboe, but my passion is the Hautbois."

Cassie smiled her first authentic smile of the encounter. She wished Mark were there in that moment—he would have loved it. "Well, keep at it," she said, stupidly, not knowing what else to say. "Thank you," she added as she accepted the bagged CD, her credit card, and her receipt.

She turned and left the shop, the heat and the street noise swallowing her up the second the door closed behind her. She stuffed everything into her straw bag and looked at her watch. Habit rather than hunger told her it was time to eat lunch. She took a deep breath, made an arbitrary choice to turn right on the sidewalk, and set off in search of a good deli.

Chapter 25

It wasn't until Cassie returned to the ship that she remembered she hadn't responded to Joel's email. As she stood in her shower washing the sweat and dust of the day away, she debated walking back into the city and finding another internet café. Propriety and a very real desire to contact Joel warred with the ungrounded feeling she had been unable to shake since her afternoon in the garden. The thought of having to pull herself together enough to be normal felt like an impossible task. Somehow, over the course of the day, it seemed as if her entire skin had been removed, leaving nothing but exposed nerve endings. Still, how could she not reply?

She stepped out of the shower, wrapped herself in the huge terrycloth robe, and sat on the little sofa by the picture window. The Opera House dominated the view in all its flamboyant splendor. After reading about it and listening to broadcasts and recordings from it, seeing it felt about as real as stumbling into Avalon. She, Mark, and Greg were the first to sign up for the special crew rate for that evening's performance of *La Boheme.* Now all she wanted to do was get into bed and not get out again until, when?

Her straw bag lay on the bed where she had discarded it. She reached over, grabbed it, and pulled out the recording of the Bach. Now that she owned it, she had no idea why she had purchased it. Her CD collection already contained several recordings of the *Goldberg.*

Too much of a good thing, she thought, as she tried to pry off the plastic wrap. It resisted her attempts, forcing her to get up, walk to the bathroom, and slice into it with the end of her nail file. The long strip of tape across the top of the recording proved even more difficult to remove. The nail file was too thick to fit under it, and not a single corner of it was loose enough to pull off the CD.

"Son of a bitch," Cassie muttered, nearly slamming the recording down on the marble counter in disgust. She pawed through her toiletry bag and pulled out her tweezers; these had a sharp enough corner to slide under the edge of the tape and work it loose. She pulled the tape, removing just a fragment of it before it split.

"FUCK!"

Picking up the CD, she slammed it against the edge of the counter, shattering the jewel case into large pieces that flew across the counter and scattered to the floor. Cassie stared, stunned, at the ruined case in her hand, then she very slowly, very carefully, put what was left of it on the counter and started picking up the pieces that had sheared off. After she threw out the projectile fragments, she extracted the disc and threw the rest of the packaging into the trash. She turned it over and checked for scratches. Miraculously, it had escaped damage. She carried it to the nightstand, where she had her portable CD player and inserted it. After starting it, she stretched out on the bed, closed her eyes, and tried to breathe deeply and evenly.

Anger sparked through her like fire. All the snapped strings inside seemed to thrash around and tangle together like the inside of Beethoven's Broadwood fortepiano—a bramble-bush, *a burning bush*. She tried to concentrate on the music, but the anger was so deep and so old that the music couldn't get in. What should have been escape and comfort sounded like a swarm of hornets. Finally, after five minutes, she sat up and turned the CD off.

The silence of the room pressed in on her. She got up, paced to the window, then paced back to the bed.

"Get a grip," she muttered to herself. "Get control."

She walked to the mirror and studied her own eyes. They stared back, frightened, wild, and grieved.

"What's the matter with you?" she asked her reflection. "Is it the miscarriage? Are you homesick?"

No answers, just more agitation. Finally, feeling like a caged animal in the small stateroom, she put on exercise clothes, went to the on-board gym, and got on one of the treadmills. The workout room was a reassuring mixture of luxury and banality, and she had it to herself. A ceiling-mounted television broadcast a gossipy celebrity program while Cassie ran faster and faster until, exhausted and drenched with sweat, she stopped the machine and stepped off with shaky legs. She had run ten miles.

She went back to her stateroom, turned on the TV and tuned it to one of the ship's on-board popular music channels, and took another shower. When she got out she felt clean, calm, and completely hollowed out. It was a casual night on the ship, but she dressed for the opera, choosing a simple knee-length black sheath, a pair of sling-back mid-high heel sandals, and her pearl earrings. She took extra time to put her hair into a chignon and apply her make-up.

The popular music began to irritate her, and she turned it off. A quick look at her watch told her she had an hour to kill before joining Mark and Greg for dinner in the city. She picked up a magazine and tried to read, but it failed to hold her interest. Finally, she grabbed her faux Pashmina shawl and her evening bag and walked upstairs to the lounge, where they played for tea every sea day. In all her time on board she had never walked in there alone and ordered a drink; today she knew it was the only way she would relax enough to enjoy the evening.

She sat at one of the small, protected tables that afforded privacy and looked out over the bow of the ship. A few minutes after placing her order, a glass of champagne appeared as if by magic. She drank it slowly, feeling the muscles in the back of her neck and her stomach start to unclench as the alcohol worked its magic.

In front of the ship lay Sydney, spread out like a movie scene. The early evening sunlight lay in long shadows across the city, giving it the magic it had possessed when they'd sailed into the harbor at dawn. All the formerly sun-bleached buildings now had a rosy glow, and streetlights were beginning to come on.

How did I ever think it was a ghost town? she thought as she watched people and vehicles move like streams of energy. Everyone seemed to move with purpose; they all had somewhere to go. Cassie imagined them going home to families, sitting down to dinner, and chatting with their spouses about work or local gossip or world events. They would be normal people, Cassie decided, watching as another wave of cars moved through the intersection--normal people with normal backgrounds and normal families. She imagined multi-generation Christmas dinners, mother-and-daughter shopping trips and lunches out, and her chest began to ache.

She shut down her thoughts, turned from the window, and ordered a second glass of champagne. By the time she finished it, the ache had receded, replaced by a warm glow. She joined Mark and Greg at the gangplank and felt witty, beautiful, and slightly euphoric as they left the ship and went to a classy waterfront French Bistro for dinner. The three of them drank a bottle of wine with dinner, and that, combined with the pre-dinner champagne, allowed her to enjoy the opera and guaranteed that she'd go right to sleep when she got back to her stateroom.

She woke at 4—wide awake with dry mouth and pounding headache. She took a couple of painkillers and sat up in bed while she sipped her way through a bottle of water. The couple in the room next door was having very noisy, very energetic sex. Outside the window, the lights still illuminated the harbor walkway, and another couple walked there, arms around each other.

The loneliness hit her hard. Chest aching, she closed her eyes and tried to think of Joel. He felt so far away—almost as if she had made him up. She thought of Maureen, but she, too, seemed so impossibly distant that it seemed she would never see her again. Flicking on her bedside light, she crawled out of bed and pawed through the desk drawers until she found the CD Dr. White had given her of the 9/11 concert. She inserted it in the player and skipped through everyone else's pieces until she came to the Brahms.

It wasn't a very good recording. The sound guy had only used the room mics, and they picked up too much audience noise and not enough of Joel's warm clarinet tone. Still, as he played the opening line, she heard it again: the beauty and yearning and passion that had captured her the first time she heard him play it all those months ago on that Roseburg stage. The notes brought it all back: the evening he took her to the winery, where he had her blind taste-test the wines and then kissed her afterward, gently brushing her hair off her face. That kiss held everything she heard in his music, and everything that followed felt as inevitable and right as breathing. She waited to cry. Her chest and her throat ached with tears, but none came.

It was the first time I dared hope since Eric, she realized. She thought again of lying on that examination table, feeling the loss of her dream as keenly as the loss of the child: Until she lost both, she hadn't known she was carrying either one.

The Brahms ended, and she turned off the player. She flicked off the light, hugged a pillow to her chest, and focused on breathing in and breathing out until eventually she fell asleep.

The second day in Sydney, she joined Mark for a trip to Bondi Beach, while Mark's boyfriend had a rehearsal. They stopped for lunch in a pub and split a pitcher of beer between them. The alcohol masked what she had privately begun to call her "snapped string" feeling and gave her a carefree, daredevil attitude entirely new to her. She and Mark did drunk body surfing until, exhausted, they collapsed on beach towels and napped for a few hours. Cassie woke sunburned, covered with sand, and slightly hung over.

"Oh my freakin' God, I need a beer," Mark groaned as he shaded his eyes from the sun and squinted at Cassie.

Cassie just nodded, her head pounding and her mouth feeling like someone had stuffed it full of rancid cotton balls while she slept.

They brushed the sand off themselves and put their clothes on over their now-dried swimsuits. The straps of her sundress rubbed against Cassie's sunburned shoulders, and she winced every time she moved. Her feet felt like sausages—fat, rubbery, with oddly shaped appendages that used to look like toes. She winced again as she forced them into strappy sandals and hobbled off the beach with Mark. They walked into the nearest pub—an overpriced tourist joint across the street from the beach—and ordered a pitcher of water and two pints of beer.

A family sat at the table next to theirs—mother, father, and two little boys. The woman wore a one-piece swimsuit cut to the navel, exposing aging pendulous breasts, a sarong tied across her ample hips, and a huge sun hat. The man had a flaming-red bald scalp, an enormous Hawaiian shirt, shorts, and the ubiquitous white tennis shoes. Both boys—Cassie guessed they were somewhere between ages seven and twelve—were engrossed in their Gameboys. When the woman spoke, the American accent came as no surprise.

"Jesus God, no wonder the rest of the world hates us," Mark muttered, staring at the exposed cleavage. "Those aren't puppies—they're full-grown Labradors!"

Cassie snorted with laughter. "Nice of mummy to let them out for a run in the park," she added nastily with a fake English accent.

Mark laughed. "Damn things need leashes!"

One of the boys overturned a glass of soda, and both parents started scolding him. His brother put down his Gameboy and watched the melee with a smirk of satisfaction. Mark turned to Cassie in disgust.

"Holy shit, Cass, they're like evil little aliens! They come into your life, ruin your figure"--he threw a significant glance toward the monstrous cleavage which was now bouncing around like silly putty as the woman tried to mop up spilled soda with paper napkins— "and then they ransack the rest of your life. I don't know why anyone would ever have one!"

Cassie froze. Everything in the room seemed to freeze with her, as if reality itself were holding its breath. No white noise, no music, just stunned silence and the feeling of being sucker-punched in the gut.

Mark's face went white. "Cass? What's wrong?" Realization dawned. "Oh, God, Cass. I didn't mean," he reached across the table and tried to take her hand.

Another string snapped. An anger Cassie didn't even know she possessed flashed through her, and she stood up so fast she nearly toppled her beer. She was shaking from head to toe.

"You never do, do you?" she hissed, grabbing her bag, and walking blindly toward the door. The tears were so thick she could barely see. She pushed through a pack of people waiting for a table, hearing "Watch it!' and "Sorry, luv, are you all right?" in her wake. She kept walking.

A queue of taxis waited across the street, and she stepped into traffic without looking. A car skidded to a stop and blew its horn. She waved her hand in its direction but kept walking. Behind her she could hear Mark yelling at her to stop, and to wait. All she could think of was going, going anywhere, getting away from him and from this place. She climbed into the back of one of the taxis, told the driver to take her to Sydney Harbor, and then began sobbing.

The radio had been playing in the taxi but the driver turned it off. All she could hear was the sound of the road and her own sobs, which humiliated her even as she couldn't make them stop.

"Are you OK, Miss?" the driver asked, timidly.

Cassie nodded, said, "Yes," and then burst into more sobs.

He pulled the cab to the side of the road. "Are you sure?"

She nodded again. "Just drive," she said. She met his eyes in the rear-view mirror. "Please, just go," she said.

He waited a second, and then nodded, reached over and turned the radio back on, and then rejoined traffic. She cried until she seemed to run out of tears, and then she sobbed dryly. Finally, it stopped. She dug a scarf out of her bag, wiped her face, and then applied some lip gloss. *Look normal, act normal*, she thought as she brushed sand off her legs. *Hold it together until you get to your room.*

When they reached the cruise terminal, Cassie paid the driver and added a 20% tip—guilt money for the crying. He accepted the cash and then studied her a second, his lined face clearly worried.

"You sure you're going to be OK?" he asked.

She nodded and gave him a brilliant smile. "Yes. Sorry. Just had a fight with my boyfriend," she lied.

He nodded, smiled, and looked relieved that it was something so minor, so typical, and so ordinary. "Well, you're a lovely girl. He'd best remember that!"

She gave him a real smile this time—sad, tender, and aching. He looked old enough to be her Dad. He probably had kids her age.

She imagined he was a great Dad. "Thanks," she said, and then turned and left as her lip started to quiver again.

She walked to the edge of the wharf and looked at the ship. It shimmered clean, white, and magnificent against the cloudless blue sky. The Opera House appeared to be in full sail right behind it. Behind her, the didgeridoo street player was doing a brisk business, and the wharf was full of sun-drenched tourists. She could smell something deep-fried and sweet being sold from a food cart, and a slight breeze lifted her hair away from her face.

It was absolutely perfect, and she wanted to die.

"Cassie?"

Mark's voice. Cassie sighed and turned. He rushed up to her and then hesitated.

"I'm so sorry," he said. "I am such an asshole."

Cassie reached out and squeezed his arm. "No, it's OK. I overreacted."

He shook his head. "It was stupid."

He looked absolutely miserable, and Cassie feared he would start crying. She opened her arms, and he gave her a grateful hug. After she released him, they stood together and looked at the harbor.

"It's perfect," Mark said. "I still can't believe I'm here, in Australia. It's like a dream."

"I know," Cassie said softly.

And inside, another string snapped.

Chapter 26

By the time they got to Melbourne, Cassie felt contained, in control, and in no danger of snapping at people or bursting into tears. The steely resolve that had got her through the first few months after The Apocalypse came back, and she played her performances with focus and professionalism. She hadn't been able to listen to the new Bach CD after her first attempt. Every time she tried she could feel the snapped strings beginning to jangle up inside and the out-of-control feeling would start coming back. At first she tried listening to other classical music—her recording of the Chopin Nocturnes, another of the Brahms Intermezzos—but the same thing happened. She didn't even try to listen again to Joel and Naomi's performance of the Brahms. She resolutely threw it in the trash the morning after they left Sydney.

When they docked in Melbourne, she left the ship with the first group of guests and took the shuttle into the center of town. She had dressed well and put on make-up and jewelry, knowing from past experience that looking good always gave her confidence. As soon as the bus arrived at its designated stop, she exited and started seeking an internet café. She found one within three blocks, purchased two hours of internet time, and sat down in front of the computer with a cup of coffee.

She opened Joel's email first and quickly reread it, willing herself to not tell him everything. *We're just casual,* she reminded herself, *he doesn't want anything heavy or any responsibility.* His comments about their last night together brought it all back—the food, the wine, and most of all the whispered conversation when he held her and told her his dream of opening his own winery someday—and she started to shake. All the snapped strings thrashed around. She feared that she would throw up. Finally, after several slow, measured, deep breaths, she put her hands on the keys and started typing.

"Joel,

Greetings from Down Under! We were in Sydney for a few days, and I cannot begin to describe how lovely the Opera House was when we sailed in at dawn. Mark, Greg, and I went to a production of La Bohème, and Mark and I did some body surfing at Bondi Beach. It's hot down here, and very dry. The locals fear a drought.

I'm glad your job is taking you to such interesting places (ha ha!!). I will be going wine tasting with a bunch of crew in a few hours. I'll be sure to let you know if I taste anything good.

Love,

Cassie

She re-read what she had written—so banal, so dismissive—and pressed "send." As the message went, she felt both freedom and a dull ache inside. She knew he would read it exactly as she meant it—friends, nothing more. *I have to survive*, she thought, unable to open her other messages for a few seconds. *Somehow, I have to survive.*

She responded to email from Maureen, and a note from Naomi telling her that she had just met a divine man and was madly in love. *How do you do it?* Cassie asked her, silently. *How do you fall in love over and over again and still have any hope that the new one will work out?* She tried to imagine her own future, and it seemed to stretch out in front of her as empty and lonely as the desert at dusk. *I will always be alone.* She thought the words and then waited for a reaction. Nothing, no feeling, no thoughts, just that huge, dark silence. She looked around the café and studied the faces of the strangers. Most were there in pairs or trios. She, and a 20-something male, were the only ones in there alone.

She logged out of her email and left the café, most of her final hour of purchased time unused. One street led into another; nothing held her interest. She kept walking, and the stream of humanity rushed past her on the sidewalks and on the streets. Strangers, all with their own lives and hopes and dreams, people she would never see again—they were here, in this place, for just a moment, and it would never be repeated. *You can't step in the same river twice.*

She walked for an hour and then went back to the bus stop, where she joined other crew members for the wine-tasting tour. They got in a small bus, and the tour guide kept them entertained with anecdotes and tips about Australian wine. Cassie, sitting three seats back, pretended to listen. *I am alone. I am alone.* A refrain, an ear worm—she didn't know what it was, but the thought became the soundtrack in the back of her mind where music used to be. She searched her mind for the music, but came up with nothing more than the regrettable lyrics to Billy Ray Cyrus' "Achy, Breaky Heart." That obligingly took up residence in her mind so that the lyrics and the refrain created a crazed composition of banality and self-loathing.

"It looks like Napa Valley!" one of the crew members noted as they left the city and started driving through acres of vines.

Cassie looked at the scenery; she had never been to Napa, and the area only resembled Oregon wine country in that it had field after field of vines. This area was dry, and the guide mentioned that there was always the threat of drought. She felt a pang of homesickness for the green of Oregon, especially the Douglas-fir-covered hills hugging the vineyards and wineries of Roseburg. Right after they got their driver's licenses, Naomi and Cassie had driven those back roads west of Roseburg in Naomi's mother's car with the sunroof open and music blasting from the speakers. She remembered one drive in late September, when the grape leaves had turned yellow and the late afternoon sunlight spilled over the valley like liquid gold. Naomi and her boyfriend-of-the-week had just "done it," and she couldn't wait to tell Cassie all about it. Cassie pretended to be worldly and sophisticated, but internally had been shocked to the core. She nodded and smiled, but could hear His voice saying that Naomi was a Jezebel, a whore of Babylon.

And what are you now? Cassie asked herself as she studied mile after mile of dusty vineyards out the window of the bus. She thought of her pitifully short string of boyfriends: Eric, Brad, Nate, Steve, Gabe, and Joel. Just six guys, and she never even slept with Eric or Steve. *Could Joel even be considered a boyfriend? Gabe?* She shook her head. *Do married men count as boyfriends or just affairs?* Brad and Nate had been brief relationships, and she didn't keep in touch with either of them. When Naomi asked, she told her the sex was great, but in truth both were inexperienced, and the sex had been hurried, and a little embarrassing. *I was always looking for the kind of connection I had with Eric.*

She could almost hear His voice—*but you weren't good enough, you little pagan whore. And you aren't good enough for Joel either.*

The memory of His voice hit her so hard that she stopped breathing. The truth of His accusation seemed dredged up from the center of her. In a rush it all came back: the compound, His charisma, and the way He played the guitar and sang. Cassie played along on the piano, but He never seemed to see her. He chose others—girls her age—to be His wives—but never looked at her.

That's because I knew you were a Jezebel and an infidel, she could almost hear Him say.

When it hit, the nausea was immediate, fierce, and inescapable. She jumped out of her seat, hand over her mouth and ran to the front of the bus. The driver took one look at her, screeched to a halt, and opened the bus door just as Cassie ran through it, her morning coffee bursting through her fingers. She made it just outside the bus where she vomited up the rest of her coffee and then, with her stomach empty, she retched, and retched, and retched until she thought she might pass out. Finally, shaking, she leaned against the bus, eyes closed.

I want to die.

The tour guide tapped her on the shoulder and handed her a couple of handi-wipes when she opened her eyes. She slowly cleaned her hands and her face and put the soiled wipes in the proffered trash bag while the tour guide babbled on and on about motion sickness, telling the bus driver to slow down, and anti-nausea medication. He handed her a couple of chewable motion sickness pills, which she ate without question, and then she climbed back on the bus.

The crew gave her a round of applause, along with some good-natured ribbing.

"What'd you do, Cass? Start drinking early?"

"Yeah, why aren't you sharing with the rest of us?"

Cassie blushed, forced a smile on her face, and mumbled, "Sorry about that" as she slipped into her seat. The bus started moving again, and she leaned her face against the window and closed her eyes.

I want to die.

She knew that most of the crew had much more spectacular tales of public vomiting—most of which seemed to take place during or after all-night parties in crew bar—but she still felt smothered in shame. *Just one more way I am not perfect; just one more way I am damaged goods.*

They reached the first winery a few minutes later, and the rest of the crew headed straight for the tasting room. Cassie stayed outside on the porch of the rustic building and looked out over a world of vineyards, outbuildings, and sunshine. A dog came up and nuzzled its snout on her lap, and she petted it distractedly. The tour guide came out with a bag of potato chips—he called them crisps—and handed them to her.

"Sorry about that," he said. "I'll tell the driver to slow down a bit."

Cassie nodded, opened the bag, and ate one of the chips. It made her feel better almost immediately. She ate another.

"I guess I should have eaten more than coffee for breakfast," she said, eating another chip. After swallowing, she continued. "I'm just sorry I'm too unsettled to try the wine."

He leaned toward her and whispered, "That's OK. The wine isn't very good here. Wait until we get to lunch. You'll feel better, and the wine will be worth drinking."

Cassie smiled gratefully. "Thanks."

He looked back at the tasting room. "I guess I'd better get back in there and check on everyone else."

She nodded, glad to be alone. He kept trying to make eye contact, and she could tell he was interested in starting a conversation, but all she wanted to do was sit, eat her chips, and stare at the vineyard. It filled her mind. It edged Him out. That felt like more than enough.

Six hours, lunch, and four wineries later, Cassie walked back on board ship, pleasantly tipsy and carrying a couple of bottles of wine. On her head she wore an Aussie cowboy hat she had been surprised to win in a wine-tasting contest. She entered her stateroom, kicked off her shoes, put the wine and her bag on the bed and walked into the bathroom. The reflection made her laugh out loud: with the hat, her tan, her blonde hair and her make-up, all she needed to look like a Dallas Cowboy cheerleader was the outfit and a boob job. She took off the hat and placed it beside the sink. While washing her hands, she picked up the hat and carried it with her out of the bathroom as she looked for a place to display it. Finally she perched it on top of the TV at a cocky angle, and then stripped down to take a shower. She could hear the anchor going up as the ship prepared to leave port, and by the time she stepped out of the shower they were sailing north.

She towel-dried her hair, wrapped herself in the bathrobe, and then turned on the TV. Flipping through the usual classic movie stations, and past the ship's programs advertising future tours and items for sale in the gift shops, she settled on a news broadcast. It was an Australian channel. Since leaving the States, Cassie had discovered that she preferred non-U.S. newscasts; they seemed to take more of an interest in what was going on all over the globe, and there weren't so many shrill comments about President Bush. All her friends loathed him—he seemed to be the far left's anti-Christ—but Cassie had never forgiven President Clinton and his head bulldog, Janet Reno, for The Apocalypse, and she felt that as a Texan, President Bush would never have given orders to murder a community of his neighbors.

The newscasters chatted about several Australian events, and seemed to spend a great deal of time discussing players from the Melbourne Victory football club. Cassie listened distractedly as she stood in front of her closet in her bra and underwear trying to decide what she wanted to wear to dinner. She had just taken her baby blue silk sheath dress off its hanger when the announcer startled her into paying attention.

"In breaking world news, fifty-seven Hindu pilgrims and activists were burned to death today on a train just as it was leaving Godhra station in the western state of Gujarat, India. A gang of Muslims are suspected of causing the fire, and India's prime minister Atal Bihari Vajpayee has appealed for calm amid fears of renewed religious tension in the country."

A picture flashed on the screen; no video, just a still shot of a burned-out train car and the terrified, angry faces of survivors. The newscaster continued.

"Initial evidence suggests kerosene was poured into four of the carriages before they were set alight. Local residents report hearing screams for help and seeing a huge ball of fire and people putting out their hands and heads through the windows, trying to escape. Schools and shops have been shut in Godhra, and a curfew has been imposed. Police in the town have been ordered to shoot troublemakers on sight."

The other newscaster, a pretty blonde, grimaced and arranged her features into an appropriate expression of care and concern and said, "What a tragedy."

Her co-anchor answered, but Cassie didn't hear him. The dress slipped from her hands and lay on the bed. She picked up the remote, and with shaking hands, turned off the TV. In the silence Cassie heard the sound of waves hitting the ship, a door shutting somewhere near her cabin, and her own rapid breathing, which she seemed unable to control.

For the second time in her life, the world came to an end, and Cassie was back in Texas with her grandmother, watching it on TV. Just like the first time, there was no question of pain, or hope, or even anger—just numbness and a blank white noise in the brain that the TV images and sounds bumped into but never permeated. She watched her life catch fire, and then she watched it burn to the ground, with nothing but the deadness of the silence behind the chaos.

Like the first time, Cassie felt no surprise, no grief, no anger, and no guilt. Instead of her grandmother's living room, she stood half-naked in a luxury cruise ship stateroom somewhere north of Melbourne. She again saw survivors stumbling out of the compound, and again knew better than to search for the faces of her parents. This time—every time—they were right next to Him, guns firing, proclaiming their Messiah with bullets and martyrdom. Once again the flames danced—red, orange, billows of black smoke—all of it visible fulfillment of the apocalypse He had prophesied was coming. Once again she knew He'd seen it, and now—over and over again, from terrorism in Northern Ireland to violence on the Gaza Strip to the twin towers in New York, to a train in India--the rest of the world saw it too.

"That's it, then" Cassie stated to the empty room, her voice flat and cold. "It's over."

Chapter 27

The second hand on her alarm clock moved unevenly. With each tick it paused for a millisecond as if gathering the strength to move, and then rushed to the next tick. It seemed to take even extra effort for it to move from that last second to the 12 where the next minute began. Cassie lay on her left side and watched seconds turn into minutes and minutes turn into hours.

Tick. Tick. Tick.

Sunlight crept into the room through a crack in the curtains. People walked by on the Promenade outside her window. The ship rocked gently, cradle-like.

Tick. Tick. Tick.

Cassie got up and took a shower. The effort exhausted her. She lay back on the bed and wondered if she should go and find herself some lunch. Somehow she had missed breakfast; she wasn't sure how.

Tick. Tick. Tick.

At 2:30 she got up again, put on a performance dress and fixed her hair and make-up. She walked to the High Tea gig in a daze. Guests smiled and said hello, and she answered from someplace outside herself. That was the shell—the animal that kept going because that's what she did. Cassie tried to surface and look normal, but it felt as though she was so far down inside herself that there was no way to climb up to the twin windows to the outside world.

At 3, she and Greg and Mark started their set. They knew it so well that Cassie could sleep-walk through the notes. Her fingers pressed the keys. Her arms moved and lifted—a puppet? Mark and Greg played—caricatures of musicians, pretending to care for music that had never interested them. Even the Mozart felt wooden.

"Bach?" Greg asked as they came to the end of the Rodgers and Hammerstein medley.

Cassie nodded, opened her score, and played the G Major French Suite. For weeks its relentless cheerfulness had been an irritant; today it was just notes, played one after another—a succession of meaninglessness in a meaningless set of music on a meaningless ship in a meaningless world.

They finished the set with their usual polished perfection. Cassie heard herself tell both of them that she was tired and would not be joining them for dinner. She watched herself pick up her music and greet guests with a smile. She watched herself walk to the poolside grill, where she ordered a grilled cheese sandwich and fries.

Her head ached. Sunlight sparkled off the water, making it worse. When the sandwich arrived, she ate it with more appetite than she knew she possessed. It was then she remembered that she hadn't quite made it out of the stateroom since returning from the wine tour in Melbourne and hadn't eaten anything since lunch the previous day. Then she remembered that she hadn't had any caffeine either, so she ordered a cup of coffee and drank it with a couple of painkillers she always carried in her music bag.

The cradle-rocking of the ship continued. Guests and crew walked past, looking to Cassie as ephemeral as ghosts. As her headache receded, she stood, picked up her music bag, and left the table. Rob, sitting several tables over, smiled and waved her over. She gave him a vague smile and just kept walking. He caught up with her by the elevators.

"Hey Cassie, are you OK?"

She could see the sincerity behind his Casanova smile, but the idea of responding to it was so exhausting she couldn't even try.

"I'm fine," she said evenly.

He looked at her, a flash of annoyance crossing his face. "You know, sometimes people just want to be friendly. You don't have to be so icy all the time."

She shrugged. "Sorry." The elevator door opened, and she got in and punched the button for her floor. She noted his startled face and then the doors closed.

Her stateroom enveloped her like a dark womb. She put the "do not disturb" sign on her door, locked it, and methodically stripped off her dress, hose, and heels. Then she ran a bubble bath so hot that she had to get into it inches at a time. But the heat failed to warm her. After getting out of the tub, she dutifully scrubbed her face and her teeth, and climbed naked into bed, pulling the covers up to her chin.

Tick. Tick. Tick.

The phone rang. She answered it, groggy and disoriented. *Is it day or night?* Her headache had been replaced with a numb fogginess.

"Cass, I'm heading into Perth. Wanna go?" Mark's voice sounded relentlessly chipper.

"What time is it?" Cassie mumbled, sitting up and pushing hair out of her eyes.

"9:30. I've got directions to a wicked beach. Wanna go?"

She tried to imagine getting into the shower, taking the time to do her hair and makeup, and choosing what to wear. She tried to imagine making conversation with guests on the shuttle bus, and then making conversation with Mark all day. She thought of her last beach trip with Mark and cringed.

"No, I'm wiped out. I'm going to rest today."

"Oh, OK. Just thought I'd see if you wanted to go. I'll go with the casino crowd. Want me to bring you anything?"

"No," Cassie said. "Thank you. Have fun."

She hung up, lay back down, and tried to go back to sleep. After ten minutes she gave up, got out of bed and took a shower. She sat on the sofa, wrapped in her bathrobe, and tried to find the energy to get dressed.

"Coffee," she told herself. "Coffee, a croissant, maybe some yogurt."

She waited. When she looked at the clock another ten minutes had slipped past.

"Coffee. I'll feel better with coffee."

With that she forced herself to stand, get dressed, fix her hair and make-up, and leave the stateroom.

Although most guests were ashore, the ship buzzed with activity. Maintenance and cleaning crews clogged most of the hallways and the Promenade deck. Alarms went off—a mandatory crew drill. Cassie felt short of breath and dizzy; the noise and light poured into her, filter free. Halfway to the Bistro, she nearly gave up and turned around. But her need for coffee overcame her aversion to the chaos and she continued. She was shaking by the time she ordered her coffee and sat down at one of the tables with a croissant and some fresh strawberries.

You need to find an internet café.

She nibbled at the croissant. It was, as always, perfect. She barely tasted it. The strawberries tasted like water. Only the coffee—a triple-shot latte—tasted good. She closed her eyes and drank as deeply as the heat allowed. It scalded, but she didn't care. She imagined the warmth working all the way through her, and she took another sip. When she finished the first cup, she ordered another one.

You need to find an internet café! This time the thought was sterner. She imagined going upstairs for her bag, coming back through the chaos, taking the shuttle into town, and then walking the streets seeking a café. *Maybe after the second cup.*

The second coffee arrived and she drank it more slowly. It gave her enough energy to eat the rest of the croissant and the strawberries, and to pick up a small carton of yogurt and eat that as well. As she finished her breakfast, she felt buoyed and determined. She took the elevator to her floor, got her purse, and then took the elevator back down to the gangplank. Several guests waited at the shuttle stop, and she stood a few feet away from them, hoping her sunglasses and hat gave her some anonymity.

One of the guests was mid-rant. "Well, I just told the Captain that this is Sterling after all, and we shouldn't be stopping in these piss-ant ports."

Cassie looked at him out of the corner of her eye. He was a bald, angry Santa without the beard.

"I mean, if we pay this sort of money, we should be brought to better ports! " He looked around in disgust. "And where the Hell is the shuttle?"

Texas, Cassie thought, listening to his accent. She looked down. Sure enough, he was wearing cowboy boots. *Probably a former oil executive.*

"Oh, Howard, just drop it already!" This came from a big-haired woman dripping with gold jewelry. She turned to the woman sitting next to her and added, "Everywhere we go, the same story. We take these damn cruises every year, and he complains about everything every year. If you hate it here so much, why worry about the shuttle?"

"Faye, watch your mouth!" Texas-Santa glared at Big-Hair woman. She dropped her eyes and shrugged.

For a second, no one spoke. Texas-Santa broke the silence. "Where the Hell is that damn shuttle?"

The fatigue enveloped Cassie. As the shuttle arrived, she turned, walked back on the ship and into her stateroom. She opened the heavy drapes to let in more light, but kept the gauzy sheers closed for privacy. She had learned early in the cruise that Promenade deck walkers liked to peer into stateroom windows, and the best way to avoid feeling like a zoo animal was to keep a veil between the window and her room.

With the veil in place, everything looked gauzy and smudged. She collapsed on the sofa, kicked off her sandals, and stared at the small chunk of sky outside her window. Her caffeinated body felt jittery; her mind felt fatigued.

I just want to go to sleep and not wake up.

She closed her eyes and tried to sleep but that proved impossible. She turned on the TV and tried to focus on an old movie, but she couldn't seem to get into it. She left it on for company and for background noise; the stateroom's silence was beginning to feel oppressive.

You've got to get a grip.

She tried to think through what had happened. The facts were there—the Apocalypse, the miscarriage, that awful incident in India—but none of the emotions. It happened. It just was. There was no meaning. Her thoughts jumped from crying on the examination table to the horrible picture of burned-out train cars, to the face of her grandmother while she watched the Apocalypse—perfectly composed, perfectly made-up, but wet with silent tears. She tried to imagine the last part of her grandmother's life. According to Maureen, Grandma never really recovered from the Apocalypse. During the last three years of her life, she rarely left the house and saw few friends. Maureen said it was probably a blessing that Grandma had a heart attack and died in the middle of a Sabbath School discussion about the Book of Daniel; had it happened at home, she might have been dead a week before anyone knew to look for her.

Cassie tried to feel some sadness for her grandmother, but felt more envious than sad. Whatever happened after death, Grandma never again had to suffer people's mock sympathy. She never again had to re-live the Apocalypse. She never again had to "keep it together" or "keep up appearances." When she died, Maureen worked with Grandma's lawyer, and they sold everything and put the money into the trust Cassie still couldn't touch. Now nothing remained in Waco. Time, death, and fire had erased everything, leaving just a smooth, bland surface.

Did it actually happen? Cassie had re-written and repressed the events so many times that nothing felt real anymore. Before she died, Grandma told Cassie that she was a miracle—the only good thing to survive Him and the fire. She told Cassie she was the future and because she was still alive, so were her parents because they lived on in her—in her DNA and in her memory.

Cassie thought again about the baby she would never know, and her throat closed. That baby carried her parents' DNA. That baby would have continued the hope Grandma placed in her. Now the baby was gone, and Grandma was gone, and Cassie had tried so hard to forget her parents and the Apocalypse that now she couldn't remember what they looked like. She tried to picture them, and all she could see was the snapshot Maureen had of the two of them when they were younger than Cassie was now. Mom wore white bell-bottoms, platform shoes, and a gauzy Indian-print blouse. Dad wore cut- off shorts and an old army green t-shirt, and his face was nearly hidden behind a bushy brown beard. By the time Cassie was born, the beard and the hippie clothes had been replaced by carefully modest church clothes, and the easy smiles wiped out by a surface piety that barely contained the tension.

Tension. I forgot about the tension. She remembered one time when she was about eleven years old. She had been outside playing with some of the other kids in the compound, and when she came back in to get a drink of water, she found her parents standing in the kitchen, speaking in heated whispers. Mom shook her head; Dad leaned in, apparently pleading. When they saw her they stopped talking, and the smooth, happy masks slid back into place. At the time Cassie had been frightened to see them angry and relieved to see their normal expressions; now, she wondered what they had been talking about.

Probably Dad wasn't enjoying celibacy, she thought, staring at the cowboy hat where it still sat on her TV. He had a hat similar to her Australian hat, Cassie realized with a little jolt of surprise. He wore it outside, especially in the summer. Sometimes, if she was lucky, she got to go with him to pick up supplies. They drove an old blue Chevy pick-up truck with board seats and a rickety shift column. If she was particularly lucky, they would take the long way back to the compound by meandering through the back gravel roads. Dad rarely spoke during these rides, but he would whistle. His face would relax, and he looked happy. She remembered one time when they stopped in the middle of the desert to watch a stunning sunset.

"You see, Cassie? That's God's paint-by-number," Dad had said, gesturing to the sky with his arm.

Cassie—had she been eight or nine?—squinted and tried to see the hand of God moving an enormous paintbrush across the sky. She had wished just for a second that they could be a normal family and live in a normal town. She wished Dad could be like this always, and that Mom wouldn't cry herself to sleep when she didn't know Cassie was listening.

What were you thinking? Cassie asked both her parents as she stared at the cowboy hat.

No answer. Outside she heard the deck crew laughing and chatting with each other as they put a fresh coat of paint on the railing. Somewhere down the hall someone was running a vacuum cleaner. Tonight they would leave Australia and sail for Bali. The water would show no trail—no trace that they had ever been here. They would stop at the next port, and the next, and the one after that, and there would be no memory of them once the ship had left.

She thought again of the young family she'd seen in Sydney. The memory tightened her throat. She pictured the little girl and felt an aching envy so strong she gasped.

Why wasn't I enough?

They had joined Him when Cassie was eight. She tried to remember something—anything—from that pre-Him time. The only memory that held any emotional significance was of a time when she and her mother made chocolate chip cookies together during a thunderstorm. The smell of the cookies, combined with the fresh, rich smell of wet earth came back in a rush. Mom abandoned chores, and they sat together on the front porch eating warm cookies, drinking cool milk, while watching the dusty ground around the house turn to mud. In order to keep her from getting scared, Mom taught her to sing "How Much Is That Doggie in the Window?"

She wasn't much older than I am today, Cassie thought. She could see her pretty blonde mother, dressed in cotton shorts and an old button-down shirt, sitting with her bare feet up on the porch railing, blue eyes shining as the heavens sent down rain, thunder, lightning, and eventually hail. *You were fearless; what made you choose Him?*

No answer. The memory faded. Cassie pulled herself off the sofa, took off her shoes, and then curled up on the bed. The second hand continued its unending quest. She followed its progress with the diligence of a bodyguard. Its constant irregularity soothed her, and finally its soothing tick carried her into sleep.

Chapter 28

With the curtains closed, Cassie found that it was difficult to tell the difference between day and night. She started avoiding the pool deck first. The relentlessly bright sunshine and party atmosphere became teeth-grindingly unbearable. Avoiding dinners came next. With bravery she didn't know she possessed, she called the dining room and asked to be removed her from the seating assignments. This left her free to order dinner in her room and to avoid having to make conversation for hours every evening. When Mark and Greg asked about her absence, she gave them a vague "female trouble" sort of answer that she knew would cause them to drop the topic immediately. It worked. Within days, she was able to whittle her public time down to performances and rehearsals, trips to the Bistro for coffee, and midnight walks on the deck.

Her days took on a sort of pattern. She slept late, and then either watched the second hand on the clock or—if she was feeling more energetic—old movies on TV. The effort to get showered and dressed was so great that only the promise of coffee pulled her through it and out the door of her stateroom.

At the Bistro, she always chose a small table in the corner, and came in with a book. If people tried to engage her in conversation, she smiled and nodded, but gave very short answers. After a few attempts, most people just left her alone.

She attended the rehearsals and played her gigs. She smiled when required, and spoke when spoken to. Inside, behind the eyes of the functioning shell, she wondered at her ability to keep going, and sometimes in her stateroom she thought of her grandmother—so perfect, so controlled, and so alone. The world had come to an end, but at least she was wearing her lipstick. A few years ago, Cassie had considered her grandmother shallow to work so hard for external perfection; now each day when she put on her own lipstick and brushed her hair into shiny waves, she understood Grandma's need to look good. It was the only controllable factor in a completely uncontrollable world.

The midnight strolls started one night when afternoon napping produced insomnia. Cassie's restlessness finally drove her out on deck, and she walked and walked until five miles later, when she'd exhausted herself enough to be able to go back to her stateroom, she got one of the best nights of sleep she had had since the miscarriage. After that, she put on her shorts, t-shirt, and tennis sneakers every night and walked the deck regardless of weather conditions.

At night, the sea shows its true mystery. During the day, Cassie could almost convince herself that the sea was safe; at night she knew differently. The sea tolerated their presence, and the abyss of moving blackness was the macro version of her internal world. There was no friendliness here. Coziness and safety proved to be as ephemeral as mist in the presence of such vast anonymity and meaninglessness. There had never been safe ground—and even the illusion of such land was now absorbed by the formlessness of moving darkness.

Lines came back from her childhood, "In the beginning, when God created the heavens and the earth, the earth was a formless wasteland, and darkness covered the abyss, while a mighty wind swept over the waters." She knew, according to the Genesis story, God hovered over the face of the waters and eventually brought forth light and life and all of creation. But a deeper knowledge told her that the "formless wasteland," the dark abyss, was still the foundation of all that was and that no creation or evolution would change it. Eventually, everything would dissolve into the wasteland that supported the illusion of meaning and solidity.

Wind, mighty and gentle, swept over the waters and the ship. During each turn around the deck, she walked either with it or into it. On rougher nights, the wind brought sea spray and rain on deck, which Cassie welcomed. When it hit her lips, it tasted like reality. *The first I've ever known?* she thought. Memories, like pictures, flipped through her mind. What had been real? Mom and Dad? Him? Grandma with her perfect façade? Maureen, saddled with a granddaughter she may or may not have wanted? She thought about the men she knew: Eric, who loved her until his mother convinced him not to; Gabe, who loved her as long as it was convenient; Joel, did he even love her? She thought about her friends: Mark and Greg, who brought her along because they were desperate for a pianist; Naomi, who just wanted someone who would let her talk and never interrupt the monologue with thoughts of her own. She thought of music.

I lived for you, she thought. The piano, which had been lifeboat, best friend, therapist, and lover, had now abandoned her as well. Now when she played, no worlds opened up. She felt nothing. She pressed the notes as absently as a typist. Even her beloved Bach had shut her out. Instead of each note leading her like stepping stones into a better world, they sank like rocks to the bottom of the abyss and left no trail to follow. There was only the chaos, and the sheer animal drive to survive in the face of meaninglessness.

Another line came back to her, this time from a college literature class. She couldn't remember who wrote it or even in what context it appeared, but she did remember the imagery, which described humanity as "maggots, clinging to a dirt clod, hurtling through space." *We live, we breathe, we procreate, and then we die. There are no threads to the other side; all we know is our wish that things were different.*

Some nights, if she walked late enough, she would see a group of Eastern European waiters who met in the crew's area of the bow to smoke. The red tips of the cigarettes, combined with whiffs of smoke and fragments of Russian became part of Cassie's midnight ship landscape. To her, the smoke smelled as lonely as the sea, and the unintelligible bits of Russian as grim as death. She felt perversely grateful to the smokers; it was as if their presence validated her own and that they were the only other humans on the planet—or at least on the ship—who saw the same meaninglessness that she saw. For their part, they left her alone, and she suspected she was as much a part of their nightly reality as they were of hers. She was grateful that other than a brief occasional nod, none of them tried to engage her in conversation.

One night, after walking a couple of miles, she stopped on the stern and watched the wake churn behind the ship. She was never able to stop in this place without remembering the crew's story about one of last year's world cruise guests who had committed suicide by jumping overboard off the back of the ship. The ship set up a search pattern for hours, but the body was never recovered. Now, as she watched the white foam on dark water, she wondered what drove that man to jump. She considered the peace of oblivion, but only briefly.

I don't want to die, she thought, gripping the railing as she stared at the water. *I want to figure out how to live.*

She stared at the water, stunned by the sudden tears flowing unchecked down her face. *I want to live. I want to live.* She half considered prayer, but didn't know whom she would pray to if she tried. Finally, she just looked up at the stars and thought it again: *I want to live.* The sound of the water, the engines, and the wind were her only answers.

They docked in Singapore a week later, and within an hour of their 6 A.M. arrival, Cassie was awakened by a knock on her stateroom door. When it didn't stop, she stumbled out of bed, pulled on her robe, and opened the door a crack. Mark and Greg stood there, showered and dressed, with matching determined faces.

"What?" she asked, not caring if she sounded rude.

"We're going into the city as soon as the ship clears through customs, and you're going with us," Greg replied.

Cassie shook her head, and turned away. "No, thank you."

Mark pushed the door open. Cassie stepped back, surprised and angry, and then stood by her bed, arms folded across her chest, as they both entered the room and shut the door behind them.

"No argument. You're coming with us."

They continued to stand with their arms crossed, and looked even more determined than they had in the hall. Cassie shrank back; they had obviously been discussing her and had decided between themselves to rescue her from herself. A flash of anger went through her, and she glared at them.

Greg reached over and flipped on the lights. "It's a tomb in here, Cassie," he said quietly.

She shrugged. Part of her felt horrified at having people see her before she had showered or brushed her teeth; the rest of her didn't care. She pulled her robe tighter and refolded her arms, trying to look just as determined as they did.

"I don't feel like it," she said.

Mark and Greg exchanged a look.

"I'm showing up for our gigs," Cassie reminded them. "And my playing hasn't suffered. If I want to be alone during my time off, what do you care?"

They exchanged another look. Finally Mark spoke.

"We're worried about you," he stated. "You never come out of your room, and you aren't eating."

Cassie shrugged again. "So?"

"It's this, or we'll get the doctor involved," Greg said.

She stared at him. He held her gaze. *Here, there, what difference does it make? It's just another part of the job.*

"OK," she said.

"We'll be back in an hour to pick you up," Greg added, more threat than promise.

After they left, Cassie sat on the edge of the bed and tried to find the energy to get in the shower. She had missed Bali—somehow she hadn't been able to get the energy to leave the ship, although she did take a walk around the deck a couple of times. Now that they were docked for a couple of days in Singapore, Mark and Greg were determined to drag her to Raffles and through the shopping centers. *Maybe I should just hide somewhere on the ship.* The thought was fleeting; even the idea of evasion took too much energy.

She forced herself to stand, strip off her robe, and get in the shower. *It's just today,* she told herself as she shampooed her hair. *Just get through it.*

Just get through it, she thought as she stepped out of the shower and towel-dried her hair. She brushed her teeth, put on some sunscreen and lip gloss, and then stood in front of her closet in a bra and panties as she tried to decide what to wear. Nothing looked right. She stood and listlessly pawed through the hanging clothes, and then went through the dresser drawers.

You have to wear something. Just put something on and be done with it!

She chose a turquoise sundress Mark had helped her choose before the cruise. She had lost weight in the past few weeks and the dress hung loosely, making her small breasts look non-existent. She looked in the mirror and shuddered. *I look twelve!* She cocked her head to the side and squinted at her reflection. Hadn't she had a sundress like this when she was twelve or thirteen? She had been the skinny, flat-chested girl with knobby knees and bony elbows. Her friend Megan had developed early; she filled out her pink sundress, and by the time she was fifteen, He had chosen Megan to be one of His wives. The only time He seemed to notice Cassie was when she played the piano.

Is He going to be here forever? Cassie thought as she sank to the bed. "He's gone," she said out loud. It gave her the energy to stand again and choose sandals and jewelry. By the time Mark and Greg returned, her hair was up in a French twist, her make-up was in place, and she was wearing what Grandma used to call her "company face."

It was close to three in the morning when they returned to the ship. After going through mall after mall, they took the tram to Sentosa—Singapore's Pleasure Island—for dinner and club-hopping. After the second waterfront bar, Cassie stopped drinking and started ordering seltzer. Mark and Greg were both so blitzed on Singapore Slings that they didn't even notice she had stopped drinking. Greg kept slapping down his credit card, and the waiters kept bringing the drinks. Mark flirted with every man who came near the table, confessing to Cassie that he had always "had a thing for Asian guys." The music blasted—American pop music at decibels that made conversation impossible. By the time they got back to the ship, Cassie's head was pounding, and her teeth ached from clenching them. *That's the last time they talk me into this shit,* she vowed to herself as they went through the ship's security checkpoint.

"We should get a nightcap," Mark said.

"Everything's closed," Cassie replied.

"Besides, we've had enough," Greg added. Cassie was surprised to hear him slur his words; in all the time she'd known him, she had never seen him show any signs of being drunk.

They took the elevator to their floor and Cassie waved good night to them as they entered their staterooms. When she got to her own door, she was surprised to see a package waiting for her, along with the usual collection of ship's newsletters and meeting announcements from the cruise director. Once inside her room, she put on the lights and peered at it.

The return address was London. *Do I know anyone in London?* Cassie wondered as she pried open the cardboard and pulled out the contents. What she found was a copy of the Bach Double Keyboard Concerto and a folded note. Dropping to the bed, she put the music aside and opened the letter:

Dear Cassie,

I hope this note finds you well and that you are having a fantastic time in Singapore. Since I returned home, my agent has been in contact with Radick and we are scheduled to play the middle movement together as part of the final show on the last segment of the world cruise. He has sent the string parts to Radick, and I hope you can convince Mark and Greg to work with the other string players on board to polish up the chamber orchestra bits.

As per our onboard discussion, I will play piano 2 and you will play piano 1. I will be joining the ship in Tokyo, and Radick is willing to set up two keyboards so we can rehearse. It is not ideal, but he has assured me that we will have access to two grands for at least a week before the performance.

Looking forward to it! Please contact me with questions or concerns.

Best,

Jessica

The note fell to Cassie's lap and she stared at the floor. *I can't do this.* No panic, no fear, just deep knowledge. *I can't do this.* She took a deep breath and looked at the cover of the music. It was the same edition she and Eric had worked out of, and the blue cover brought it all back—Indian summer sunshine, the feel of his hands on her bare arm, the shock wave that went through her the first time he kissed her. Back then she knew all she had to do was be normal, be perfect, play gorgeously, and get out of Roseburg. Now she knew that normal was unattainable, perfection could not be reached by such a flawed girl, the playing could desert her, and the wasteland wasn't Roseburg but the desolate landscape she carried with her everywhere on the planet.

She thought of Eric, trapped now with his fat, crabby wife and that dreadful child. He looked defeated and old, and he wasn't even thirty. She thought of Naomi, still strutting, still seducing guys, still talking tough, but beginning to get a shrill edge to her. She thought of herself—a fake, a phony, a shell of a loser sitting in a luxury stateroom on a top-rated cruise ship and knowing that she didn't belong here any more than she belonged anywhere else. Everything was gone, and her place of belonging was a burned-out charnel house that everyone wanted to forget ever existed. For the rest of her life, she would be sixteen years old, sitting in front of the TV in Grandma's house, and watching her world go up in flames.

She slowly took off her sandals and then curled up on her side still dressed, lights still on. The clock's second hand continued its relentless journey as it marked seconds, minutes, and eventually an hour. Finally, a little after four, she fell asleep.

Chapter 29

The children danced. The hot Cambodian sun beat down, and the children danced. The monks practiced their English on members of the crew. Other crew members visited the Buddha shrine. Cassie stood under a tree on the temple grounds, silent and watchful.

"You're going on the crew tour with us," Mark had told her the night before.

They had already dragged her out for one of the two days they spent in Thailand. She avoided touring the second day by claiming she needed to stay on board and practice the Bach. Mark didn't know she hadn't played a note of it. She had spent the day trying to avoid looking at it. The Bach sat on her coffee table, a mute accusation. Every time she opened the cover and looked at the notes, bleak exhaustion flooded her, and after a few minutes she gave up and closed the score. Every couple of hours she considered taking the score to a piano and playing a bit of it, but somehow it never happened.

"I don't want to go," Cassie had told Mark. "I have to practice."

He shook his head. "You will have plenty of time for that later. When will you get to see Cambodia again?"

Now, sweating and feeling the beginning of a headache, Cassie watched the children and the monks and her fellow crew members as though she was watching a movie. Graveyards surrounded the temple grounds. *And these are just the ones that are marked*, Cassie thought as she remembered everything she had read about Pol Pot and his massacre of his own people.

This temple was just one stop among many on their whirlwind tour of Cambodia. She thought of all the places they had visited on the cruise and knew she would remember just as little about this place as all the others. It was always the same: show up, see a few cultural sights, get some local eats and drinks, and then rush back to the safety and familiarity of the ship.

I won't remember the people, and they won't remember me. We are here, in this temple, and it is the only moment when all of us will be here in this place like this.

She looked at the temple grounds and at the children. They were smiling. Another tour bus arrived—this one full of cruisers— and the guests were handing money to the kids. The dancing became even more energetic in response to the money and applause.

Do they know they're dancing on the graves of their ancestors?

She studied their faces. They were too young to be the children of those slaughtered: maybe they were the grandchildren? Did they know of anything before Year Zero? Had they been to the killing fields or seen the piles of anonymous skulls? The tour literature Cassie had read the night before said that Pol Pot killed over twenty percent of Cambodia's population. When she stepped off the ship this morning, she hadn't known what to expect from Cambodia, but the dancing surprised her.

"There are lots of ghosts here," the bass player from the ship band told Cassie as they rolled through the countryside in their air-conditioned bus. He said it as calmly as if he had pointed out the presence of trees, and his conviction chilled Cassie to the bone.

Cassie closed her eyes a moment and tried to sense the ghosts. Was he right? Were they here, in this temple, or at least in the graveyards surrounding the temple? She could almost feel something brushing against her arm. She opened her eyes just a little--nothing. *But they're here,* she thought. *Maybe they're out there, dancing with the children.*

She studied the tourists, the children, and the monks. They were real. If any ghosts were present, they had no interest in showing themselves to her.

Maybe I'm spiritually dead, she thought. *I just don't get it.*

During their freshman year in college, Naomi had started seeing auras and reading tarot cards for everyone. Every time she read the cards for Cassie, the death card and justice, which Cassie secretly named "our-lady-of-the-sword," always came up. After a few of these readings, Cassie refused to have Naomi read her cards for her again.

She studied the faces of the children—the living progeny of a generation of death. Did they see ghosts? Were the ancestors as present for them as the Texas dust was for her? She remembered playing in the corner of her bedroom on a sunny afternoon when she was six years old. The light came through the window in golden shafts, and a whole world of magic and fairy dust sparkled on the light. At six, she sat transfixed, knowing in her gut that she was seeing a window into forever; now, at twenty-six she knew it had just been plain old household dust, transformed by sunlight and a child's imagination.

She looked across the temple grounds and briefly considered walking over to join the rest of the crew near the entrance of the shrine. The heavy heat convinced her that she preferred to stay in the shade of the tree and pray for a breeze. It was so still the whole country seemed to be holding its breath.

She remembered wondering about an afterlife a couple of months after The Apocalypse. She had asked Maureen, and Maureen told her something vague about possible reincarnation. Cassie found that idea terrifying—He would come back, just as He promised. A week later, during one of her weekly calls to Texas, she had asked Grandma if they would ever see Mom and Dad again. Grandma went silent a moment before she replied.

"When Jesus returns, you will see your Mom and Dad again," she had told Cassie, her voice firm.

In retrospect, Cassie knew Grandma had meant it to be comforting. But at the time, all she heard was that He was the Messiah He claimed to be, and He would do exactly what He had promised to do—come back from the dead—and that was the only way she would be able to see her Mom and Dad again. She had never told anyone of that conversation with Grandma—not Maureen, and not either therapist. She had pushed it as far to the back of her mind as she could and put her parents there too. He was gone, and they were gone. The end. But now, in a Cambodian Buddhist temple, Cassie knew the blinding truth:

They had to stay dead so that He would stay dead. I buried them to keep Him away.

First, the staggering truth. Second, a chill so deep her hands went icy. Third, shortness of breath. She leaned against the tree as the memories, flashes and pictures, came at her as fast as a flip book. Mom holding her and braiding her hair in the shade of one of the compound's trees. Dad giving her a piggy-back ride around Grandma's house sometime before they joined Him. Mom comforting Cassie when He ignored her. Dad driving with her to get groceries each week--their little quiet time when no words were spoken, but so much was said. The smell of her mother's shampoo and the shape of her father's hands. The water fight her parents got into one hot day when He was off the compound and they were washing windows. The exact shade of her mother's blue eyes. How had she forgotten Mom's eyes? They stared back at her every morning in the mirror. How had she forgotten Dad's hands? They were her own.

Cassie stuffed her fist into her mouth to keep from crying out. The children kept dancing, and the tourists kept handing out money; the monks kept talking, and the wind held its breath. The memories kept coming.

She was sitting at the old upright piano at the compound, working through a tricky passage in a Brahms Intermezzo. It was early spring, and the windows were open. Cassie sat on the piano bench in shorts and a t-shirt, her hair in a high pony-tail on top of her head. She played the passage over and over again, trying to hear the sound she sought in the clunky piano she played. She didn't hear Him until He spoke:

"It's almost time for meeting," He said, just a foot behind her.

She jumped and squealed. He put His hands on her shoulders and gave her a gentle massage. She leaned against Him and closed her eyes, thrilled at His touch. She imagined being chosen. She imagined being His wife. His hands had just caressed the backs of her ears when her father walked into the room.

He froze, and His hands dropped from her shoulders. Cassie's father stared at Him with an intensity Cassie had never seen. No one spoke. Her father's right fist clenched and unclenched several times, and then he spoke.

"Cassie, your mother needs your help." He didn't look at her as he spoke.

Cassie grabbed her music and ducked out of the room, cheeks burning. She found her mother taking a nap and felt horrified that her father had lied to Him. When she saw her father later in the day, he said nothing about the confrontation, and she was afraid to ask. Two weeks later she left the compound; several months later, everyone was dead.

Why did you stay? she asked her father. *If you knew enough to protect me, why did you die for Him?* She thought of how angry she had been with her mother right after the Apocalypse and felt shame that she always assumed her father was as much a victim as she was. *At least Mom had the excuse of being depressed. Why were you so weak? Why didn't you stand up to her? Why didn't you care enough about yourself and me to tell her no?*

No answer, only the present with its heat, tourists, monks, and kids. The children, flush with cash, huddled together in the shade of the shrine and compared their spoils. The tourists climbed back on the bus. The bass player came up to Cassie as the rest of the crew got on their tour bus.

"You OK?" he asked. "You look like you've seen a ghost."

She just nodded, and followed him back to the anonymous, air-conditioned safety of the bus. As the cool air surrounded her, she sipped on a bottle of water and watched the temple recede as they drove to their next stop. The ghosts—if there had been any present—were sealed off from the bus, and the door shut on Cassie's memories as well. The casino crew handed out cheap local beer, and after drinking half of the can, she felt almost normal again.

This is real, she thought as she traced condensation trails down the side of the beer. She ignored the bleakness that accompanied that thought and took another swig of beer.

That night she dreamed of Waco. The Apocalypse raged, and she stood naked and barefoot at the edges of the compound watching it burn. The Feds weren't there; neither were the reporters or gawkers. She stood alone, the smoke and flames ferocious in their intensity. She knew she was supposed to put out the flames, but she had no water. She heard no screams and saw no people, but knew everyone was still inside and that she was the only one who had gotten out.

"It's your fault, you know," He said. He appeared before her, a semi-transparent being with glittering green eyes. "If you believed in Me, you could have saved them all."

Cassie cried out and tried to grab Him. He dissolved under her fingers, leaving nothing but His mocking laugh behind Him.

Mom! Dad! She tried to scream, but had no voice. She tried to push her way into the flames but wasn't brave enough to get burned. *I'm sorry!* she tried to scream. *I'm sorry, I'm sorry, I'm sorry!*

Her failure robbed her of breath. All the evasions and lies she'd told rose like bile; all the blame she heaped on her parents followed. Hate—at them for following Him and for dying, and at herself for failing to rescue them or die with them—came next. The grief that followed came from a place so deep within her that she was sure she would never be able to cry it all out.

She stayed at the edge of the compound until the flames became cold ashes. She couldn't stay, but couldn't leave. Some sort of strange paralysis kept her feet trapped, and she had the sense that if she could break free, no matter where she went she would be forced back to this place. Waco was everywhere. He was everywhere. When the twin towers came down, He was there. When bombs blew up on the Gaza Strip, He was there. When that train burned in India, He was there. He kept His word; He came back over and over and over again and would until the end of time. He took and took and took, and He never let His victims go.

Through her grief, Cassie felt the first flames of anger. *You evil, evil monster*, she thought. She remembered the lives He stole and the lies He told. She thought of those who burned with Him and those, like herself and Grandma, who died inside but kept walking outside. She thought of her loss of Mom and Dad, of Grandma, of Eric, of the baby, and of Joel, and the ferocity of that flame of anger became an inferno of rage. She looked at her arms, and they were radiating red heat like a fireplace poker. She knew beyond doubt that she was capable of murder. With every fiber of her body, she wanted to grab Him by the throat and choke the breath out of Him.

"You've taken enough! You can't have them!" Cassie tried to scream at the blackened compound. "They aren't yours. You can't have them, and you can't have me!" Her voice came out a hoarse whisper.

She thought of Beethoven shaking his fist at God just before he died, and she clenched her fists and shook them with just as much passion at the ruins. She tried again. "You can't have them, and you can't have me!" Her voice disappeared and it was as though she had never had a voice.

She raised her arms to the desert sky, heat and light flashing from them as she clenched her fists and held them with every bit of strength she possessed.

"You can't have them, and you can't have me!" Rage forced the words through the barrier that seemed to block her throat. Her voice didn't have the strength she felt, but for the first time, it could be heard.

At first, silence. The ashes and ruins and sky were without sound. The anger drained away, leaving just the grief, and Cassie put her fists to her eyes and sobbed. Then, as if coming from a child's music box, she heard a thin thread of music. Cassie's crying stopped as she strained to identify it. It grew louder, and she soon recognized it as the 19th *Goldberg Variation,* played on the piano. The sound swelled and seemed to morph into an orchestra, then an orchestra with chorus. As it played, Cambodian children came out of the ashes and started to dance. With each note, Cassie felt a fragment of her grief dissolve into warm light. With each of the children's steps, the ashes transformed into green grass and flowers—life springing up with every footfall. The grief dissolved, and the grass grew, and Cassie stood and silently watched the transformation.

At first the children didn't seem to notice Cassie. After a few minutes, however, one little girl came up to her and took her hand. With a tug, she pulled Cassie into the group, saying "You have to dance."

Cassie stared at her and at the other dancers. "But I don't know how," she said.

The girl smiled and pushed Cassie to get her moving, and Cassie tried to dance. As she stepped, others seemed to join them—kids she remembered from the compound, and even some of the adults. She searched the faces for her parents. *Mom?* The little girl tugged her hand. Cassie glanced down, and in the child's face saw her own face, then the face of her mother, then the face of the child Cassie knew she'd lost, before the beaming face of the Cambodian girl reasserted itself.

"You must dance," she said, tugging harder. "I'll show you how."

She first became aware of the gentle rocking of the ship— movement as gentle and rhythmic as a mother rocking a cradle. Her stateroom was dark, but around the edges of the curtains she could see the beginning of early morning light. The dream lingered. In her ear, the notes of the Bach; in her legs, the movement of the dance; in her hands, the desire to caress piano keys and release the music trapped in each note. The Bach Double sat on the coffee table, its blue cover beckoning. Cassie got out of bed, opened the curtains to the morning light, sat on the sofa, opened the score, and entered the notes.

Chapter 30

From backstage, the audience couldn't be heard over the sound of the storm. Cassie stood in slender high heels and braced herself against the wall. The ship had been in rough weather all day, and the floor pitched drunkenly every few minutes. Jessica groaned, opened a package of sea sickness pills, and ate two of them.

"This is out of control," she said. "And I do hope they've bolted the pianos down!"

Cassie grimaced; she feared the same thing. In dress rehearsal that afternoon, a rogue wave had hit the side of the ship, pitched it starboard, and then rolled it port. Jessica's piano charged across the stage and almost fell off into the front row of seats. She had just enough time to jump back to avoid being hit as it skidded past her. Cassie's piano had been better secured, but her music had gone flying all over the stage. Several of the string players fell off their chairs, but miraculously the instruments and the players were unharmed.

"I'm sure they've bolted it down now," Cassie replied, with more hope than conviction.

It was the first really rough weather they had encountered on the cruise, but two days of it more than made up for months of smooth sailing. Guests were complaining. Mark told Cassie that the dining room had lost sixty thousand dollars of wine, as well as much of its china and stemware, when the rogue wave hit. There was discussion as to whether or not the show would be canceled, but when the seas went back down to twenty-foot waves, Radick decided to go ahead.

"I can't fathom why they're running the tango number," Jessica said.

In dress rehearsal that afternoon, the entire orchestra had been terrified that the dancers would break limbs doing lifts and leaps on a careening dance floor.

"They took out the lifts," Cassie replied, parroting what she had overheard at dinner in the officer's mess earlier that evening. She smiled at Jessica. Since Jessica had rejoined the ship, they'd been practicing together every day, and now, a week from the end of the cruise, they had plans to play some duet and two-piano concerts together in the future.

The ship's orchestra started the opening number: a John Williams medley arranged by the cruise line's entertainment director. From where she stood, she could see Greg's face, and the back of Mark's head. She knew both of them were drugged up on anti-seasickness pills and that both were worried about being alert enough to make all their entrances. She had eaten a maximum dosage as well, but somehow it just seemed to make her really calm.

She looked down at her shoes and smoothed her dress over her hips. She wore her favorite black sheath dress—the same one she was wearing for the post-9/11 concert before she sailed. The dress fit well again; after Cambodia, her appetite for food increased with her appetite for music. Once she started practicing, the notes came back easily—so easily that she wished Radick had time to let them play the entire concerto rather than just one movement. To satisfy her need for music, she worked her way through everything she had brought on board with her. She started with the *Goldberg Variations* Dr. White had given her, and she learned #19 first. Every morning she began her practice with that variation. *A reminder of her dream?*

The medley ended, and the band master took his bow. Radick walked out on stage and began his comedy routine and warm-up for the tango number, which was next. Dancers, in full costume and make-up, pushed past her.

"Sorry," one of them whispered as Cassie stumbled to get out of the way.

"It's OK," she whispered back.

The costumes were stunning—red and black scraps of fabric barely covering perfect bodies. The women wore fishnet stockings. Cassie wished she had the nerve to wear fishnet stockings. With their hair slicked back, heavy eye-liner, and lipstick, Cassie hardly recognized the girls she had accompanied on crew tours or drunk with at crew parties. In their costumes they were like smoldering sex. Radick announced the number and walked off-stage. The lighting changed, the smoke machine started, and the orchestra started playing the first strains of the Piazzolla tango.

Cassie wanted to dance with them. In the past months, she had learned to waltz, foxtrot, cha-cha, swing, and tango. Several of the elderly guests had welcomed the opportunity to teach her to dance, and as they patiently bore her missteps and stumbles, she learned to laugh and relax with them. The dancing brought her into the world cruise "family," and she quickly found herself invited to specialty dinners, birthday and anniversary parties, and even a private tour of Kyoto when they visited Japan.

"You're their pet," Mark grumbled more than once.

Cassie gave his arm a squeeze. Mark and his dancer had split when the dancer left for his vacation, but Mark still preferred to be with the crew rather than the guests. Greg spent much of his free time squiring the widows around the dance floor, and there was some talk that he might be invited back as one of the cruise line's Ambassador Hosts. Cassie never stopped marveling at his ability to make conversation with anyone. Even her newly found popularity among the guests did little to lift her shyness. As in the past, this earned her the reputation as being a great conversationalist. When she mentioned this to Mark, he snorted, "That's because you let them do all the talking."

The lighting shifted, and the dancers moved through soft red lights and shadows. Each couple's moves mirrored the others, yet each one seemed to be in his or her own world. One deep bend was so stunning Cassie sighed.

"They're so beautiful," Jessica said, looking at the dancers.

Cassie nodded. "They live the music."

And they did. Every note and beat moved through their bodies, and the entire story of love and loss and eternal longing came through each movement. They ached for the consummation of that desire, but it was the desire itself that gave the dance its power.

Cassie had always felt completely connected to music through the keys of the piano, but watching dancers made her realize that while she was co-creator of a sound world, she would never embody it so completely. Yet that consummation—the complete melding of self with sound—was the Holy Grail she sought every time she played. She remembered her teenage belief that music could connect her with the dead. In college she dismissed it as sentimentalism, but the idea had kept coming back to her over the past month. If she and Bach could communicate through notes written nearly three hundred years earlier, was communication with other dimensions really that far-fetched?

The tango ended with the female dancers woven like vines around the male dancers. They held the pose for a second until the stage went dark. Then they moved again, all sexiness and longing gone as they raced off stage to change costumes for their next number. Radick told a few more jokes to the audience. She couldn't tell, over the sound of the storm, if he was getting any laughs. She had to wonder if the audience was as tired of his comedy routine as she was; after months of the same tired jokes about the band master and false, self-deprecating humor, Cassie found she gritted her teeth every time he picked up a microphone.

He would not be one of the people she would miss after the cruise ended.

Several crew members, quite a few guests, and even Mark were thrilled that the cruise was ending in a week. Greg said he looked forward to being able to eat breakfast in his bathrobe again. Cassie felt ambivalent about returning to land life. After so many months on board, the ship felt more real than Oregon. She missed Maureen and Naomi, but she hardly dared ask herself if she missed Joel. She had told none of them about losing the baby. She had told none of them about Cambodia and the gut-wrenching experience of discovering and sorting memories she had never looked through before. She knew she would have to start visiting a therapist again, and the thought fatigued her.

Where would I even start explaining? And Naomi and Joel don't even know anything about my life before Oregon.

She tried to imagine telling them the truth, but every time she visualized it, she felt panicked and ill. She decided to tell them when she got home, provided they gave her the chance. *Maybe a therapist could tell me how to talk to them about this?*

The lights came back on, and the lead ensemble singers stood in the middle of the stage facing each other. The orchestra played the introduction, and they started the first lines of "Somewhere" from *West Side Story*. Months of playing and listening to show tunes had numbed Cassie to the sentiment in musical theater, but she still loved *West Side Story*.

"...somehow, somewhere, we'll find a new way of living, we'll find a way of forgiving, somewhere."

Cassie had heard that melody and those words so many times before, but tonight they seemed even more poignant than usual. Her throat closed. She shut her eyes and willed herself to stay calm. *It's just theater, it's not your life,* she told herself firmly. But she couldn't stop hearing every phrase as if it was written for her. Even the ambiguous ending felt personal. *Is there hope? Or is all of it just youthful fantasy in the face of experience?*

The song ended, but the question remained. While everyone else seemed to be talking about where they were going and what they were doing after the cruise, Cassie looked into a void. She could visualize leaving the ship, going to the airport, and flying home. She could even see Maureen meeting her in Portland and driving her home to Roseburg. But after the welcome-home dinner and late-night chat, her visualization faded to black. She couldn't even imagine waking in Maureen's house and drinking coffee with her, much less what to do that day and the day after that.

But Naomi seemed to have it all worked out. When Cassie had called her from Seward, Alaska, she told Cassie they would get an apartment together in Portland, Cassie would get gigs and teach some piano, and they would live lives dedicated to art and music, eschewing love and using men for sexual purposes only. But after years of Naomi's enthusiasms, Cassie knew it was only a matter of weeks before Naomi would find another man who was the one. And she knew that if she got an apartment in Portland, it would have to be one she rented by herself. She tried to muster some enthusiasm for being a career pianist in Portland, but all she could see was the drudgery of months of rain and piano students who didn't practice. *And therapy, probably years of therapy.*

"You could get a ship band gig," Mark suggested one night when she confessed she didn't know what she would do after the cruise ended.

She nodded, but inside knew she had no interest in working on ships again. It was too terrifying to live in a culture of instant friendships and glossy personas. She always felt that she was just one word from an unrecoverable social blunder, and the stress of trying to be perfect meant it took every ounce of energy to mingle with the guests.

Jessica gave her the only glimpse of a future she looked forward to living. She promised to book a small concert tour for the two of them in England, and Cassie promised to do the same for them in Oregon. They planned a program of 2-piano pieces, as well as a 4-hand concert, so they could book themselves at a variety of venues. Cassie still didn't know why Jessica wanted to work with her. She stole another look at Jessica, who stood regal in a long silver gown. Her hair was pulled back into a jeweled clip, and she wore sapphire chandelier earrings that caught the light every time she moved.

She looks like a goddess, Cassie thought.

The "goddess" caught her gaze and smiled. "We're next," she said, and then started to do some neck rolls. Cassie nodded, took a deep breath, and then leaned forward into a deep forward bend, her arms hanging heavy. All thought stopped—now her world was Bach and breathing. She straightened, closed her eyes, and entered the music. As she opened them, she met Jessica's gaze and knew Jessica was in the music as well. The audience started applauding. Jessica gave her a nod, and then walked out on stage. Cassie followed with more confidence than she felt. She walked carefully across the moving floor and tried to keep from stumbling as the ship moved. The band master picked up his baton, the audience fell silent, and the orchestra waited.

Jessica looked at Cassie and nodded, and then nodded to the band master. The first notes floated out of Jessica's piano and the pizzicato strings. Past and present collided in the labyrinth of notes—for a split second Cassie could hear Eric's hands on the keys, feel Maureen's support, and in an odd way, could feel the shape of the compound's piano keys under her fingers. The audience felt huge. In it she sensed all her cruise friends, all her land friends, the shadows of her parents and her grandmother, and the promise of a new life to come. They were there, in the Bach, participants in the joyful present of notes and love and transcendence.

Cassie lifted her hands to the piano, played her entrance, and entered the dance.

Aria da Capo

From the first note, the Bach Double Concerto had been the soundtrack of Cassie's life. She loved it the first time she played it years ago with Eric, and she still loved it when she and Jessica performed it in London and Portland. Each phrase wound its way through every thought and experience. Now, sitting beside Dr. White as they listened to students play the second movement in a master class, she breathed each line with the performers and felt the satisfaction of having come full circle.

They were in Jacoby, both concert grand pianos side by side on the stage, the auditorium dark except for a few stage lights. Two students played the Concerto with all the passion and hopefulness Cassie remembered bringing to the piece when she first learned it. Dr. White's other students sat in a semi-circle beside the pianos. Some of them looked engaged in the music; some looked bored. They made Cassie feel old; she could see that they dismissed her as an adult, not one of them, and she wondered when she had stopped being relevant to teenagers. Joel, who would be thirty on his next birthday, joked that she was still just a kid and said she didn't look a day over eighteen. She loved him for that little white lie. Maureen told her she still had her whole life ahead of her, and when she looked at her music, at Joel, and at her expanding circle of friends, she sensed they were right. Her therapist encouraged her to trust those she loved, and to forgive those she had lost. Some days were easier than others.

The movement drew to a close, and the group applauded. After the performers bowed and sat again on their piano benches, Dr. White looked at Cassie and nodded. He had introduced her to everyone at the beginning of class as a guest artist and concert pianist. It sounded like hyperbole to Cassie. She felt a flutter of her habitual nervousness and had to take a couple of deep breaths before she started speaking. After praising both players for the passion they brought to the piece, she heard Dr. White's words come out of her mouth as she addressed the main problem she heard in the performance.

"A double concerto is an intimate conversation," she began. "This one—which you both know is a transcription of the famous Bach Double in D Minor for two violins—is the most intertwined of Bach's concerti." She looked at both of them a second. "It is a conversation between two people who know each other intimately."

They nodded and waited. She sighed, realizing in that instant how difficult it was to put intangible concepts into words.

"When you are really close to someone, you don't just hear the words he or she says, but you hear the deeper meaning in the words," she continued. "It is only then that you can respond deeply to what the other person is telling you. When you play this music, you must hear the deeper meaning in each phrase, and you must answer with your own depth of understanding. "

She walked over and opened one of the student's scores to the first page of the second movement. "You two need to have one mind when you play this. You must be in a place where you know what the other is thinking and feeling, so you can communicate, not just push the notes."

She turned to one of the students and smiled at her. "Your partner said some lovely things in this phrase. Did you hear it?"

The student nodded

"What did you hear?" Cassie asked.

The student looked confused. "It was really pretty," she said.

Cassie nodded. "Yes, but what was behind the beauty? What was the meaning?"

The student thought a moment. "It was a question. I heard her ask a question."

Cassie smiled. "So how are you going to answer?" She turned to her small audience of pianists and grinned at Dr. White before she continued. "When I learned this piece, Dr. White reminded me that in this section the orchestra is playing pizzicato. The orchestra is the heartbeat, the passage of time. And the two pianos trade each phrase back and forth like caresses. The lines connect, but there is an essential loneliness that never goes away."

Dr. White smiled, and the two student performers nodded. "Take it from the beginning of the Largo," Cassie told them. "This time, reach beyond the notes and listen to what your partner is saying."

As the performers played the opening lines, Cassie closed her eyes. She heard confidence and tenderness. The notes held none of the pain she had brought to the piece years ago, and little of the redemption she found in it when performing with Jessica. It was as fresh and new as the young players who created it. In the caress of notes, Cassie knew nothing of fire, death, loss, or fear, just love plucked from Bach's hands, to the performers, to her own— spoken of in a language too deep for words.

About the author

Rhonda (Ringering) Rizzo has crafted a career as a performing and recording pianist and a writer. A specialist in music that borrows from both classical and jazz traditions, Rizzo has released four CDs and appears as both a soloist and a collaborative artist. Her numerous articles have appeared in national and international music magazines. She has a Bachelor of Arts degree from Walla Walla University and a Master's of Music Education degree from Boston University. She lives in Portland, Oregon.
www.rhondarizzo.com

Acknowledgements

This story came to me long after I'd decided I wasn't a fiction writer, and it has had many literary "midwives" in it's birthing process.

Without the vision of my editor, Arnold Dolin, this book wouldn't exist. Arnold, you saw the potential in the story and worked with me through several edits and you've spent the last few years helping to promote it to literary agents. Thank you for your faith in this story, and for your friendship.

I owe a great deal of thanks to the late Barrie Wellens who loved the book enough to edit it twice for me. "Mama Barrie," I miss your guidance and humor every day.

Karen Sade, thank you for being an enthusiastic early reader and for referring me to Arnold Dolin. Dr. Jill Timmons, thank you for your thoughtful reading of the book, for sharing your love and knowledge of Bach with me, and for always believing I was a pianist and a writer.

And, of course, gratitude and love to my husband, John Grosshuesch, who read and edited the book numerous times, encouraged me when I wanted to give up, and never stopped believing in me or in this book.

This is a work of fiction. All of the characters, organizations, and events portrayed in this novel are either products of the author's imagination or are used fictitiously.

ISBN 9781982930028

Made in the USA
San Bernardino, CA
21 June 2018